AWAYDAY

Or

Which don did it?

Judy Ford

Bernie Fazakerley
Publications

AWAYDAY

Published by Bernie Fazakerley Publications

Copyright © 2015 Judy Ford

All rights reserved.

Front cover design by Acepub.

ISBN-10: 1-911083-06-6
ISBN-13: 978-1-911083-06-1

DEDICATION

To the staff of the North West Stroke Research Network 2006-2014.

CONTENTS

1 THE BURSAR

'All set to reveal the dire state of the college finances?' Tom Carrington asked cheerily as he entered the room and saw the bursar sitting in a chair close to the screen on the wall, apparently leaning back and contemplating the graph displayed there.

The Master of Lichfield College had summoned senior members of the college to spend a day at a local hotel, away from their normal duties, so as to be free from distractions while they made strategic plans for the development of the college. They were about to re-convene after lunch and Anthony Bridgefield, the bursar, was to start the afternoon proceedings with a presentation of the accounts. He had excused himself from the group in the hotel restaurant about half an hour earlier, to go and set up his talk. Now he sat, strangely silent, gazing up at the screen on the wall.

Suddenly Tom realised that something was wrong. The bursar had not reacted at all to his voice. Now that he looked properly at him, Tom could see that his head was inclined at a most unnatural angle and his eyes were staring lifelessly into space. Tom put down his laptop bag on a chair and hurried over to where his colleague was sitting.

'Are you alright?' he asked futilely, shaking him by the shoulder. The bursar slumped forward and Tom had to grab at his arms to prevent him from sliding off the chair. Then he noticed a red line around his neck. This could not really be happening. College officials did not really get strangled to death while sitting in a chair in a respectable Oxford hotel.

The door opened and two more people came in. They were Plant Sciences tutor, Beverley Greenhalgh, and President of the college alumni society, Charles Brampton.

'Of course, in *my* day,' Charles was saying, 'we didn't have any compunction about simply taking the best students, and if they came from the best schools that was only to be expected. You can't expect-'

He broke off as he noticed Tom, who was still gripping the bursar by the arms, and stood staring at him.

'What's going on?' demanded Beverley, pushing past Charles and hurrying over to help Tom. 'Has he had some sort of seizure?'

'No. I don't think so. I think he's been strangled. Look!' Tom pointed at the line around the bursar's neck.

'Don't be daft! Who would want to garrotte Anthony?' Beverley's Lancashire accent could still be discerned, although it was less pronounced now than when she had first left the Western Pennines some thirty-five years previously. 'No, don't answer that! I can think of plenty of people who might have *wanted* to, but nobody who would actually have done it.'

Between them, Beverley and Tom managed to settle the body back on the chair. Tom closed the staring eyes and then wondered whether he ought not to have done. Weren't you supposed to touch nothing at the scene of a crime? They were still standing there, wondering what to do next when the door opened again and the rest of the party entered.

Featherstone Grainger, the Master of Lichfield College, strode into the room and then stopped abruptly when he saw the limp body of the bursar slumped awkwardly in his chair, with Tom and Beverley standing over it. A cluster of people collected behind him as the others crowded into the room.

'I found him like this when I came back from lunch,' Tom explained. 'It looks as if someone came at him from behind while he was loading his presentation and strangled him with something.'

'Are you sure?' the Master demanded, coming closer and peering down at the bursar's neck.

'Are you saying that Anthony's dead?' asked Ann Lambert, the Dean, who had followed the Master into the room together with the chaplain, Simon Sutcliffe.

'That's awful!' the Master's secretary gasped, pushing her way through from the back of the crowd to see the body for herself. 'Why would anyone want to do that?'

'I could give you some suggestions,' muttered Damien Ogden, the marketing officer.

'It seems to me that we ought to call the police.' The calm voice of Graham Weldon, the senior chemistry tutor, caught everyone's attention and they all stood looking expectantly at him.

'Quite right!' agreed the Master, recovering from his shock and taking charge. 'I'll go to reception. You'd all better wait here – and don't touch anything!' he added, turning to look at them as he opened the door.

He went out, closing the door behind him. For a moment, they all remained standing, looking at each other. Then Beverley resumed the seat that she had occupied during the morning session and got out her iPad. Gradually the others all followed her lead and sat down around the large boardroom-style table.

Tom took out his laptop and plugged it in, leaving a trailing cable lying dangerously across the floor in clear breach of health and safety guidance. While it was booting up, he sat looking round at his companions.

Graham Weldon, a large man in his fifties with steely

grey hair and dark brown eyes, sat impassively at the end of the table furthest from the screen, apparently unperturbed by the discovery of his colleague's body. Was that just his naturally calm disposition, or could he have been expecting it?

Next to him sat the chaplain, looking suddenly very young and inexperienced, talking in a low voice to Ann, the dean. They both looked shocked and anxious. Tom remembered that Anthony had been living with Ann in her house in Jericho until only a few months previously. Was there any possibility that the breakup of their long-term relationship had anything to do with the bursar's sudden death?

The chair on the other side of Ann was empty. The Master had been sitting there, in the middle of one side of the table, chairing the meeting; so next, Tom's eye fell on young Jessica Stevens, the Master's secretary. She seemed to have got over her initial shock at seeing the body and now appeared more excited than distressed. She glanced round the room before picking up her pen and starting to make notes on an A4 pad, which she had brought for taking minutes of the meeting. Tom tried to see what she was writing. He strongly suspected that she was trying to work out which of her colleagues could have killed the bursar.

Charles Brampton got up from his chair and paced around the room with his hands in his pockets. Tom had not met him until today and was not sure what to make of him. He was a retired civil servant of indeterminate age, who, Tom presumed, had devoted himself to the Lichfield Society, as the college alumni association was called, as a way of filling the empty days now that he had no full-time job to occupy him. He was a typical old-school Oxford graduate: Eton, then a third in Greats, followed by a moderately successful career in the Civil Service. His white hair and moustache reminded Tom of the stereotypical military gentleman from television situation comedies.

On Tom's side of the table there were Damien Ogden the college's marketing officer – a position of which Charles Brampton had been openly scathing during discussions that morning – and Plant Sciences Fellow, Beverley Greenhalgh. Tom liked Beverley's down-to-earth and practical approach to life. He watched her now, her head bowed so that the dark brown curls fell over her face as she concentrated on reading a research paper on her iPad. She had evidently decided that, there being nothing further that she could do for their dead colleague at present, the sensible thing was to get on with her work.

Tom turned to his own computer, which was now ready for use, and wondered whether to do the same, but he could not stop both his mind and his eyes being constantly drawn towards the lifeless figure on the chair at the front of the room. He opened his inbox to see whether there were any emails that he could deal with. At least that did not require a high level of concentration. Nothing new had arrived since he had last checked his mail in the hotel bar fifteen minutes earlier. Tom hesitated for a minute then began typing a message to one of his colleagues.

'Hi Ben,' he started, 'this Awayday has suddenly become like no other I've ever known! In fact, I can hardly believe that it's really happening. We all came back from lunch a few minutes ago to find the bursar lying dead in his chair – apparently strangled! Old FG has gone off to Reception to alert the police. I don't-'

'The hotel have called the police and an ambulance,' the Master's voice interrupted Tom's train of thought and he looked up to see Featherstone Grainger standing in the doorway. 'They should be here soon. Meanwhile we are to wait in here.'

He walked round the table and resumed his seat next to Jessica, who quickly turned over the sheet on which she had been writing, confirming Tom's suspicions that it had been nothing to do with her work. He turned back to his email, glad that the Master was sitting on the opposite side of the table so could not see what he was typing.

'I don't know what will happen after that,' he resumed. 'I don't imagine the Master will try to carry on with the meeting, so I may get back earlier than we thought. But, on the other hand, we'll presumably have to hang around while the police ask us questions to try to find out what happened to him; so if I'm not there by 4.30, better scrub our meeting and catch up tomorrow. Let me know what time suits you...'

2 THE POLICE INSPECTOR

The door opened again and the hotel receptionist came in, followed by two uniformed police officers: a woman in her late thirties and a younger man. Tom hastily clicked 'send' on his email client as the woman cleared her throat to signal that she was ready to address them.

'My name is Sergeant Tracy Burton,' she said, looking round at each of them to check that she had their attention. 'We've notified CID, and a senior officer will be here soon to conduct an investigation into the death of your colleague. I'm afraid that you will all need to stay so that they can speak with each of you. I've asked the hotel manager and they've found another room where you can wait, while our doctor examines the deceased and the scenes of crime officers check over this room. So now, please, will you come with me and I'll show you where to go.'

'Is it alright to bring my laptop with me?' Damien asked. 'If we're going to be stuck here for some time, I'd like to get on with my work.'

'Was it in this room while you were at lunch? Or did you take it with you then?'

'I left it here. They said that the room would be locked

while we were away, so I didn't bother to take it with me.'

'In that case, please leave it behind.' Sergeant Burton instructed. 'And that goes for the rest of you,' she added, raising her voice to indicate that everyone was included. 'I want you to leave this room exactly as it was when you left for lunch this morning. Anything that you took out with you should come with you to the other room; anything that you left behind should be left here, and as far as possible, left where you left it then. Constable Appleton will be standing outside the door to make sure that nobody comes in until CID arrive, so anything you leave here will be quite safe.'

There was a short period of confusion while everyone tried to remember how the room had been left when they had gone for lunch that morning. Tom shut down his laptop and packed it into its case. Beverley slipped her iPad into her handbag and slung it over her shoulder. Jessica carefully tore off the last two sheets of her pad of paper, where Tom had seen her jotting down notes, and stuffed them into her pocket, leaving the final page of the morning's minutes exposed on the top. They all trooped out after Sergeant Burton. The young police constable who had accompanied her tripped over the trailing power lead attached to Damien's laptop and collided with the Master as he brought up the rear.

'Sorry, sir,' he apologised, steadying himself by grabbing hold of the door. 'I should have looked where I was going.'

The Master gave him a look of disapproval, but said nothing.

The hotel receptionist led them downstairs and into a room that looked eerily similar to the one they had just left. Just as before, there was a large screen at one end, a large table in the centre with 12 chairs arrayed around it, and a smaller table at the side of the room under the window.

'Make yourselves comfortable here,' Sergeant Burton

said, waving her arm in the direction of the chairs.

'Would you like me to send in some tea and coffee?' the receptionist asked tentatively.

'That's a very good idea,' the sergeant agreed. 'Yes: please do that.'

Once they were all sitting down, she handed out sheets of paper and instructed them to write down their names and addresses.

'This will save time when the CID officers arrive,' she explained. 'Please include a telephone number where we will be able to get hold of you if we need to ask any more questions later.'

They obediently started writing. After a few minutes, Sergeant Burton came round and collected in the pieces of paper, checking each one carefully, asking a few supplementary questions of each person and noting down the answers. Then she gathered the papers together into a neat pile and sat down at the head of the table with the papers in front of her.

A few minutes later, the door opened and the receptionist appeared again.

'There's a Detective Chief Inspector Porter asking to see you,' she said to Sergeant Burton.

'Thank you. I'll come.' Burton got up to go. As she reached the door, she turned and addressed the company: 'You shouldn't have much longer to wait. Now please stay here and be patient.'

They sat looking at one another, wondering what to expect when the CID man came to question them. Charles got up and started pacing the room again, like a big cat in a zoo.

'I wish they'd get it over with,' Ann said nervously. 'All this waiting about makes me feel as if I must be guilty of something even though I know I've done nothing wrong!'

'I suppose there are things they have to do before they talk to us,' Jessica suggested, 'viewing the body and that sort of thing.'

The door opened and a woman entered. She was in her fifties with grey hair cut very short and grey-blue eyes behind metal-rimmed glasses. She wore green trousers, a yellow polo shirt and a green zip-up cardigan. She came into the room and stood silently, holding the door wide open. Tom gazed in amazement as he recognised her as Dr Bernadette Fazakerley, commonly known as 'Our Bernie', a former colleague of his from the university Mathematics department, who had taken early retirement the previous year.

A man in an electric wheelchair followed her in, accompanied by a younger man, whom Tom judged by his dark complexion and frizzy black hair probably included some Afro-Caribbean within a mixed-race heritage, wearing a rather ill-fitting navy blue suit. Sergeant Burton followed them in and Bernie Fazakerley closed the door behind them before hurrying to clear a path for the wheelchair to pass behind the chairs on the left-hand side of the table to reach the front of the room. Its occupant steered it expertly across the carpet, nodding briefly to Jessica, who had leapt up to help by moving aside a flipchart.

Tom turned in his chair to watch the man's progress, wondering who this might be. He was dressed in a dark grey suit with a pale blue shirt and navy tie. His hair was brown, turning to grey, and his eyes were a clear blue. His right hand lay motionless in his lap, while his left controlled the wheelchair by means of a small joystick. There was a computer screen attached to the right-hand arm of the chair. As it passed close to Tom, he saw that it was displaying a list of names, his own among them. It looked as if the information that they had given to Sergeant Burton must have already been transcribed to a computer to enable this man to read them. But who was he?

The man took up a position at the front of the room and surveyed the assembled group with an air of authority.

They immediately fell silent, waiting for him to speak.

'Good afternoon,' he began. 'I'm Detective Chief Inspector Jonah Porter and this is Detective Sergeant Andrew Lepage.'

He inclined his head towards his companion who stood towering over him, a lean, gangling man of about thirty, looking rather awkward as he glanced round at them acknowledging his identity.

'I'm leading this investigation,' the inspector went on. 'Sergeant Lepage and I will need to interview each of you. We'll try to do that as quickly as possible in order to let you go home, but we may need to talk to you again at a later date, depending on how things progress. Please be open and frank with us. You can be confident that nothing you say will go any further unless it's needed as evidence in a prosecution.'

He paused and looked round the room, as if sizing up his audience.

'Try not to be put off by the wheelchair,' he went on. 'To save you from asking, it's the result of a bullet in the back of my neck five years ago. I'm not embarrassed to talk about it, so you shouldn't be either. I have lots of clever gadgets to help me, but even so there are some things I can't do for myself, so wherever I go I take along my right hand man, Dr Bernadette Fazakerley.'

He stopped talking and Bernie stepped forward from the inconspicuous seat that she had taken at the corner of the table. She looked round the room, catching Tom's eye briefly and giving a smile of amusement as she noticed his surprised expression. He hastily looked down, unsure what to make of her unexpected appearance in this unfamiliar role. Bernie sat down again and Inspector Porter resumed his speech.

'Dr Fazakerley is a Senior Member of the university and used to be a tutor at St Luke's College,' he continued, 'so you can rely on her to understand where you're all coming from.'

'And not to be intimidated by academics trying to throw their weight about,' Tom thought silently to himself, admiring the subtle way in which they had been warned off any attempt to claim privilege by virtue of their seniority or scholarship.

'Now,' the inspector continued, 'I've been told that you are all senior staff from Lichfield College attending a meeting here. Sergeant Burton has given me a list of your names and addresses so next I'd like to-'

He broke off as a knock on the door was followed by the appearance of the receptionist, who stepped apologetically into the room.

'I'm sorry to interrupt, but there's a journalist at Reception wanting to know what's going on. I thought I'd better let you know.'

'Thank you. I'll go and have a word with them,' Inspector Porter said, making for the door, accompanied by Sergeant Burton. 'I won't be long. Just talk amongst yourselves while I'm gone.'

'You can't help admiring him,' Jessica observed, as soon as he was gone. 'I remember seeing about him on the news. I was just starting my second year at Uni. All the girls thought he was a real hero. He was in hospital for over a year and then had to fight to get his job back. He's completely paralysed apart from three fingers on one hand.'

Tom joined in the general murmur of agreement with this sentiment, which went round the table. Then he got up and hurried over to where his ex-colleague was sitting impassively. He pulled up a chair and seated himself next to her.

'Bernie! What on earth are you doing here?' he demanded, speaking in an undertone to avoid Sergeant Lepage overhearing.

Bernie smiled back at him, clearly amused at his agitation.

'Tom,' she replied calmly in the tone that one might

adopt when speaking to a four-year old who was proving rather slow on the uptake, 'you *know* what I'm doing here: it's my job; I'm DI Porter's personal assistant.'

'But what sort of job is that for someone like you?'

'And what exactly do you mean by "someone like me"?' Bernie asked, her Liverpool accent growing more marked and making her sound somewhat aggressive.

'You know: someone with your qualifications and experience. I mean, it can't be exactly intellectually challenging running round after a man in a wheelchair, opening doors and moving things out of his way. It seems such a waste.'

'It's the best move I ever made,' Bernie declared decisively. 'Oh, come on Tom! You must be aware of my long association with the Police Service. It's the most natural thing in the world for me to get more involved; and it's far more interesting than tutoring undergraduates.'

'Of course! I'd forgotten: your husband was a policeman. Wasn't he killed in the course of duty?'

'That's right. Jonah Porter used to work with him, so I've known him for years.'

'And didn't you marry again?' Tom asked, dredging up from the recesses of his mind snippets of information, which had gone the rounds of the mathematics department over the last ten years or more. 'And wasn't he a policemen too? He wasn't ...?' Tom glanced meaningfully towards the door through which the inspector had recently left the room, as a disconcerting idea occurred to him. 'That's not your second husband?'

'No, no,' Bernie smiled reassuringly. 'Yes, I did marry another policeman, but not Jonah Porter. He's just a very old friend of the family.'

'Good. I mean – I was thinking it would be incredibly bad luck if you'd had one husband killed and another seriously injured like that.'

'Now Tom,' Bernie chided gently, 'just you stop worrying about me and try to remember that I'm here in a professional capacity – nothing to do with my former life as an academic. All you need to be bothered about at the moment,' she went on, conscious that she should be using any influence she might have with the witnesses to encourage full co-operation with the enquiry, 'is making sure you answer all the questions honestly and as fully as you can.'

3 THE MATHEMATICS TUTOR

The door opened and Detective Chief Inspector Porter reappeared.

'I'm sorry to keep you waiting,' he apologised, 'but I had to make sure that the press had something that they could report and knew that they'd be in trouble if they started asking any of the hotel staff – or indeed any of you – for information about this incident. And while I'm on the subject, I'd like to make it clear to all of you that you must not discuss what's happened with any of the media. Is that understood?'

He looked round at each of them in turn, checking that they were paying attention.

'Right! Now we'd better get started. I think I'd like to talk to ... Dr Thomas Carrington first,' he said, looking sharply towards where Tom and Bernie were sitting together. 'I think that's you, sir. And I believe that you were the first one back after lunch and discovered that Mr Bridgefield was dead. Is that right?'

'Yes. That's right,' admitted Tom.

'Good. So we'll have a little chat about exactly what happened, and Bernie here will take some notes for me. Meanwhile, Lepage!'

'Yes sir.'

'You start with Dr Grainger. He's the senior person here and will be able to give you an overview of the day. Set yourself up at the other end of the room, so we won't be overhearing one another's conversations. When you've finished with Dr Grainger, start working through all the other witnesses in turn. Is that clear?'

'Yes sir.' The tall detective sergeant turned to face the Master. 'If you wouldn't mind coming with me, sir?'

Bernie silently handed over to Lepage a sheaf of papers, which Tom recognised as the pages on which he and his colleagues had written their names and other details. Clearly the three of them were a close-knit team with an established routine for working together.

The inspector turned his wheelchair so that he was facing Tom. At the same time, Bernie reached down and took out a notebook computer from a pocket at the side of the chair. She set it down on the table in front of her, opened it and prepared to take notes.

'I gather that you two know each other,' Inspector Porter began.

'Yes,' Bernie admitted. 'Tom here is another mathematician, so our paths used to cross quite regularly. In fact, I seem to remember we even co-authored a couple of research papers, years ago.'

'Did we?' Tom asked, trying to remember.

'Yes. Don't you remember Gerard's thesis?'

'Gerard? Oh! Of course! Numerical modelling of the flow of melted chocolate.'

'That's right. You were co-supervisor on the project.'

'So I was! What became of Gerard? I don't remember hearing anything of him after he graduated.'

'He's doing OK. He's back in Ireland now – Galway, I think it is or maybe Cork – and still talking nineteen to the dozen: the typical "tongue-tied Irishman from the land of the bogs and the little people."'

'Much as I enjoy listening to your reminiscences,'

Porter broke in, 'I have to ask you to address your attention to the more recent past. Dr Carrington: tell me about today. This was a meeting of senior staff from Lichfield College: is that right?'

'Yes. It was what the Master describes as an Awayday: getting everyone out of college so that we can't sneak off to our rooms part way through if we get bored.'

'I see. And what exactly was this meeting about?'

'It was supposed to be strategic planning for the future of the college. We're not as far up the Norrington Table as the Master would like; and apparently we're in some sort of financial crisis. I don't know the details: Anthony was supposed to be going to *reveal all* this afternoon.'

Porter glanced briefly in Bernie's direction.

'I'll see that we have a copy of all the presentations before we go,' she assured him. He nodded and turned back to Tom.

'And what was your role in this strategic planning? Why were you there?'

'I'm currently Undergraduate Admissions Tutor, so I suppose the Master holds me responsible for the fact that we don't get as many applications per place as some of the other colleges. And I also run a summer school for bright sixth formers whose schools don't have the resources to teach double maths A' level. We're under pressure from HEFCE to demonstrate that we're making an effort to increase the proportion of state school students that we take.'

'And "heff-key" is?'

'The Higher Education Funding Council for England,' Tom and Bernie said together.

'I see. Now, what time did the proceedings start?'

'It was half past nine for ten o'clock.'

'And you got here at what time?'

'About twenty to, I think. Beverley Greenhalgh was already here and Jessica was busy setting up the room: putting out agendas round the table, that sort of thing, and there was an IT guy from the hotel fiddling with the display screen.'

'And was there anyone else there when you arrived?'

'No. I don't think so. I think everyone else came in after me.'

'Good. Now, can you remember what order the others arrived in?'

'I'm not sure,' Tom said slowly, trying to remember. 'Simon was late – I do remember that. We'd already started. He's always late for meetings and someone remarked that it was good going for him to be arriving when we were only up to item two on the agenda. I think probably, after me, the next person was the bursar and then the Old Boy-'

'Old Boy?'

'Sorry! I mean Charles Brampton, the Lichfield Society president. I always think of it as the Old Boys' Club.'

'I see. And after that?'

'I think the Master must have come in not long after that, but I wasn't really taking any notice. I got myself a cup of coffee and then went and sat down. I remember now: when I sat down Ann was already there sitting opposite. So she must have come in while I was getting my coffee. Oh, yes! And then Graham and Damien came in together. They'd met in the lobby.'

'That's everyone,' confirmed Bernie, who had been marking off the names on a list as Tom spoke.

'Good. Now, you say there was a man doing something with the display screen when you arrived: can you remember how long he stayed? Was he still there when Mr Bridgefield arrived, for example?

'I'm not sure,' Tom said slowly. 'I *think* … oh! I remember now. He was just leaving when the Master came in with his presentation on a data stick. The IT guy stopped behind to see that he managed to load it up OK; then he went out.'

'So, by ten o'clock you were all assembled ready for the

off: all, except the reverend Simon, that is.'

'That's right.'

'And how did it go? Were there any differences of opinion? Heated debates? Swords crossed?'

'Not really. It was all rather boring really. The Old Boy kept bemoaning the fact that things had gone downhill since he was an undergraduate, and Damien complained that he never seemed to get any support from the SCR for his marketing initiatives-'

'SCR?'

'Senior Common Room. I mean the fellows, the academic staff of the college.'

'Thank you. Go on.'

'Well, that's about it. There was nothing particularly contentious and no one got angry with anyone else. So if you're thinking that the bursar was murdered because of something he said ...'

'At the moment I'm not thinking anything. I'm just collecting information. Now, let's move on. You broke for lunch at what time?'

'Twelve-thirty prompt. One thing the Master *is* good at is keeping a meeting to time. Damien left a few minutes early, because he had a teleconference to attend. He was going to take it on his mobile in the bar.'

'And the rest of you went to the dining room for lunch? Did you all go together?'

'All except Jess: she stayed behind to sort out the room for the afternoon session. We were going to have a brainstorming session with flipcharts and post-it notes,' Tom said disparagingly. 'You know the sort of thing.'

'I do, indeed,' Porter admitted. 'Even the Police Service has been known to resort to such antics. So you went to lunch together; and did you stay together until it was time to return for the afternoon session?'

'No. I finished my lunch first and went off to the bar to catch up on my emails.'

'Why didn't you return to the meeting room to do

that?'

'It was locked. I tried the door, but I couldn't get in, so I went to the bar. Damien was sitting there in a corner talking on the phone. So I found myself a seat well away from him and set up my laptop.'

'Could you see Mr Ogden from where you were sitting?'

'No, he was round the corner.'

'So, you wouldn't know what time he left the bar?'

'No. I didn't see him go.'

'And about what time did you leave the dining room?'

'Ten to one – something like that.'

'And when you left, all the others, with the exception of Miss Stevens and Mr Ogden, were still eating their lunch?'

'Miss Stevens? Oh, of course! Jess. That's right.'

'Did you see Miss Stevens on her way to the dining room, as you were leaving?'

'No – not that I remember.'

'So, as far as you can recall, she didn't get to the dining room until after you left at 12.50?'

'That's right.'

'Thank you. I'm sorry to ask so many questions, but I want to get a clear idea of where everyone was throughout the lunch hour.'

'It hardly matters where people were until after the bursar went back to the meeting room,' Tom objected.

'Perhaps not, but we don't know when that was yet,' Porter pointed out calmly. 'Now, let's go back to you and your emails in the bar. Did you stay there for the whole time until you went back to the meeting room?'

'Yes. I got rather engrossed and suddenly noticed it was nearly one-thirty, so I closed down the laptop and raced up to the room thinking I'd be late.'

'So you were surprised to be the first back after lunch?'

'Well, I *would* have been: if I hadn't been too busy being surprised at finding the bursar lying dead in his chair.'

'And, when you got to the meeting room, the door was unlocked?'

'Yes, I went in and saw the bursar sitting in the chair in front of the screen. I thought at first he was leaning back to get a better look at it. But he didn't seem to hear me when I spoke to him and then, when I looked closer, I saw that he was dead with this red line round his neck.'

'And what did you think then?'

'I didn't know *what* to think. I mean, you don't expect to find people strangled in a hotel meeting room. Anyway, I wasn't sure at first, so I tried to rouse him by shaking him, but he just started to slip off the chair. Then Bev came in and we got him back on to it again, and then everyone else started coming back.'

'Can you remember what order they came back in?'

'No. Everyone seemed to be there at once.'

'And then the Master went off to give the alarm?'

'That's right. After all: he *is* in charge.'

'So what did the rest of you do?'

'We just sat down and waited for the police to arrive.'

'I see. And how did everyone seem? Was anyone *particularly* agitated or upset – more than the others?'

'I don't think so. We were all pretty shell-shocked I think. We didn't know what to make of it all.'

'Thank you. I think that's all for now. I'm afraid that I'm going to have to ask you to wait again while Sergeant Lepage and I finish talking to everyone. Try to make yourself comfortable; we'll be as quick as we can.'

4 THE PATHOLOGIST

'Excuse me, sir,' Tracy Burton put her head round the door of the room and addressed Jonah. 'The pathologist has arrived and he thought you might like to be there while he examines the body.'

'I certainly would. Who is it? Atherton, I suppose'

'No, it's Dr Carson,' Tracy said, smiling. She knew that her superior found Dr Leonard Atherton's rather pompous bearing and cautious approach to saying anything definite about such things as cause or time of death intensely irritating. The easy-going Irishman, Michael Carson would be a much more welcome sight at the scene of a suspicious death.

'Lead on MacDuff!' declaimed Jonah, clearly delighted at the news.

Bernie opened the door wide and Tracy led the way out to the lift, which took them all up to the first floor, where the ill-fated Awayday had been taking place. They could immediately identify the room because Constable Malcolm Appleton was there, keeping vigil outside the door. He opened it to allow Jonah and Bernie to enter. Tracy returned to Reception to intercept any more journalists who might attempt to come in and talk to the hotel staff.

The body of the bursar was lying awkwardly in a chair at the other end of the room, its head leaning over the back of the chair so that the curly brown hair stood out a little behind it.

'Jonah!' the pathologist greeted his friend, looking up from his position bending over the corpse, examining the mark round its neck. 'It's good to see you. How're you keeping?'

'I'm on fine form, how about you?'

'Oh, you know how it is: wrecked after Patrick's stag do last night, but otherwise just fine. And Bernie! It seems a long time since our paths crossed. How's old Peter doing? Has he got bored with this house-husband lark yet?'

'Peter is doing extremely well, thank you,' Bernie laughed. 'And house-husband is still suiting him down to the ground. I think he's wishing he'd thought of retiring sooner.'

'And how about Lucy? Is she still set on becoming a pathologist?'

'Indeed she is. She's been on at me to talk to you about doing her Year Ten work experience with you.'

'I'm sorry to interrupt,' Jonah broke in, 'but could we possibly all get back to work?'

'Very well,' the doctor grumbled, grinning mischievously at him. 'I know you are always very keen for me to estimate time of death. I think I can offer you quite a nice short window on this occasion. I'd say he was killed sometime between, say,' he looked down at his watch, 'twelve noon and two pm.'

'Thank you, Mike,' Jonah said sarcastically. 'That's incredibly helpful, seeing as we have seven witnesses who can vouch for him being alive at twelve fifty, and at least three who can confirm that he was dead at one thirty!'

'There you are then. My estimate was spot on.'

'Yes, but it doesn't really add much to the sum of human knowledge, does it?' remarked Jonah drily.

'There's no pleasing some people,' said Mike, shaking his head. 'Moving on then: my preliminary thoughts on cause of death are that it was by strangulation with a fairly thin ligature. You'll no doubt have noticed the marks on the deceased's neck?'

Bernie and Jonah both nodded, looking down at where the doctor was pointing.

'The line is narrow, suggesting that the ligature was thin, but the skin isn't broken, so I'd say it was not as thin as, say, piano wire: probably some sort of thin electrical cable …'

He looked round the room and Bernie and Jonah followed his gaze, taking in several laptop power cables, a smart phone recharging cable and cables connecting the keyboard and mouse to the computer at the front of the room, which controlled the display screen. There seemed to be an abundance of potential weapons available to the amateur strangler.

'When we get him back to the mortuary, we'll have a good look to see if there are any traces of the ligature left on the body,' Mike continued, 'but I rather doubt we'll find anything that will help you much.'

'How strong would you need to be to strangle someone like that?' Jonah asked.

'It's difficult to say. Strangling someone isn't as easy as it looks, so you would need a certain amount of upper body strength; but if he was taken unawares and the murderer had a firm grip on the ligature then maybe you wouldn't have to be particularly strong.'

'Could a woman have done it?'

'It's difficult to say,' Mike replied cautiously.

'Force yourself,' Jonah encouraged.

'Well, I'd say it was more likely to have been a man; but if you had me in the witness box I'd have to give it as my opinion that it *could* have been a woman. After all, the victim was sitting down, so you wouldn't have to be particularly tall to reach his neck and women often have quite strong arms, particularly if they have caring responsibilities which involve lifting elderly relatives, say. Bernie here, for example, would have no difficulty strangling you, if she had a mind to.'

'How very reassuring,' Jonah observed.

'I'll be able to say more confidently after the post mortem,' Mike went on. 'You never know, he may have had some underlying morbidity that would have made strangling him easier than usual; or it may turn out that strangulation wasn't the cause of death at all!'

'Ever the optimist,' Jonah commented. 'All right: you can take the body away now.'

While the medical team transferred the body to a trolley and manoeuvred it out of the room, Jonah looked round, taking careful note of the layout.

'Make a plan of the table,' he instructed Bernie, who obediently sat down at the table and opened the notebook computer. 'I want to know where everyone was sitting. I'd better get the secretary up here. She'll probably know and she'll be able to fill us in on the running order for the morning.'

He pressed a button on the left-hand arm of his chair to operate a mobile phone built into his computer screen and spoke to Tracy Burton. A few minutes later, the sergeant ushered in Jessica Stevens, who was clearly thrilled to meet her hero on a one to one basis.

'The sergeant said you wanted to see me,' she said earnestly. 'What can I do to help?'

Bernie, who had heard Jessica's declaration of esteem earlier, smiled to herself at the young woman's eagerness. A quick calculation in her head had told her that Jessica must be twenty-three or twenty-four. That was still young enough for her to have something of a crush on a man like Jonah for whom she could feel both admiration and pity.

'I think you're fantastically brave,' Jessica rushed on, without waiting for Jonah to reply. 'I saw the report on your first day back at work after you were shot. I remember particularly the picture of you with your little daughter coming out of the hospital in your wheelchair.'

'I'm afraid I have to correct you there,' Jonah said mildly. 'I don't have a daughter.'

'But, I remember it so well,' Jessica sounded confused. 'There you were at the entrance to the hospital, and there was a little girl with a load of yellow curls standing next to you with her arm round your shoulders.'

'She's thinking of Lucy,' Bernie said, thinking back to the occasion. 'Don't you remember? She insisted on coming to the hospital the day you were discharged to say a final goodbye to the ward staff. There *were* some press photographers waiting for us when you came out. I expect they thought Lucy was more photogenic than the rest of us! Lucy is *my* daughter,' she explained to Jessica. 'Jonah's an old friend of the family. Lucy's dad died before she was born and she's managed to accumulate quite a number of men who consider themselves to be surrogate fathers to her!'

'Oh! I see,' Jessica said in a rather dissatisfied voice, sounding rather as if this explanation had only served to raise more questions in her mind.

'But to get back to the matter in hand,' Jonah said firmly. 'First, I'd like you to see if you can remember who was sitting where during the morning session.

He looked round at the litter of personal possessions on the table.

'Perhaps you could start at the front and work your way round. Dr Fazakerley will take notes.'

'Charles Brampton was there,' Jessica began, pointing at a place on the left-hand side of the table, close to the chair which had, until recently been occupied by the dead body of the bursar. 'That's his diary.'

Jonah looked and saw a small electronic organiser in an imitation leather case lying on the table, on top of a thin pad of paper with the hotel's logo on it.

'And I was sitting next to him,' Jessica went on,

indicating the unfinished minutes lying in the place next to the diary. 'The Master was next to me, because he was chairing the meeting and I was taking the minutes. Then, next to him was Ann Lambert. That's her iPad. And the chaplain was sitting next to her: he came in late.'

'So I've been told. Can you remember what time it was?'

'Not off-hand, but I wrote it in the minutes. Would you like me to have a look?'

'If you don't mind. And, I'd like to take the minutes away with me – and the agenda too.'

'And we'll need copies of all the presentations,' Bernie added.

'No problem. I can let you have all those,' Jessica assured them. 'Now, let's see … yes! Here it is: Simon arrived at twelve minutes past ten.'

'Thank you. You're very efficient,' Jonah said.

Jessica blushed with pleasure at the compliment.

'Graham was sitting at the end of the table,' she continued, 'then Tom Carrington, Bev Greenhalgh and the bursar down the other side, with Damien Ogden nearest the front on that side and an empty place near the front.'

'I see from the minutes that, in addition to the people who were here in person, there was a Martin Reiss attending by telephone?' Bernie said, looking up from the notes, which she had picked up from the table.

'Yes. That's right. He's with a group of students on a field trip today, so he couldn't come; but the Master wanted his input so he agreed to dial in on his mobile.'

'And what time did he dial in?' Jonah asked.

'According to these notes,' Bernie said, 'ten thirty. It says here that he gave an update on Schools' Liaison.'

'That's right,' agreed Jessica. 'He leads on schools' liaison: that means he organises for people to go out into schools and give talks about the college, and he arranges meetings with teachers to encourage them to put students forward to apply. He called at ten thirty for that item and then stayed for the rest of the morning.'

'So he dialled out when?' asked Jonah.

'Twelve thirty: just before everyone went for lunch.'

'And was he expected to dial in again this afternoon?' Bernie asked, suddenly becoming aware of the possibility that there was someone outside the group at the hotel who might be wondering what was going on.

'No. He didn't have time. Actually,' Jessica confided, 'I don't think he was best pleased at the Master insisting he took part in the morning session. I half expected him to "forget" or to find that there wasn't any mobile signal where he was.'

'Thank you, Miss Stevens-'

'Jessica, please!'

'Thank you, Jessica. That's all very clear. Now, if you could just check that we've got the seating plan right ...'

With a slight movement of one finger of his left hand, Jonah made the screen in front of him swivel round to face Jessica, so that she could see the diagram that Bernie had drawn.

'How did you do that?' she asked in wonder. 'I mean ...'

She looked from Jonah to Bernie and back again, unable to work out how Jonah had managed to produce the plan.

'It's all just a matter of digital technology,' he explained. 'Bernie here took it all down while you were talking and there's a wireless link between her computer and the one in my wheelchair which enables them to display information from either machine on either screen. She's got two hands, so she types faster than me, which is why I use her to take notes, but given time I can do quite a lot for myself too. Let me show you. Come round behind me, so you can see.'

Jonah turned the screen back to face him and became very busy with the first two fingers of his left hand, manipulating the joystick on the arm of his chair and pressing buttons next to it. Jessica peered over his shoulder and saw that the screen was now displaying a keyboard and a few lines of text above it. It reminded her of the touch screen display on a tablet computer, but of course, Jonah could not move his hand to touch the screen. Instead, a pointer was moving around selecting keys from the keyboard, which then produced letters in the lines above. As she watched, Jessica worked out that Jonah was controlling the pointer with his joystick and selecting characters using the buttons. It was painstaking work, but he was remarkably efficient and it was not long before he had completed a sentence.

'Show Jessica how we communicate behind people's backs.'

Jonah's fingers stopped moving and he looked towards Bernie, expectantly. Bernie seemed intent on something on her own screen and did not look up. Then Jessica saw a new line of text, in a different colour, appear beneath the one she had just read:

'Show her yourself!'

She looked up and saw both Jonah and Bernie smiling at her.

'So now you know our secret,' he said, conspiratorially. 'People sometimes remark on what a wonderful rapport we have with one another: almost telepathic, they say. But it's all down to modern wireless communication.'

'That's wonderful,' Jessica declared in tones of awe. 'And you're so quick! With your left hand too!'

'Aah!' Jonah smiled. 'Now there you are mistaken. I was extremely fortunate in that respect, having been born left-handed.'

'But still,' Jessica insisted admiringly, 'to manage so much with only one hand ...'

'Stop massaging his ego,' Bernie broke in. 'He's quite full enough of himself without having attractive young ladies eulogising over him and turning his head!'

'I'm sorry, I didn't mean ...' Jessica turned rather red

and looked round at them both in confusion. Seeing them both smiling, she eventually smiled nervously back.

'Thank you, Jessica,' Jonah said decisively. 'You've been a great help. Now I think we've finished here. I'll go back down to see how Lepage is doing with interviewing your colleagues. If you could just hand over all the meeting papers and presentations to Bernie, and then join us downstairs.'

Bernie went with him to the lift, leaving Jessica to assemble the papers that they wanted.

'You've got a fan there,' Bernie observed with a smile, as they waited for the lift to come.

'So it seems. I hope it doesn't cause trouble.'

'What sort of trouble? I'd have thought you'd be delighted to have young ladies swooning over you!'

The lift came and Jonah manoeuvred the wheelchair into it. Bernie followed him in and pressed the button for the ground floor before stepping out again.

'I'm sure this is contravening Health and Safety,' she observed. 'Be sure to send me a message when you're safely out at the bottom, or I'll feel obliged to come down and check you're OK.'

She went back to the meeting room where she found Jessica busily assembling a folder of paperwork for her. She looked up as Bernie entered.

'Is he OK to go down on his own?' she asked anxiously. 'You could have gone with him and let me bring the stuff down to you.'

'I try to give him as much independence as possible – and not to think about what would happen if the lift doors didn't open when it gets to the ground floor. And it wouldn't do for me to have an argument with him about it in front of you!'

'It must be very frustrating for him, having to rely on other people so much. I mean, for example, it had never occurred to me what it would be like not to be able to open doors for yourself.'

'Yes,' agreed Bernie. 'That's a bigger problem than you'd imagine. We've got voice-activated doors at home, but you can't expect that sort of thing everywhere you go.'

'At home?' Jessica queried. 'Do you mean you live with him?'

'Well, to be more precise, *he* lives with *us*; but only during the week. At weekends, he goes back to his own house in South Oxfordshire and his son, Nathan, stays there to look after him. Nathan's a trainee barrister in London and works long hours during the week, so Jonah stays in our house in Headington. Now, I've got a USB stick here: can you copy all the presentations on to it for me?'

'Yes, of course.'

Jessica took the proffered device and inserted it into the computer at the front of the room. For a few minutes, there was silence as she concentrated on finding all the files and copying them from the desktop. Then she ejected the data stick and handed it to Bernie.

'That's the lot. You should be able to tell from the agenda which ones were given in the morning and which were going to happen in the afternoon. Do you really think they'll tell you anything about who killed Mr Bridgefield?'

'It's not for me to think about it one way or the other. I'm not the detective. My job is just to follow orders, as a humble assistant.'

'But you must sometimes get ideas.'

'Yes. I have to admit I do. In fact, I've got an idea right now about you. There were a couple of pages missing from the pad you were using for taking the minutes. I was wondering whether you might have made some more notes *after* the morning session finished and then removed the pages when you had to leave everything in this room and go downstairs.'

She waited silently for a few moments, before going on.

'I'd be very interested to see those pages; and I rather fancy Chief Inspector Porter might like to see them too.'

'I'm not sure,' Jessica said hesitantly, blushing bright red. 'It was just some thoughts I put down about which of the staff might have killed Mr Bridgefield. I mean – it *must* have been one of us, mustn't it? Really. It wouldn't make sense for a complete stranger to walk in and do it.'

'You might well think that. I couldn't possibly comment. Now, are you going to hand them over or what?' Bernie demanded, becoming suddenly the archetypal aggressive scouser.

'I don't know that I ought to,' Jessica pleaded. 'I mean – it's only my ideas.'

'Look: you don't have to worry,' Bernie reasoned with her. 'It isn't evidence that could be used in court, but it might give the police some ideas of where to *look* for the evidence. You know these people a lot better than they do, so your hunches just might be a help in pointing them in the right direction.'

'Oh, OK!' Jessica pulled out two crumpled pieces of paper from her jacket pocket. 'Here they are. But please, don't let the Master know about them. He wouldn't be pleased at the idea of me writing things about the fellows.'

'Thanks.' Bernie flattened out the sheets of paper and slipped them into the folder with the other papers. 'Inspector Porter will appreciate it. Now we'd better join the party downstairs.'

As they walked down the stairs, Jessica returned to the subject of Jonah's living arrangements.

'It's very generous of you,' she suggested, 'taking him into your home as well as looking after him at work all day.'

'Not at all. In many ways, it's more convenient for me than having to pick him up from his house to take him to work each morning. That's what I used to do, before his wife died.'

'How awful! When was that?'

'April of this year.'

'You mean, just a couple of months ago?' Jessica

sounded appalled.

'Yes. We're still working out how to manage things. It's been a bit of a shock to the system, even though we had plenty of time to prepare.'

'It wasn't a sudden death then?'

'No. Margaret was diagnosed with cancer getting on for a year and a half ago, so we had about a year to make plans.'

'You know, when I saw you together, I rather thought that maybe *you* were Inspector Porter's wife.'

'Oh no!' Bernie laughed. 'Even if I'd been in the right place at the right time to meet him, I could never have competed with Margaret. She was a one-off: a trauma surgeon who rode a motorbike. Imagine! You'd think she'd see so many tragic injuries it would have put her off.'

'She was a doctor? Was Inspector Porter treated in her hospital? It must be strange for doctors when that happens.'

'No. He was whisked off to the spinal injuries unit at Stoke Mandeville.'

'But even they couldn't do anything for him.'

'That's not true. Nobody could repair the damage to his spinal cord, but they operated to fix the damaged vertebrae so that his spine was stable and then he got a lot of rehab. And – well you can see for yourself, he gets on very well now. Look: Inspector Porter doesn't want your pity, you know. All he wants from you is co-operation in finding out who killed your Mr Bridgefield.'

'Did they ever find out who shot him? I don't remember ever hearing about it.'

'No. There are a depressingly large number of unsolved crimes about, I'm afraid. It's not like the police dramas on the television, where at the end of two hours all the loose ends have been tied up and the criminals have been banged to rights – usually as a result of a maverick police officer having broken all the rules in order to get the perpetrators to confess!'

'And does Inspector Porter break the rules?'

'Absolutely not! Well, except for things like going down in the lift unaccompanied!' she laughed. 'In real life, the rules are there to help us. It doesn't do to flout them and it wouldn't help anyway because it would just give the defence lawyers a way of getting their clients off on a technicality. And you just have to face it: in an awful lot of cases, either the police have no idea who did it or they know full well who it was but don't have the evidence to prosecute. In Jonah's case, everyone assumes that it must have been some sort of revenge attack to get back at him for putting some criminal behind bars, but it's never got any further than that.'

'Doesn't it make him angry to think that whoever did it has got away with it?'

'No. We're all pretty much resigned to it by now. The thing that worries me is the thought that there's a gunman out there who wanted him dead. I just hope whoever it *is*, is satisfied and doesn't get any ides of coming back and finishing the job.'

They reached the bottom of the stairs and Bernie held open the fire door to let them both out into the corridor.

'It just seems so unfair!' Jessica blurted out.

'Whatever made you think life was supposed to be fair?' Bernie said, smiling. 'We all just have to make the best of whatever's thrown at us, that's all. Mostly we manage to muddle through OK.'

They entered the downstairs room where the others were all assembled, waiting for the interview process to be over. Lepage handed his notebook over to Bernie and she started typing up his interviews with the Awayday attendees so that Jonah would be able to read them on his screen. While she did this, Jonah addressed them.

'Thank you all for your patience,' he began. 'I know that you all want to get off, so I won't keep you much longer. We'll be using what you've each told us, together with forensic and other evidence, to try to work out exactly what happened to your colleague Mr Bridgefield. We'd appreciate it if you could refrain from speculation on that subject, especially to the press. If any journalists approach you, please refer them to me. We may well need to speak to each of you again in the course of the next few days, so don't be surprised if we get in touch. Now are there any questions before we disperse?'

'Just one thing,' said Simon the chaplain nervously.

'Yes?'

'Has anything been done about informing his next of kin?'

'A police officer has been sent to talk to his ex-wife. We aren't aware of any other relatives, but I assume that she will be able to tell us if anyone else needs to be informed. Do you know of anyone else?'

'Well,' Simon hesitated, seeming to be about to say something then changing his mind. 'No. I don't.'

Jonah looked at him for a few moments as if hoping that he might go on, but did not press him.

'Right then!' he resumed. 'If that's all then you're free to go. You can collect your things from the room upstairs. We've finished with it now.'

5 THE SCHOOLGIRL

'And *you* are free to come home,' Bernie added in his ear, speaking low but forcefully, as everyone started to move towards the door. 'So don't start getting any fancy ideas about going back to the office for a conference with young Andy Lepage!'

Jonah opened his mouth to protest and then thought better of it. Reluctant though he was to admit it, ever since Bernie had taken over as his daytime carer, her firm handling in respect of keeping regular hours and not overdoing it had improved his health. In some ways, that was the worst aspect of his condition: not being able to push himself beyond the call of duty whenever an interesting or challenging case came up, without repercussions in the form of exhaustion, digestive problems or infections.

'Right then!' he said brightly. 'Let's make an early start tomorrow. Eight-thirty prompt in my office.'

'Right you are, sir,' his sergeant answered, holding out his hand towards Bernie. 'If you give me my notes back, I don't mind finishing the typing overnight.'

'I'm not sure I ought to be encouraging you to burn the midnight oil like that, Andy,' she observed. 'And that's my

36

job really. Anyway, your writing's good enough, why not just scan them in, in the morning?'

'She's right,' Jonah intervened. 'You do that. Now you get off home and I'll see you bright and bushy-tailed first thing tomorrow.'

Bernie walked ahead out into the hotel car park and opened up the adapted people carrier in which she transported Jonah around. She fixed the ramp and he drove the chair up into the back. Then she climbed in and fastened him in securely.

'I've got something to show you,' she confided as she adjusted the straps. 'While she was waiting for the police to arrive, young Jessica, the secretary, whiled away the time making notes about which of her colleagues might have done away with the bursar. I thought it might make interesting bed time reading for you.'

'And how did you winkle that out of her?'

'Oh, I played shamelessly on her adulation of you. She was only too pleased to be helping the Master Detective who is so terribly brave in his troubles!'

'Did I ever mention that you were incorrigible?'

'Practically every day: I'm getting used to it by now.'

Bernie's husband, Peter, was waiting for them when they got home.

'Tea'll be ready to dish up in forty minutes,' he announced as they came in.

'Just time for you to show me those notes from the secretary,' Jonah said eagerly to Bernie.

'Oh no you don't!' she contradicted. 'It's just enough time for your physio session. The notes can wait.'

They made their way into the ground floor bedroom, which housed an array of equipment to help with his care and daily activities. Bernie began the task of removing Jonah's business suit to prepare him for the functional electrical stimulation, which enabled him to exercise his muscles despite being unable to move them himself.

'I'll take over now Mam.' Bernie's daughter, Lucy, put

her face round the door, her yellow curly hair standing out around it like a halo. 'I'm on duty this week.'

Bernie looked up from where she was engaged in detaching Jonah's urine bag from his leg.

'OK, love,' she agreed. 'You carry on. I'll just empty this and then I'll leave you to it.'

Fourteen-year-old Lucy worked methodically, taking Jonah through a range of exercises by means of electrodes attached to his skin. She was extremely fond of him and insisted on taking an equal share, with her mother and stepfather, in his care. Since he had moved in with them on a permanent basis, they had agreed a rota system whereby they each took over primary responsibility for his care for a week at a time.

'How was your day?' she asked conversationally. 'Any good murders to report?'

'Well, as it happens, we *are* investigating a murder. Someone's done away with the bursar of Lichfield College and it looks suspiciously as if it must have been one of the dons wot dunnit!'

'Lichfield? That's Martin's college.'

'Martin?'

'Martin Riess. Oh, come on Jonah, you *must* know Martin. Hasn't he ever called while you're here?'

'D'you mean Martin with the narrow boat that you're always talking about going out in on the canal?' Jonah queried. 'I thought you said he'd been a refugee from East Germany.'

'Yes. That's the one. He and his mother made it to the West but his father was killed trying to get across the border to join them. And now he's a fellow at Lichfield and a lecturer in the Earth Sciences Department and a great friend of us all.'

'But, the name?' Jonah queried, still puzzled. 'Rhys is a Welsh name.'

'R-I-E-S-S,' Lucy spelled out. 'It's a German name, but you wouldn't know he was German. He's been here since

38

he was eight. Are you *sure* you've never met him?'

'Quite sure, but I'm eagerly awaiting the opportunity.'

'He's not a suspect, is he?' Lucy asked anxiously, remembering what Jonah had said about the murderer being one of the bursar's own colleagues.

'Not unless he's solved the problem of how to be in two places at the same time. He apparently spent the day blamelessly escorting students on a field trip. We'll have to check it out, but on the face of it there's no reason to suspect he could be involved.'

'That's good. It'd have been a bit awkward if my Mam had had to help you investigate him, especially seeing as half the university think she and Martin are having an affair!'

'You can't be serious?'

'Oh yes, I am. Martin and Peter have this really weird relationship-'

'Hang on! I thought you said people thought Martin was having an affair with *Our Bernie*?'

'Yes. That's right. As I was saying: Peter and Martin have got this sort of standing joke that Martin is madly in love with Mam and always trying to seduce her away from Peter. They pretend that they've got a bet on whether or not Martin will succeed in persuading her to run off with him. I don't know how it all started; it's been going on since I was seven.'

'And your mam goes along with it?'

'Oh yes! She finds it amusing to think that people suspect her and Martin of having an adulterous relationship when there's nothing in it at all. It's completely ludicrous. It just goes to show what dirty minds people have got. I mean, for a start Martin's eight years younger than Mam and his mother's an old friend of hers. It would be like your Nathan falling for one of Margaret's friends!'

'I shall certainly look forward to meeting this Martin,' Jonah said, his face clouding momentarily at the mention of his late wife's name. 'I will need to interview him about this case, because he was on the other end of the phone, talking to the victim and the chief suspects only a short time before the crime was committed.'

'I don't suppose you're allowed to tell me about it?' Lucy asked, curious to know what had happened, but well aware that what Jonah and her mother did in working hours was confidential and could not be discussed at home.

'Only as much as we're telling the general public; which is that the death of the bursar of Lichfield College occurred at lunch time today in a hotel on the outskirts of Oxford where he was attending a meeting with other senior members of staff from the college, and that we are treating the death as suspicious.'

6 THE ATTENDEES

After they had finished their evening meal, which Jonah referred to as 'dinner' but Bernie insisted on calling 'tea', he returned to the subject of the notes which Jessica Stevens had made and which Bernie had inveigled out of her.

'Don't you think you might as well leave it to the morning?' Bernie asked, looking up at the clock and reflecting on how short the evenings were when you took into account the length of time it took to go through the routine of getting Jonah ready for bed. 'You ought to take some time off to relax.'

'You told me it was bed time reading,' Jonah insisted. 'If I promise to go to bed like a good boy afterwards, will you show them to me?'

'Very well,' Bernie conceded, adopting the tones of a nanny who has just given way against her better judgement, 'But Lucy is to come in prompt at nine to give you your shower and there are to be no arguments. You've promised Andy that you'll be there for an early start tomorrow, remember.'

'OK. OK,' Jonah grumbled. 'Stop pontificating and let's get started.'

He led the way into the small study adjacent to his bedroom, where he and Bernie would be able to discuss his work without being overheard. Bernie took out the two A4 sheets, which Jessica had handed over to her, and smoothed them out in front of Jonah. He looked down and read out what was written there.

'*TC. Motive: funding for computer lab. Opportunity: yes, found body.*'

'Presumably "TC" is Tom Carrington,' Bernie said, 'typing the information into her computer. I wonder what Jessica means about the computer lab.'

'Make a note to ask Dr Carrington about it,' Jonah instructed. 'It looks as if she went through all the people at the Awayday, writing down what motive they might have for killing the bursar and whether or not they could have done it. The next is "BG". Presumably that's Dr Greenhalgh.'

'Well, there aren't any others with those initials.'

'*BG. Motive: blackmail, question mark. Student visa scam, question mark. Opportunity: question mark. Not in dining room.* I suppose that means that Dr Greenhalgh had left the dining room before Jessica got there. Does that fit in with what the other witnesses told us?'

'Of course, I haven't got all the notes that Andy took away,' Bernie pointed out, checking through computer files, 'but that doesn't contradict anything as far as I can see.'

'And what d'you think she means by "student visa scam"?'

'Well, I suppose she could have been involved in some sort of racket getting visas for non-EU citizens to come into the country as students when they weren't really. I've never been involved in dealing with it, but I know that universities have to provide confirmation to the Border Agency or the Home Office or someone that they are bona fide students on a real course. If she was somehow getting people in by falsifying that declaration, she would be a potential target for blackmail if anyone found out.'

'Right. So that's something to look into. We'll need access to Mr Bridgefield's flat and his room in college so we can check out whether he left anything in writing about whatever hold he had over Dr Greenhalgh – if any. It may all be a figment of young Jessica's fevered imagination.'

'Possibly, but I don't really think her imagination is fevered exactly. She seems quite level-headed to me. Apart, that is, from her idolisation of you as the great hero fighting to succeed against all the odds!'

'*FG. Motive: question mark. Opportunity: where did he go when he left the dining room?*' Jonah resumed, ignoring her. 'What d'you think she means by that? Do we know about him leaving the dining room?'

'According to Andy's notes, he admits to going to see the bursar in the meeting room after he'd had lunch,' Bernie answered, after checking. 'But he says that he left him alive and well at about ten past one. I suppose Jessica must have met him coming out of the dining room as she went in.'

'Good. So at least we haven't got any inconsistency so far. It looks as if the Master could have done it – unless anyone else saw the bursar after one-ten. Tell you what: will you draw up a timetable of who was where throughout the lunch break, ready for tomorrow? Then we'll be able to see at a glance if people's stories don't agree with one another. Now let's see … *AL. Motive: exclamation mark, exclamation mark, exclamation mark.* What d'you think she means by that?'

'I can only assume that she thinks Ann Lambert has reasons for wanting Anthony Bridgefield out of the way.'

'Precisely what I was thinking. Make a note to ask her about that.'

'Do you mean a note to ask Jessica what she means or to ask the dean why she would want to do away with the bursar?'

'Both. *Opportunity: question mark.* It looks as if Jessica

43

didn't know where Dr Lambert was during the lunch hour. Do we have any idea?'

'Not that I can tell. Andy interviewed her, but I didn't get the notes typed up. We can check with him tomorrow.'

'OK. So, moving on. *CB. Motive: not "people like us" question mark exclamation mark. Opportunity: question mark.* Do I gather young Jessica thinks the Old Boy is a snob?'

'Looks like it. And I'd say she's got him exactly right there. Did you see his face when he heard my scouse accent? But surely you wouldn't do away with someone just because you thought they were vulgar?'

'Perhaps he thought the bursar was lowering the tone of the college!' joked Jonah. 'He must care about the place or he wouldn't be president of the old boys association.'

'In that case, it's a good thing I got out of my job at St Luke's before anyone noticed that they'd allowed the working class to invade the SCR!'

'*DO. Motive: wants more money for marketing. Opportunity: sneaked back from his telecon, question mark. SS. Motive: divine retribution, exclamation mark.* Why would the chaplain want to bring retribution down on the bursar?'

'Search me,' Bernie shrugged. 'Although I do get the impression that the bursar wasn't a particularly nice person. And nobody really seemed that upset that he was dead.'

'And finally we come to *GW*. That's the Chemistry tutor, isn't it? *GW. Motive: wants more money for accommodation, question mark. Opportunity: question mark.* Not a lot there.'

'No,' Bernie agreed. 'It looks as if all we've really learnt from these notes is that there is something sinister about the relationship between the dean, and the bursar but we don't even know what sort of thing that is.'

'Whatever it is, Jessica considered it worthy of three exclamation marks, which must make it worth following up. And on the subject of exclamation mark-provoking relationships: why didn't you tell me you knew Martin Riess?'

'What d'you mean?' Bernie asked, puzzled.

'The don on the end of the phone at the Awayday: Lucy tells me he's a family friend.'

'Yes – but surely you knew that? Come on, Jonah, he's round here so often, you must have met him.'

'No. I'm sure I haven't. I do remember you talking about this Martin, who's a geologist and keeps a narrow boat on the canal, but I never knew his surname and I absolutely never met him. It was only when Lucy told me he was at Lichfield that I twigged he was the same Martin as we'd been hearing about this afternoon.'

'Well, I'm sorry. I wasn't trying to conceal anything. I just assumed you knew. It doesn't matter, does it? I mean, I don't need to declare a conflict of interest or anything?'

'No, I shouldn't think so. He's not a suspect, and it isn't as if he's *my* friend. Now, explain what Lucy meant when she said that you are pretending to be having an affair with him.'

Bernie laughed.

'Oh dear! You're going to think we're all very childish. It's all Peter's fault really. He doesn't usually like academics, as you may have gathered'

'Present company excepted,' Jonah put in.

'I'm not even sure about that. Anyway, against all the odds, he and Martin really hit it off and they somehow started up this ridiculous fiction that Martin was madly in love with me. And then, later, Martin and I got thrown together a lot, one way and another. I got a discipline-hopping grant to work with him applying mathematical methods to his earth sciences research; and we're both on a university committee for promoting the recruitment of more working class students. So, anyway, people at the university saw us and started putting two and two together and making five.'

'And you didn't rush to deny it?'

'That would only have made them all the more convinced there was something going on. Anyway, it was fun seeing them all trying to look as if they weren't thinking what they *were* thinking. And nobody who really knows us was taken in for a minute. You must meet Martin. You'll like him, I guarantee.'

'I intend to. He's on my list to be interviewed. I will now be paying particular attention to his attitude towards you. And I warn you: I'll be reporting back to old Peter, if I think you've not been entirely honest about this relationship!'

'Do your worst,' Bernie laughed. 'There's nothing in it, I promise you. If Martin does have a crush on anyone in this family, it's Lucy. Of course, I don't suppose she told you about all the afternoons they spend together aboard his boat, or about how he's been teaching her to speak German?'

'Lucy!' Jonah exclaimed in mock dismay. 'But she's *my* girlfriend! I must say, you could have been a bit more diplomatic about the way you broke the news to me that she's seeing someone else behind my back. Haven't you ever heard of letting people down gently?'

He caught Bernie's eye and they both burst out laughing.

'And talking about Lucy,' Bernie said, picking up the sheets of paper containing Jessica's notes and putting them away. 'She'll be here any minute to help put you to bed.'

Right on cue, Lucy came in. She came up behind Jonah and put her arms round his shoulders, as she had done on so many occasions ever since, at the age of nine, she had first visited him in hospital and had it explained to her that he could feel nothing below that level of his body. She pressed her cheek against his and spoke softly in his ear.

'Time to get started on your bedtime routine, I'm afraid.'

7 THE PARALYSED MAN

The alarm went off in Jonah's room at six the following morning. Lucy reached out from the narrow bed under the window, where she was sleeping, and switched it off. She groaned silently as she got out and stumbled across the room in the semi-darkness to check that Jonah was awake. She gently rolled him over to face her.

'It's morning,' she said, trying not to sound as reluctant as she felt towards the prospect of getting up. 'I'll just have a shower and get dressed and then I'll be back.'

She disappeared into the adjacent bathroom, leaving Jonah reflecting on what a nuisance it was that his spinal injury made everything so laborious and take so long. He heard sounds of movement overhead, which told him that Bernie and Peter were also awake and preparing for the day ahead. He was very lucky to have such friends, but it was frustrating in the extreme to be so dependent on them.

Lucy returned, dressed in her school uniform: black trousers, white shirt and a green and yellow striped tie. She expertly transferred him into a sitting posture in the bed, carefully positioning the backrest and pillows to ensure that his body was well supported.

The door opened and her stepfather appeared, wearing

a green towelling dressing gown and carrying a plastic cup with a long straw protruding from the lid.

'Your morning tea, milord,' he said, imitating the tones of a PG Wodehouse butler. Peter Johns was a retired Detective Inspector, who had once worked alongside Jonah. Since Jonah's injury, they had become close friends and, indeed, it had been Peter's idea for Jonah to move into their home after his wife died. He advanced into the room and put down the cup on a tray table next to the bed. He swivelled the table round to bring it into a position from which Jonah could reach the straw with his mouth.

'I'll leave you to it,' he said, addressing Lucy. 'Let me know if you need any help with lifting or anything.'

'OK,' she nodded, 'but I'm sure I'll be able to manage. The new hoist is really easy to use.'

Jonah sipped his tea. He knew that starting the day with a warm drink was important for keeping his digestive system working correctly. Passing a bowel motion before leaving for work each morning was essential in order to avoid risking the embarrassment of an unscheduled evacuation during the day. Leaving sufficient time for that tedious but necessary process was the main reason that he needed to start getting up so early.

Lucy rolled up her sleeves and busied herself with getting ready the equipment that would enable her to take him into the bathroom for his morning ablutions, proud to be considered mature enough to take responsibility for his welfare. She had long since got over any embarrassment that she might have felt over dealing with his most intimate needs and cheerfully performed tasks which most of her school friends would have considered quite disgusting. Once Jonah had finished his drink, she started on the business of removing his pyjamas, having first disconnected and emptied the urine bag, which was attached to the side of the bed. Then she continued working methodically through his early morning routine.

'Can I help at all?' Bernie appeared in the bedroom, just as Lucy was transferring Jonah back on to his bed after the ninety minutes or so that he had spent in the bathroom. 'It's getting late, if you're still aiming to be in the office by half past eight.'

'I can manage,' Lucy argued, reluctant to relinquish her position as Jonah's prime carer for the week.

'I know you can, love, but it'll be quicker with two and we've got a murder to solve.'

'Just cut the cackle and get on with it,' Jonah growled, annoyed with himself for not having kept to the schedule that he had set himself and anxious at the prospect of arriving late to work. He was determined never to allow himself to perform his job less well than his able-bodied colleagues.

Bernie stepped forward, and she and Lucy proceeded to put on his clothes, working quickly but taking care not to damage his skin by rubbing the fabric against it too roughly, and checking that there were no folds in the cloth that would cause chafing. Then they transferred him into the electric wheelchair and Lucy placed his left hand on to the controls. Jonah experienced the usual feeling of relief at being back in control of his own movements after a night of complete dependence on others.

Bernie bent down and put on his tie, adjusting it carefully, knowing that he set great store by his smart appearance. At the same time, Lucy combed his hair and brushed a few flecks of dandruff off his collar. Then they both stepped back to allow him to manoeuvre the chair out of the bedroom, through the study and out into the hall. They followed him to the kitchen where Peter was sitting down at the large table eating his breakfast.

Jonah joined him and Lucy sat down at his side. She poured cereal into a bowl and started spoon-feeding him. Without speaking, Peter poured more tea into the plastic cup, which Bernie had brought through with them from the bedroom, and placed it within Jonah's reach. For several minutes nobody spoke. They were all anxiously watching the clock and concentrating on completing the morning routine so that Jonah would be in time for his early meeting. They all knew how much he hated being late for anything.

Breakfast over, Jonah headed for the front door, but Bernie intercepted him, insisting that he wait while she brushed his teeth.

'For goodness sake!' he exploded, uncharacteristically giving way to his frustrations. 'Why do you have to insist on treating me like a two-year-old? One day can't make any difference-'

'No, but if we let it go for one day, just because we're a bit late, then it'll happen again and again and before you know it you'll have serious problems,' Bernie argued, standing her ground. 'You know that mouth hygiene is important for your general well-being.'

'Well, if it does cause any problems, that's up to me. I'm not a child. It's my decision what I do with my own body.' Jonah was angry with himself for having set an unrealistic start time for the day and was consequently annoyed at being thwarted in his efforts to keep to the schedule regardless.

'Actually, it's not,' Peter said calmly, breaking the awkward silence, which had followed this outburst. 'If you develop a chest infection as a result of inhaling some rubbish that's caught on your teeth or develop ulcers in your mouth or whatever, it'll be *us* that have extra work to do sorting you out afterwards.'

Jonah turned his chair to face Peter, who was still sitting at the table gathering up the cereal bowls in readiness for the washing up. His face was thunderous and he seemed about to bawl him out. Then he changed his mind and turned back towards Bernie.

'Oh very well,' he said ungraciously. 'I can see I'll get no peace until I give in. Just get on with it will you?'

A few minutes later they were both in the people

carrier heading out of the drive and on their way to the meeting with Sergeant Lepage. Jonah was still angry – more with himself than anyone else – and maintaining a stony silence. Bernie tried to think of something to say to restore normality.

'I've been thinking,' she ventured at last. 'I assume you'll be wanting to interview the dons from Lichfield again?'

'Yes,' Jonah replied shortly.

'I thought,' Bernie continued, wondering whether she would have done better to have kept her peace and waited for him to come out of his foul mood through the passage of time, 'maybe it would be a good idea to contact the ever-helpful Jessica before we go, and ask her to organise a room for them to meet you in.'

'I'd rather see them in their own rooms. You can learn a lot about someone by seeing how they organise themselves and what sorts of things they collect around them.'

'But Lichfield is one of the old colleges,' Bernie explained, now wishing heartily that she had not embarked on this particular line of thought, 'so the tutors' rooms are liable to be at the top of inconveniently narrow and winding staircases.'

'Which I won't be able to get up,' Jonah finished for her with bitterness in his voice.

'Yes,' Bernie admitted. 'That's why I thought …'

There was a long silence. Bernie hardly dared to breathe for fear of adding to his feelings of anger, frustration and inadequacy. Then Jonah spoke, his voice sounding strangely small.

'I'm sorry, Bernie,' he said penitently. 'Old Peter's quite right: I had no business claiming that you don't have the right to expect me to look after myself properly. And I was out of order taking my frustrations out on you.'

Bernie sighed with relief.

'Oh Jonah! If we're going to continue to spend the best

JUDY FORD

part of twenty-four hours a day together, five days a week we're going to have to get used to the idea that sometimes we're going to get on each other's nerves. The main thing is whenever we fall out to know how to kiss and make up afterwards.'

'And you're quite right,' Jonah went on, as if he hadn't heard, 'it's a good idea of yours to get Jessica to arrange an interview room for us at Lichfield. Give her a ring as soon as we get to the office and ask her to get it set up for this morning from, say, ten thirty.'

'OK. I'll do that,' Bernie agreed, as they turned into the car park, relieved that Jonah seemed to have become his usual calm and business-like self again, 'But it'll have to wait for a little while: I doubt if Jessica'll be in college before nine.'

'What time is it now?'

'Twenty-nine minutes past eight,' Bernie replied, parking the car and turning off the engine. 'I reckon Andy'll just about have time to get the kettle on before you arrive.'

'Which means that it was exceptionally stupid of me making such a fuss about being late,' Jonah commented, as Bernie made her way round to the back to help him out.

She fixed the ramp then stepped into the vehicle to release the straps that held him secure. As she undid the last fastening, she bent over him, took his head gently in her hands and kissed his face.

'I said we had to learn to kiss and make up,' she said tenderly, 'and that means not going on about things afterwards either.'

'You know,' Jonah observed, trying to make a joke of the situation in order to avoid becoming emotional, 'I'm going to be tempted to lose my temper with you more often, if this is the result!'

'Don't push your luck,' Bernie warned, smiling. 'I remember, when I was a child, Father O'Malley telling us that he wouldn't give absolution to anyone who kept coming to confession week after week with the same sin, because you had to have a sincere intention to amend your life in order to qualify.'

'My father was a Baptist minister, remember. We don't hold with all that papist confession stuff!'

'Alright then, remember what St Paul said to the Romans about not sinning all the more so as to increase the amount of God's grace in forgiving it. Is that protestant enough for you?'

'I repent in dust and ashes!' Jonah declared, in an extremely unrepentant voice, clearly back on his usual cheerful form.

When they entered the office, they saw Sergeant Andrew Lepage seated at the table in the centre of the room with a laptop computer in front of him. A document was displayed on the large screen on the wall in front of him. He looked up as they came in.

'I've got all those interview notes in the computer, sir,' he said. 'Shall I transfer them across to your machine?'

Jonah looked intently at the document on the screen.

'I thought, we agreed you were going to scan in the handwritten notes.'

'Yes, I know sir,' Andy agreed apologetically, 'but I thought it would be better to have them as Word documents, so that we can search them and things. I was at a bit of a loose end last night, so I thought I might as well type them up. I've also made a table summarising where everyone said they were at five minute intervals through the lunch hour,' he added.

'Are you trying to impress me with your inordinate diligence?'

'No sir. I just didn't have anything much else to do and I thought it would help us get on.'

'He's only doing what you would have done at his age,' Bernie pointed out, anxious not to give Jonah another opportunity for reflecting on the way his paralysis was impacting on his ability to do his job in the indefatigable way that he would have liked to have done it.

'Yes I know,' Jonah sighed, thinking to himself that this was what he would have done at any time up to the day he was shot and not only when he was as young as his colleague. 'Well done, Andy. Why don't you take us through what you've got there while Our Bernie makes us all a cup of tea?'

'Well sir,' Andy began, moving the mouse to bring up a spreadsheet on the screen, 'I think it'll be easiest if we start from my table. I've got the time down the left-hand column, then the name of each of the suspects across the top and a final column for comments. I've highlighted, in yellow, places where people disagree and, in pink, where someone might have had an opportunity to do the murder.'

He looked up anxiously.

'Very systematic,' Jonah said encouragingly. 'Carry on.'

'I've started at twelve twenty-five, when Damien Ogden leaves the meeting to go to his teleconference. He left the meeting room and went down to the bar, where he was seen arriving and on and off during the lunch hour, but he could easily have slipped back to the room at some point, killed Bridgefield and slipped back to the bar. He gave me the name of the person who chaired the teleconference. I was thinking of getting on to them today to find out whether he was an active participant throughout or if there were times when he could have fitted in a bit of strangulation on the side.'

'Good. You do that. Go on.'

'Now we come to twelve thirty,' resumed Andy, 'when the morning session finished and everyone made their way to the dining room.'

'Except for Jessica Stevens, the secretary,' put in Jonah. 'According to Dr Carrington, she stayed behind to put up flip charts.'

'That's right, sir. She says that it was about ten to one by the time she left the room. She had the key card, which the hotel had given to the group, so after she'd closed the door the room was locked and nobody else could get in. She says that she met Bridgefield as she was on the way down to the dining room and handed it over to him so that he could get in and load up his presentation. She called in at the Ladies on the way down and thinks it might have been after one by the time she got to the dining room. But, going back to the timetable, the others all went down together and sat at the same table to have lunch. Dr Carrington finished first and went off somewhere.'

'According to him, he went to the bar and sat there with his laptop, checking his emails,' Jonah put in, looking at the notes that Bernie had entered up on his computer the previous day. He claims to have tried the door of the meeting room first and found it locked.'

'So that probably means he got there between when Jessica left the room and when Mr Bridgefield got back there with the key card,' surmised Andy. 'Presumably he must have missed meeting her while she was in the Ladies. So let's put him down as leaving the dining room at, say, twelve fifty and getting to the bar at twelve fifty-five. Did he say whether he saw Ogden there?'

Jonah consulted his notes again.

'Yes. He noticed him sitting in the corner when he arrived, but says he wasn't in view from where he sat down to check his emails, which presumably means that Ogden couldn't see him either.'

'Ogden didn't say anything about Carrington being in the bar,' Andy observed. 'So it's a good bet he didn't notice him come in – always assuming that he *did* go to the bar.'

'I notice that you've got both Ogden and Carrington highlighted in pink for the period from twelve fifty-five to one thirty.'

'That's right, sir. That's from when Bridgefield got to the room to when Carrington claims he found his body. What you've just told me only confirms that either of them could have slipped into the room during that time without being noticed.'

'So we need to check out whether either of them had a reason to want him dead. According to Jessica's notes, they both had things that they wanted more money for and Bridgefield held the college purse strings, but I can't see that as a motive for murder.'

'Apart from anything else,' Bernie put in, unable to resist the temptation to join in the discussion, although she knew it was not part of her job to have ideas about the case, 'it probably wouldn't make any difference. Funding for a new computer lab, for example, would have to get through a committee; it wouldn't be just down to the bursar.'

'Precisely,' Jonah agreed, 'so all that Jessica's notes tell us is that these two didn't see eye to eye with Bridgefield, which may or may not be symptomatic of a more general dislike of the man. Go on, Andy, what happened next?'

'Dr Greenhalgh says she left the dining room just after Dr Carrington and went for a walk in the grounds alone. She doesn't remember meeting anyone else out there and nobody saw her until one twenty-five when she came back in and found Mr Brampton finishing a cigarette by the entrance.'

'So she could have slipped back inside, nipped up to the room, strangled Bridgefield and sneaked off outside again,' Jonah mused.

'But how did Beverley Greenhalgh know that the bursar was going to be in the meeting room?' asked Bernie. 'She left the dining room before he did. Had he already told the others that he was going to go back to sort out his presentation?'

'He may have done; or she may just have gone back to the room – to get something perhaps – and found him there by chance. According to Jessica, Bridgefield may have been blackmailing Greenhalgh over something to do with student visas, which makes her the first person we've found with any sort of viable motive for killing him.'

'That sounds interesting, sir. Would you like me to contact the Border Agency?'

'Not just yet. I'd like to ask Dr Greenhalgh for her side of the story first. Go on with your timetable. Did anyone else leave the dining room before Bridgefield did?'

'No. He left next, picked up the key card from Jessica on the way out of the dining room and went upstairs. It's a bit strange that Dr Carrington didn't meet him on the way back down to the bar.'

'Not if one of them went in the lift and the other used the stairs,' Jonah pointed out. 'So that leaves Lambert, Sutcliffe, Grainger, Brampton and Weldon still in the dining room.'

'Grainger went out shortly after Bridgefield. He says that he followed Bridgefield up to the meeting room and had a few words with him before going back downstairs to look for Jessica. He said he had some college business to discuss with Bridgefield and some appointments that he wanted Jessica to organise for him in his diary. He claims that he left Bridgefield alive at about ten past one. Miss Stevens remembers him coming into the dining room just as she was finishing her lunch.'

'Which suggests that either she eats very quickly or we have a few minutes of Dr Grainger's time unaccounted for,' observed Jonah, 'but maybe he nipped to the Gents on the way to find Jessica and didn't mention it to you.'

'Anyway, sir, it looks like he was the last person to see Bridgefield alive – if he *was* still alive when he left him. After that, nobody admits to having been in the meeting room until Dr Carrington found the body at about half past one. Reverend Sutcliffe and Dr Lambert say that they left the dining room together and went and sat on the easy chairs in the hotel reception area; Dr Weldon stayed in the dining room until it was time to go back up to the meeting room; and Brampton went outside for a smoke. They all say they didn't go upstairs again until it was time to start the afternoon session.'

'But, apart from Sutcliffe and Lambert, who were together, any of them *could* have nipped upstairs, strangled the bursar and slipped away again.'

'Yes sir.'

'You talked to some of the hotel staff. Did they confirm what the dons said they were doing?'

'As far as I can tell, sir. The receptionist remembers seeing Reverend Sutcliffe and Dr Lambert sitting together, but she wasn't there for the whole time, because she went off to her own lunch and a colleague took over for a while, so they couldn't be sure that neither of them went off anywhere for a few minutes. Some of the staff in the dining room remember Weldon sitting on his own drinking a cup of coffee after the others had left, but they couldn't swear to him having been there for the whole time either. I couldn't find anyone who had seen Mr Brampton or Dr Greenhalgh outside, but that's probably just because none of the staff went out into the grounds.'

'Did you check whether there were any gardeners or security staff outside? Or any CC-TV cameras?'

'No.'

'Right. Well you go back to the hotel and see if there are any, while we go to Lichfield and probe the dons on the subject of why they might have wanted to kill the bursar.'

8 THE BOTANY TUTOR

When Bernie and Jonah arrived at Lichfield College, they found Jessica Stevens waiting for them in the porters' lodge. She led them across the quad to a door which opened into a small vestibule, beyond which was a room containing half a dozen tables, each with two chairs facing towards a whiteboard which covered most of one of the walls.

'This is the Pendleton Seminar Room,' Jessica informed them. 'I've booked it out for the whole day. There's water over there.'

She pointed towards a table on which stood four bottles, two labelled 'Lichfield college pure sparkling mineral water' and the others entitled 'Lichfield College pure still mineral water', and about a dozen glasses.

'Would you like me to get you tea or coffee?'

'No thank you. The water will do fine.'

'This is my telephone number if you want anything,' Jessica went on, handing a piece of paper to Bernie. 'My room is just across the quad, so it's no bother for me to get things for you.'

'Thank you. Perhaps you could act as our runner and fetch people here when we want to talk to them.'

'Yes of course. I'd be delighted.' Jessica's eyes lit up at the prospect of helping with the investigation. 'Are you ready now? Who would you like me to send first?'

'Give us five minutes and then we'd like to see Dr Greenhalgh.'

'Are you seeing her first because of what I wrote?' Jessica asked anxiously. 'I don't have any real evidence; it was just something I overheard and I probably got it all wrong.'

'And what exactly did you overhear?' Jonah asked with interest, while Bernie made notes on her computer.

'You have to go through my room to get to the bursar's office. There's a suite of four rooms for college admin. Mine's the first and everyone has to go through it to get to the others. So I'm a sort of gatekeeper for the bursar and his assistant and the Master. He has an office there, as well as his lodgings where he lives and where he does his academic work. One day Bev – I mean Dr Greenhalgh – came in with an invoice that she needed the bursar to authorise. As she was coming out, I heard him say something about how valuable international students were and had Bev made up her mind about his proposition yet? And then Bev said something to him that I didn't hear and he said in a nasty way that he might have to speak to the UK Border Agency if she didn't co-operate. It was probably nothing. I didn't think anything of it at the time. It was only when Mr Bridgefield was killed and I was trying to think of all the possible reasons someone might have for doing away with him that it occurred to me that it could have been blackmail. You won't tell Bev that I told you about it, will you?'

'Don't worry. I won't say a word to anyone about what you wrote. Now, could you ask her to come here?'

Bernie rearranged the furniture so that she and Jonah could sit across a table from the interviewees. Then she opened one of the bottles and poured glasses of water for the first suspect and for herself and filled Jonah's plastic cup, which she placed in a holder attached to his chair. She sat down on his left and put the notebook computer down on the table in front of her.

'Jess said you wanted to see me,' Beverley Greenhalgh said, entering the room a few minutes later. 'I'm not sure what I can add to what I told your sergeant yesterday.'

At the sound of her accent, Bernie looked up enquiringly and studied her face. The don was in her mid-fifties – about the same age as Bernie – with dark curly hair, showing grey at the roots, and brown eyes. She wore jeans and an open necked shirt. Large pendulous earrings glittered as she moved her head.

'We'd like to know a bit more about the background to this case,' Jonah explained. 'So, for example, you were at the Awayday in your capacity as tutor for overseas students. Can you tell me what exactly that involves?'

'Well, I work with the marketing department – Damien Ogden and his team – to promote the college overseas; and I oversee the selection process when they apply; but my main work is as the point of contact after students arrive to make sure that they're OK. For some of them it's quite a culture shock coming to Britain and they find it hard to fit in.'

'I see. And I suppose your work will sometimes bring you into contact with the bursar? You'll have expenses that he'll have to authorise and a budget to agree and so on?'

'Yes.' Dr Greenhalgh replied shortly, without elaborating.

'So presumably you got to know Mr Bridgefield quite well?'

'Not really. We were colleagues; that's all.'

'Can you think of anyone who might want to kill him? Did he have any enemies?'

'He wasn't exactly a pleasant person, but it's a long way between disliking someone and strangling them to death.'

'In what way was he unpleasant?'

'Oh, I don't know: he just seemed slimy, well oily, I

suppose.'

Jonah continued to look at her enquiringly, so Dr Greenhalgh marshalled her thoughts and began again.

'He fancied himself as an old-fashioned ladies man,' she said at last. 'He was always opening doors and pulling out chairs for them and paying silly compliments on their appearance. I just found it irritating, but it's surprising how many women fell for it. I understand that when he was younger he left a whole string of broken hearts behind him. After his wife finally got shot of him, he moved in with Ann Lambert-'

'The dean?'

'That's right. They stayed together for years – I can't think what she saw in him. And then a couple of months ago, he left her – just like that!'

'Like what, exactly?'

'He just told her one day that he was moving out and setting up home with Martin Reiss's post doc.'

'Penny Green?' Bernie asked.

'That's right. Do you know her?'

'No, but I do know Martin, and he's mentioned her. She sounded very level headed and sensible. I wasn't expecting to hear that she was having a liaison with an older man.'

'That's what he was like. He somehow managed to make all sorts of people do things you wouldn't expect.'

'Such as contemplating murder?' Jonah suggested.

'So it would seem,' Dr Greenhalgh agreed drily.

'Do you have any idea what caused the rift between Mr Bridgefield and Dr Lambert?'

'He just decided to trade her in for a newer model, I think,' Dr Greenhalgh answered dismissively. 'She was pretty cut up about it, but at least she owned the house and everything – not like when he got divorced and his wife had to move out because they'd been living in a college house, which came with *his* job.'

'Have you ever heard of Mr Bridgefield trying to

blackmail anyone,' Jonah asked.

'How do you mean, blackmail?'

'If he found out something that someone else wouldn't want to be widely known – someone fiddling their expenses, for instance. Would he threaten to tell if they didn't do something for him in return?'

'What are you implying?' Dr Greenhalgh asked suspiciously. 'Are you suggesting that he had some sort of hold over me?'

'I don't know. Did he?'

'No, of course not!'

'Getting back to the events of yesterday,' Jonah said, moving on to safer ground, 'you went for a walk in the hotel grounds after lunch: did you meet anyone at all while you were outside?'

'No.'

'And when you came back in: Mr Brampton says you met him on the hotel steps – is that right?'

'Yes. He was smoking just outside the entrance. I told him that it was time to go back. The Master likes to keep meetings to time.'

'And then you both went inside and back up to the meeting room?'

'That's right. He stubbed out his cigarette and put it in the bin just outside the door, and then we both went inside.'

'And that was at what time?'

'Well, I came in when I saw it was twenty-five past, so it must have been between twenty-five past and half past one.'

'Good. That fits in with what Mr Brampton said. I think we're just about finished with our questions for the moment. There's just one last thing ...'

'Yes?'

'I was wondering about the international students that you look after. Do they ever have trouble getting visas to stay in Britain?'

'Sometimes,' Dr Greenhalgh said cautiously, looking from Jonah to Bernie and back again.

'And then, do you help them with their applications?'

'Of course we always do what we can to help. Often it's just a matter of making sure they've ticked the right boxes on the forms.'

'And you've never been tempted to help when someone wanted to stay when they didn't have a legitimate reason for doing so? A student who'd finished his course and didn't want to go home, for example?'

'No. That would be illegal.' Dr Greenhalgh looked Jonah steadily in the eye.

'Yes. Of course. Well, thank you for your time; we won't keep you any longer.'

'I've just got one question,' Bernie put in unexpectedly. 'I was wondering about your accent: is it Blackburn or Burnley?'

'Darwen.' Beverley Greenhalgh smiled for the first time that morning. 'So you were very close. I'm surprised you recognised it; every time I go home they all tell me I speak "dead posh" since I moved to Oxford.'

'Oh, you can take the girl out of Lancashire, but you can't take Lancashire out of the girl!' Bernie declared, smiling. 'And no prizes for guessing where I come from,' she added, in the exaggerated Liverpool accent which she frequently adopted for effect. 'I'm surprised we've never met before – while I was a tutor at St Luke's. I'd have expected someone to have pointed you out to me as a kindred spirit. There aren't so very many women from THE NORTH in Oxford.'

'My wife came from Horwich,' Jonah said, becoming unusually conversational now that he had finished the formal interview. 'That can't be far from your neck of the woods.'

'Not far at all,' Beverley Greenhalgh smiled, 'but I suspect she'd have been persona non grata in our house: I bet she's a Bolton Wanderers supporter!'

'Strangely enough, no,' Bernie answered, before Jonah could reply. 'Her game was rugby league and she followed Wigan.'

'And I gather from your use of the past tense,' Beverley said, looking solicitously at Jonah, 'that she is no longer with us.'

'She died about two months ago,' Jonah answered. He spoke calmly, but avoided meeting Beverley's eye.

'I'm sorry.'

There seemed to be nothing more to be said. Beverley muttered something incoherent about leaving them to get on with their enquiries and left the room. Bernie consulted briefly with Jonah and then went across the quad to ask Jessica to summon the next interviewee.

9 THE DEAN

Ann Lambert, the Dean, was about ten years younger than Botany Fellow Beverley Greenhalgh and created a very different impression when she entered the room. She was small and slight, with long, fair hair falling loose down her back and wide blue eyes surrounded by thick black eyelashes. Her lips were glossy red and her eyebrows were thin and arched. Her ears were adorned by small gold studs with a diamond set in each. She wore a blouse with a low neckline and a close-fitting skirt, which clung, to her legs.

Jonah was struck by how vulnerable she looked, like a child in a strange place. Bernie speculated in her mind on how long it must take her each morning to apply her makeup.

'Thank you for coming, Dr Lambert,' Jonah greeted her. 'Please take a seat; we'll try not to keep you any longer than necessary.'

'Ann, please,' she replied, looking directly at him, wide-eyed. 'Formality makes me feel rather nervous.'

'Very well, if that's what you prefer. I just want to cross-check what you told Sergeant Lepage yesterday with what the others said in *their* statements and then I'd like to ask you a bit about Mr Bridgefield's background – to get an idea of why someone might have wanted to kill him.'

'Of course. I understand.' Ann favoured Jonah with another nervous smile.

'You said in your statement that you were with the chaplain for the whole of the lunch break, is that right?'

'Yes. We sat next to each other at lunch and then afterwards we went and sat in the lobby together.'

'Talking about college business?'

'No. It was a personal conversation.'

'And you were together right up until you returned to the meeting room at one thirty? You didn't pop to the Ladies, for example?'

'No. We just sat and chatted until it was time to go back to the meeting.'

'Did you talk about your relationship with Mr Bridgefield?' Jonah asked, suddenly more incisive.

'What do you mean?' Ann asked, opening her eyes as if astonished to hear such a suggestion.

'Apparently it was common knowledge that he had been living with you for several years up until a few months ago. I thought that you might have been seeking advice and support at a difficult time.'

'Simon has been a great help,' Ann admitted, 'but that wasn't what we were talking about. That was personal and of no relevance to Anthony's death.'

'Alright. Now tell me about your relationship with Mr Bridgefield. It had been going on for, how long?'

'He moved in with me fourteen years ago.'

'And his divorce was thirteen years ago,' Jonah commented, having checked the file before starting the interview. 'Were you expecting him to marry you when that came through?'

'Yes, I suppose I probably did.' Ann said, gazing thoughtfully into the distance as if dreaming of happier times that would never come again.

'So why didn't he?'

67

'It never seemed to be the right time. At least that's how he explained it to me; but with hindsight, I suppose he preferred to have his freedom. And he'd lost a lot of money in the divorce, so he probably didn't want to have another ex-wife making demands on him.'

So you were living together in your house in Jericho?'

'Yes, that's right. I gave the address to your sergeant.'

'So what happened to make you split up?'

'I finally got fed up with the way he couldn't keep his eyes – or his hands – off other women. I told him that he couldn't expect to go off with every new post doc that came along and still be able to come back to my house whenever he chose.'

'Was there any post doc in particular?'

'I suppose someone's told you about Penny Green?'

'I'd like you to tell me. Who's Penny Green?'

'She's working on a research project with Martin Riess. He's in Earth Sciences. He's got a grant from NERC-'

'The Natural Environment Research Council,' Bernie put in, seeing Jonah's blank face.

'Anthony was involved in sorting out the financial side, from the college point of view, and that's how he met her; and of course he had to prove to himself no woman could resist his charms; and they ended up in bed together – predictably enough. She was the last straw, as far as I was concerned, and I told him to get out of my house.'

'So where's he living now?' Jonah asked. 'Did he go back to the college house that he had before he moved in with you?'

'Oh, no! That was strictly for married staff. He had to give that up when he got divorced from Mandy. He made a big show of looking for lodgings and then, all of a sudden, he and Penny were sharing a flat in Kidlington: quite a nice place, much better than she could have afforded on her RA salary.'

'Research Assistant,' Bernie translated helpfully.

'How did you feel about that?'

'I felt sorry for Penny. She's got her whole life in front of her, so why does she want to lumber herself with a parasite like Anthony?'

'Perhaps she just sees it as a temporary measure until the end of the project?'

'I hope for her sake she does. If she's looking for permanence, Anthony's not going to give it to her.'

'I see. Now, you said that Penny was the last straw. That suggests there had been others. Can you give me any names – particularly if any of them might have parted company with him less than amicably?

'I shouldn't think there's a woman in the university that he hasn't tried it on with,' Ann said in a weary voice that somehow suggested that she was speaking more in sorrow than anger. 'And he could be very charming, so I'm sure there were a lot of women who may have been taken in by him – as I was.'

'But can you think of any in particular?' Jonah pressed her gently.

She looked at him wide-eyed and anxious, seeming very vulnerable. She made as if to speak and then appeared to change her mind.

'Was there anyone at the Awayday who might have resented his behaviour?' Jonah suggested. 'Perhaps a man who was jealous of his success with women, for example?'

'Well, I don't really like to say,' Ann murmured, looking Jonah in the eye and then dropping her gaze suddenly. 'I mean – I wouldn't want you to think I was suggesting that they could have been the murderer.'

'Just tell me the facts and let me decide whether they're relevant.'

'Very well,' Ann said, looking up as if she had just come to a decision. 'Well, as I said, Anthony just couldn't resist flirting with every woman he met. It didn't make any difference to him who they were or whether they were unattached or not. He even tried it on with Ruth Sutcliffe, Simon's wife.'

'And what was her reaction?'

'I imagine she gave him pretty short shrift, but, well, you never know: he could be *very* charming.' Ann looked meaningfully at Jonah and then at Bernie.

'Is that what you and Simon were discussing yesterday lunchtime?'

'No!' Ann said, rather too quickly and forcefully. 'It's none of my business what his wife may have got up to. That's something that Simon and Ruth will have to sort out between themselves.'

'Of course.' Jonah agreed equably. 'OK then. What about the women at the Awayday? Beverley Greenhalgh, for example: how did she react to him?'

'I think that Anthony had given her up as a bad job. They've both been at the college for years – longer than me – and I imagine she made it clear, in ways that even Anthony could understand, that she wasn't interested in him. She's very much a career woman and a feminist and doesn't approve of women being treated differently to men.'

'I see. So I suppose she would have tried to avoid coming into contact with him, but presumably she would often have to have dealings with him in her work – with the overseas students, for example?'

'Yes, I suppose she would. As bursar, Anthony had to sign off anything with financial implications for the college.'

'I see.' Jonah paused, knowing that most people would speak rather than allow silence to continue. After a few moments, his patience was rewarded.

'If you're looking for a motive for killing Anthony,' Ann continued darkly, 'you could do worse than to investigate Beverley Greenhalgh's student visa applications.'

'Why's that?' Jonah asked innocently.

'Well,' Ann continued conspiratorially, bending down to put her head close to Jonah's face and looking him straight in the eyes, 'Anthony told me that he thought she was selling visas to students who weren't real students. He didn't have any proof, but he was convinced there was something wrong. Suppose he found his proof and told her he was going to report her?'

'Now that *would* be a motive,' Jonah agreed. 'Thank you very much. We'll look into it. Now, getting back to Anthony and the women at the Awayday, how about Jessica?'

'Well, of course Anthony did his usual God's gift to women routine yesterday. You could see he was expecting her to fall for him, but I'm not sure she was even aware of it. She's so young. I think she probably just thought he was this strange old man who kept insisting on doing things for her and complimenting her. I saw Beverley pulling a face when he congratulated her on having all the meeting papers in order and said that it was a good thing that they had a woman to look after them, because no man would be so organised; but I think Jess just thought he was being old-fashioned.'

'I see. Well, thank you for your time. If you think of anything else that might help us, please ring me.'

Jonah looked towards Bernie and she handed a business card across the table to Ann, who took it in her hand and looked down at it thoughtfully. Then she got up and walked to the door. She opened it and then turned back and favoured Jonah with a shy smile.

'I'm sure we can rely on you to find whoever killed Anthony,' she said. 'I know he wasn't popular, but it's difficult to imagine anyone actually wanting him dead.'

Then she was gone and Bernie and Jonah looked at one another without speaking for a few moments, waiting for the sound of the outer door, which led out to the quadrangle. When they were sure she was out of earshot, Jonah gave a low whistle and raised his eyebrows in a gesture of disbelief.

'Does she really think I'm going to fall for all that wide-eyed innocence and long-suffering martyrdom?' Jonah asked. 'It's as if she's expecting me to be bowled over by her fluttering her eyelashes at me and behaving like the poor defenceless little woman who needs me to protect her against the Big Bad World! I can't think what Anthony Bridgefield saw in her. Give me Beverley Greenhalgh any time!'

'Ah! But you always did go for strong women from the North West,' Bernie teased. 'Naturally you take to Beverley more easily than to Ann; but there *are* men who like to play the role of the great protector standing up for the weaker sex. Richard, for example, might well have felt sorry for poor put-upon Ann.'

'Richard?' Jonah said incredulously. 'You mean *your* Richard? My old boss?'

'Oh yes, he was very old-fashioned in that way. That's what made it so very odd that he asked me to marry him. He'd have been much more comfortable with someone like little Ann Lambert who would presumably have enjoyed being worried over and mollycoddled. I just found it irritating. He did try very hard though to get it right. Unfortunately I didn't realise that until about four years after he died, so I gave him rather a rough time.'

'You still miss him a lot, don't you?' Jonah said, detecting a wistfulness in her voice, which most people would have missed beneath the glib, jokey tone of her comments.

'I'm not sure,' Bernie murmured thoughtfully. 'I wish he was still here to be a father for Lucy – although Peter is the best Dad that she could possibly hope for – and I regret that I didn't really get to know him until after he died, and that consequently I wasn't the wife he deserved to have … but he was only part of my life for four years, so I never got the chance for living with him to become the norm. So I don't know whether "miss" is the right word, but …'

'But it still hurts like hell,' Jonah finished for her. It was a statement, not a question.'

'I wish I could tell you that it gets better as time goes on,' Bernie said regretfully, 'but really it just changes to a different sort of pain.' She paused before continuing, 'I can't imagine what it can be like to lose someone after thirty years of marriage.'

Bernie put out her right hand and laid it on top of Jonah's left; he gripped it as hard as he could between his first two fingers and thumb, which were the only parts of his limbs that he could move. They sat in silence for a minute or two before Bernie shook herself and began busily scanning through the notes she had made of the last two interviews.

'Ann and Beverley gave different accounts of the breakdown in Ann's relationship with Anthony Bridgefield,' she observed. 'Beverley seemed to think that *he* walked out on her, whereas Ann was keen to claim that *she* chucked *him*.'

'Either way, I suspect Ann must have been rather more sore about it than she makes out. She must have resented having given him so many years of her life and then finding she'd been displaced by your friend Martin's post doc.'

'So you think she may have killed him? She doesn't look strong enough to me – either physically or mentally.'

'It's probably mostly put on,' Jonah said dismissively. 'She was deliberately trying to look weak and defenceless to get my sympathy. Don't forget, she's a psychologist by training. She's working on my subconscious.'

'With singularly little effect,' Bernie observed drily. 'I have yet to meet a psychology graduate who knew the first thing about how people's minds work – although I have to admit that yours is more convoluted than most, so it would probably present a challenge to the most seasoned people-watcher. You should, however, not allow your understandable antagonism towards Ann to cloud your judgement. She clearly has a motive for murder, but I'm still not convinced that she's capable of strangling anyone and she has an alibi in the person of the chaplain no less.'

'That is a very good point. I think we ought to talk to him next. Don't forget: he also has a motive for wanting Anthony Bridgefield out of the way, if there's any truth in Ann's hints about the chaplain's wife possibly falling under his spell.'

10 THE SECRETARY

There was a knock at the door and Jessica Stevens came in.

'The Master says you're welcome to have lunch in Hall,' she said, 'at the college's expense.'

'That's very generous of him,' Bernie answered, knowing how much Jonah hated being fed in public, 'but we've got our own sandwiches, thanks.'

'OK, if you're sure. Would you like me to bring you some tea or coffee to go with them?'

'Yes please,' Jonah took charge again. 'Tea would be very nice. And could you find out for me whether the chaplain is in college today? I'd like to speak with him next.'

'But not until after lunch,' Bernie put in firmly, determined to keep Jonah to the strict meal schedule which was important to his continued well-being.

'I'll check for you.'

'Before you go,' Jonah called her back, 'perhaps you could answer a few questions yourself. Sit down, please.'

Jessica sat down opposite him and looked eagerly across the table at the man whom she considered to be something of a hero.

'We've been hearing that Mr Bridgefield fancied himself as a bit of a ladies man and that included making advances on you. Is that true? How did you feel about him?'

Jessica hesitated for a moment before replying.

'Well,' she said at last, 'I wasn't going to say anything, but if you've already been told ...'

Jonah looked at her encouragingly.

'Actually, I thought he was creepy,' Jessica admitted at last. 'A couple of times I ended up sitting next to him in meetings and he used to put his hand on my leg under the table. I made sure yesterday that I sat on the other side of the table from him, but that meant that he kept *looking* at me, all sort of ... I don't know, sort of *suggestive* somehow. I didn't like him. I mean, he was so *old* and still he seemed to expect me to fancy him.'

'Did you complain about his behaviour – to the Master, for example?'

'I thought about it, but then I thought people would just think I was making a fuss about nothing. And it would have been my word against his and it might have been even more unpleasant working with him afterwards. So I just tried to avoid him as much as I could.'

'What did you know about his relationship with other women – Ann Lambert, for example?'

'Everyone knew that he had been living with her for years – since ages before I came to the college. They broke up about six months ago, just after I started work here.'

'Was it an amicable split?'

'I don't know. They didn't shout at each other in public or anything.'

'What about Beverley Greenhalgh? Did he try to force his attentions on her, d'you know?'

'I don't think so. I suppose he might have done years ago. They've both been at the college for donkey's years.'

'She sat next to him yesterday,' Jonah commented, having brought up a plan of the seating arrangements on his computer screen, 'which suggests that either he wasn't in the habit of directing his wandering hands towards her or else she didn't mind if he did.'

'She probably gave him what for if he tried it on,' Jessica said with a grin. 'Bev could be quite fierce sometimes. She'd probably pinch his fingers or something if he put his hand on *her* leg!'

'Alright, I think I get the picture. So, moving on, did you know Penny Green at all?' Jonah asked.

'You mean the girl that Mr Bridgefield's living with now – I mean that he *was* living with?'

'So that was common knowledge was it? They made no secret of it?'

'No. I think he was rather proud of himself for still being able to attract someone as young as she was. I mean, she can't have been much more than thirty, maybe even younger than that. It's really weird her going off with him. I mean, it's not even as if he was good looking for his age.' Jessica paused and looked at Jonah's clear blue eyes, brown hair turning a distinguished grey and endearingly lopsided smile. It was clear which of the two older men she found the more attractive.

'So it wouldn't have been surprising if Ann resented the way he cast her aside and went off quite ostentatiously with a younger woman?'

'I suppose not,' Jessica agreed cautiously.

'Now, the other person I wanted to ask you about was the Master. Being his secretary, you must have got to know him quite well. How did he get on with Mr Bridgefield?'

'OK, I think,' Jessica said vaguely.

'Was he aware of his behaviour towards women, d'you think?'

'Well, everyone knew he liked to chat them up, but …'

'But you didn't, for example, tell the Master about him putting his hand on your leg in meetings?'

'No. Like I told you, it would have been my word against his and I didn't want any trouble.'

'It looks as if the Master was the last person to see Mr Bridgefield alive. Do you know what he went to talk to him about after lunch?'

'I didn't even know he'd done that.'

'So you didn't meet him as you were going down to the dining room? He went up to see Bridgefield at about the same time as you were on your way down.'

'But, like I said yesterday, I went to the Ladies on the way,' Jessica pointed out.

'Yes, of course. He told us that he had some college business to discuss with the bursar. Were you aware of anything in particular that they might want to talk about?'

Jessica shook her head.

'And the Master hadn't had any arguments with the bursar recently – any disagreements, about the college finances, for example?'

'Not that I knew about. And if you think the Master killed Mr Bridgefield, you're wrong,' Jessica went on, becoming animated in defence of her boss, 'He wouldn't do anything like that. He was always sorting out disagreements between people. He was very good at seeing everyone's point of view.'

'So when he says that Mr Bridgefield was alive when he left him, you think we ought to believe him?'

'Definitely. He just wasn't that sort of person.'

'And which of the attendees at the Awayday would you say *was* that sort of person?' Jonah asked innocently.

''I – I don't know. I mean, it's not the sort of thing you expect anyone you know to do, is it?'

'But it looks as if one of you must have done it, so why are you so sure it couldn't have been Dr Grainger if everyone else is equally unlikely?'

'I suppose Mr Ogden always seemed very, well, sure of himself and not bothered much about other people,' Jessica said slowly. 'And Ann might have gone a bit mental with the shock of Anthony leaving her after all those years.'

'So you're definite that *he* left *her*? She didn't tell him to get out of her house?'

'That's what I heard – but I may be wrong.'

'Thank you. You've been a great help. Now, maybe we could have that tea?'

Jessica nodded and then disappeared again. Bernie got out a plastic box of sandwiches and laid it on the table. Jonah called his sergeant, using the mobile phone utility that was part of the computer system attached to his wheelchair. He arranged for him to join them for lunch and to report on his morning activities.

11 THE SUSPECTS

A few minutes later Jessica returned with a tray containing a large white bone china teapot, a jug of milk and two matching cups and saucers. She put them down on the table in front of Jonah and Bernie.

'The chaplain is working at home today,' she reported, 'but I can give him a ring and ask him to come in this afternoon if you like.'

'Thank you, but there's no need for that. We can go out to see him at home. Perhaps you could ring him and let him know we'll be there at about one-thirty.'

'OK. I'll do that. Will you be coming back again afterwards? I mean: will you still be needing this room?'

'Yes, if it's not too much trouble. We still have some other people to speak to. Will the Master be free to see us later?'

'He has to leave at about three for a meeting in London, but I know he's keen to see you and hear whether you've made any progress. Shall I tell him you'll speak with him as soon as you get back from Simon's?'

'Yes. You do that. Thank you.'

As Jessica closed the door behind her, Bernie reached into a large bag, which she had set down under the table when they arrived, and got out a second plastic cup for Jonah's tea. She took off the lid and picked up the milk jug. Then she hesitated and looked at Jonah and their eyes met. Drinking tea from a china cup was a secret pleasure of his, which he had revealed only to Bernie. Most of the time he was content to use the plastic cup and drinking straw, which gave him a degree of independence, but occasionally he would ask Bernie to help him to a 'proper cup of tea'. He had even concealed this indulgence from his late wife, knowing that she would have insisted on gratifying his preference every time she made tea for him.

Bernie poured milk into one of the china cups and added tea from the pot. Jonah was sitting on her right, so she held the cup in her left hand and carefully lifted it to his lips. She put her right arm round his shoulders to make it easier for her to hold the cup steady for him to drink. For several minutes they sat together in companionable silence while he enjoyed this rare luxury.

There was a knock at the door. Bernie put down the cup, turning it round to position the handle on the right. Then she started pouring milk and tea into the plastic cup. Andy Lepage came in carrying a briefcase. He put it on the chair opposite Jonah and took out a notebook, a pocket folder and a bulging paper bag bearing the name of a local bakery.

'Would you like some tea?' Bernie asked, indicating the unused cup and saucer.

'Yes. Thanks.'

Bernie poured tea for Andy and then re-filled the cup that Jonah had been using and started to drink from it herself.

'The post mortem report has come through.' Andy opened the pocket folder and took out a thin sheaf of papers. 'But it doesn't really tell us anything we didn't already know.'

'Take me through the edited highlights,' Jonah instructed, taking a bite from the sandwich that Bernie was offering to him.

'Cause of death: strangulation with a ligature, which could have been a plastic-coated wire, such as the numerous electrical cables lying around the room. The assault was probably from behind while he was sitting down, judging by the angle of the mark on his neck from the ligature. The deceased had no other injuries and no obvious pre-existing medical conditions. Death was soon after consumption of a meal of chicken, potatoes, peas-'

'Yes, we know he'd just had his lunch,' Jonah broke in impatiently, 'and it hardly matters what he ate. Is there anything to suggest what sort of person his murderer must have been? How strong would they have had to be, for example?'

'No.' Andy shook his head. 'Because he was sitting down, the killer wouldn't have had to be particularly tall and it looks as if he was taken by surprise and didn't fight back at all, so they probably didn't need to be exceptionally strong. The fact that he wasn't expecting to be attacked suggests that it was probably someone he knew, but then we already thought it was one of his colleagues.'

'Alright, let's leave the post mortem for the moment. Tell me how you got on at the hotel. Did you find any witnesses who saw Dr Greenhalgh in the garden?'

'No. I spoke to a gardener who was working out there, but he doesn't remember seeing anyone. On the other hand, he was busy planting out bedding plants and he was listening to music on his headphones, so he admits that he probably wouldn't have noticed anyone unless they actually spoke to him. I *did* find out that there's a side door, which leads from the gardens into the passage that goes to the stairs and the ground floor toilets. So anyone could get in and go upstairs to the meeting room without coming past Reception.'

'But we've no reason to believe that Beverley Greenhalgh knew about that entrance,' Jonah observed. 'And, of course, she isn't the only person who went outside at lunch time. Did anyone see whether Brampton stayed by the entrance for his smoke or walked about a bit?'

'No. The receptionist says he wasn't visible from where she was standing, but that only means that he didn't stay right in front of the door. It would be natural for him to step to one side, so that he wasn't blocking the way in.'

'What about CC-TV?'

'There's a camera by the entrance, but it's facing outwards to catch people approaching along the path from the car park. Brampton was probably standing against the wall under the camera, so wouldn't have been visible. There's also a camera on the corner of the building, which caught Dr Greenhalgh walking round in the direction of the side door at one thirteen and walking back again at one twenty-four. The second time, she looked as if she was in rather a hurry and she looked at her watch just as she turned the corner.'

'Probably just worried that she was late for the afternoon session,' Jonah suggested mildly. 'Going back to Brampton, presumably he could have got to the side door without going past the camera on the corner – by going through the gardens in some sort of loop?'

'Yes. The camera is directed at the path round the side of the building, so anyone could avoid it by skirting round the other side of the shrubbery, but that would take them right by where the gardener was working.'

'Alright. Let's leave the outside route for the moment. Have you been able to confirm what the others said about where they went during the lunch hour? Ann Lambert, for example: can we be sure she didn't leave the reception area for long enough to get upstairs and strangle her ex-lover? She has by far the best motive for wanting to punish him.'

'Not to mention the fact that you'd like her to be the murderer because you find her very obvious attempts at flirting with you and getting your sympathy by pretending to be the poor put-upon little woman irritating,' Bernie suggested mischievously. She did not add her other thought: *and you don't want to consider Beverley Greenhalgh capable of murder because she reminds you a bit of your late wife.* 'Young Jessica had the much better idea of playing on your vanity by undisguised admiration for your detective abilities and great bravery. I bet she wouldn't be complaining if it had been *your* hand squeezing her leg during meetings!'

'Chance'd be a fine thing!' Jonah muttered, pretending to be affronted.

Andy, who would never have dared to call into question his boss's objectivity, still less to make fun of his disability, remained silent, waiting for the banter to run its course. He had long since given up trying to fathom the relationship between Jonah and Bernie, which was clearly much closer than simply that of client and caregiver. Jonah allowed Bernie to take liberties that he would have quashed instantly in any of his police colleagues, and she often seemed to know instinctively what he wanted without him having to ask. Jonah's disability precluded the possibility that they were having an affair in the normal sense of the word and in any case, up until her recent death, Jonah's wife Margaret had clearly been a close friend of Bernie's and very much in favour of her taking on this role as his full-time assistant. She would hardly have been so positive about it if Bernie had been in any sense a rival for her husband's affections.

Bernie's husband too seemed extraordinarily happy with the arrangement. Andy had been Detective Inspector Peter Johns' sergeant before his retirement three years previously and he had been aware then that much of Peter's spare time was taken up with helping a disabled colleague from another area of the Thames Valley police service, but he had never met the officer in question. After Peter retired, his post remained vacant for nearly two years and Andy had found himself attached to various different teams as the caseload required. Then, after Jonah's wife was diagnosed with terminal cancer, he applied to move to Oxford to be closer to his new weekday home. Peter's old post was revived for him to move into. That was when Andy was assigned to work with Jonah, who, despite his physical limitations, turned out to be more dynamic and less easy-going than Peter had been. Andy liked and admired him, but sometimes missed the words of praise that Peter would have given for actions which Jonah tended to take for granted.

'If you're so clever,' Jonah went on, 'why don't you tell us who *you* think did it?'

'Well, unless we assume the chaplain was in it with her,' Bernie began, 'we *have* to rule out Ann Lambert, because they were together for the whole time. Jessica could have killed him and then gone down to lunch, if she was lying about leaving the room before he got there-'

'Except,' Jonah pointed out, 'the Master saw him alive after she left.'

'He could be lying to protect her. She *is* his secretary after all.'

'And people always perjure themselves for the sake of their secretaries, I suppose?'

'It's as likely as the chaplain lying to save Ann Lambert. But, alright then, let's assume he was alive when Jessica left. Then that makes the Master the most likely killer, because he was the last person to go into the room until Tom came back and found the body.'

'But why?' Andy asked, glad that the conversation was now back on safe ground. 'What reason could he have for killing one of his staff?'

'To stop him molesting all the female employees?' Bernie hazarded. 'Or maybe *he* was being blackmailed, the way Beverley Greenhalgh is supposed to have been. But basically, you've got that same problem with all of the men, apart possibly from the chaplain: they don't have a decent motive to make them take the risk.'

'Why the chaplain?' queried Andy. 'You're not

suggesting Jessica's idea that he might see himself as the instrument of God's punishment, are you?'

'No,' Bernie laughed, 'I was thinking more about Ann's suggestion that our friend Bridgefield might have been having it off with the chaplain's wife – or trying to, at any rate.'

'Or,' Jonah put in, seeing a way of furthering his favourite hypothesis, 'Ann could have convinced Simon that Anthony had got his eye on his wife, in order to get him to conspire with her to do away with Anthony!'

'I'm still not sure that Ann would have had the strength of arm or the strength of will to strangle a fully-conscious, largish man in perfect health,' Bernie argued.

'But what if she and Simon did it together?' Jonah asked triumphantly.

'OK, I give in,' Bernie sighed. 'Little Ann is number one suspect, in conjunction with holy Simon; but I insist on making Beverley Greenhalgh number two, followed closely by the Master, seeing as he is the one with the best opportunity of having done it. So let's hope that Simon gets a crisis of conscience when we meet him this afternoon and confesses all. Then we'll be able to put this case to bed today and win all sorts of brownie points for such a quick result!'

'Alright, that seems a reasonable summary,' Jonah agreed, smiling at Bernie's flippant attitude. 'I certainly think we need to question Simon Sutcliffe about exactly what he and Ann were doing yesterday lunchtime. And to show I'm not biased against Ann, I want you, Andy, to get on to the Border Agency and get details of any student visas that have been issued to Lichfield students going back over the last five years, especially any that have Beverley Greenhalgh's signature on the forms. And go through the files looking for anything we may have on all of the suspects – especially any signs of violent behaviour. Oh – and see if you can get permission to check out the bank accounts of *all* the Awayday attendees looking for any suspicious activity – large cash withdrawals or in-payments, for example.'

He glanced down at the time on the computer screen in front of him.

'Time we were off,' he declared. 'We don't want to keep the reverend Simon waiting.'

'I'll go back to the office and start making those checks,' Andy said, getting up. 'Will you be going back there after you've finished your interviews?'

'Yes. I want to touch base with you before the end of the day, so don't go home until we've had a chance to compare notes.'

'We've got a pretty packed programme this afternoon,' Bernie said doubtfully. 'Couldn't the debrief wait until tomorrow?' Then, seeing the determined look on Jonah's face, she tried an alternative way of ensuring that he would be home at the right time for his evening meal. 'Or how about Andy coming to our house for tea? Lucy's going to be out at a friend's all evening, so you can talk shop quite happily. Peter might even have some suggestions to make, you never know.'

'Things must be pretty bad if we've got to the stage of having to rely on old Peter for inspiration,' Jonah said, with his customary disparagement of his friend's detective abilities, which, Bernie was well aware, should not be taken seriously. 'But, if that's OK with you, Andy, it sounds like a good plan for maximising the use of our time this afternoon.'

'If you're sure you don't mind,' Andy said, looking towards Bernie.

'We'll be delighted to have you,' she declared firmly. 'Peter will love to see you again and show off his new culinary skills. I'll text him to cater for one extra for tea.'

'That's settled then,' Jonah pronounced with satisfaction. 'Now run along and check out those records.'

12 THE CHAPLAIN

Simon Sutcliffe was evidently watching out for them when they arrived at his house, just off Banbury Road. He came out as they approached the front door and helped Bernie to set up the portable ramp to enable Jonah to drive his wheelchair up the step into the house. He led the way down the hallway, calling out as he did so to his wife, who emerged from a door on the right, wiping her hands on her apron. She was closely followed by a small girl, aged about three, who took one look at Jonah in his wheelchair and burst into tears. Her mother picked her up, whispering reassurances in her ear.

'I'm sorry,' she said to Jonah, sounding rather flustered and apologetic, 'she's frightened. She's never seen anything like this before. Now, Imogen, there's nothing to worry about. This gentleman won't hurt you.'

'No need to apologise,' Jonah assured them, speaking softly so as not to alarm the little girl further. 'It's not an uncommon reaction. It must be scary to have someone coming at you, gliding along like a dalek!'

'I'll take you in my study,' Simon said hastily, opening a door on the other side of the hall. 'Make yourselves comfortable,' he added, waving vaguely towards two rather worn and sagging easy chairs.

Bernie moved the chairs to make room for Jonah's wheelchair next to them before sitting down and getting out her notebook computer. Jonah manoeuvred the chair through the door and into the space next to where Bernie was sitting. Simon followed them in and sat down behind the desk facing them across it.

'What can I do for you?' he asked, sounding slightly nervous.

'Just some routine enquiries,' Jonah assured him. 'I want to check that we've got the sequence of events yesterday lunchtime correct, and I also want to know as much as I can about Mr Bridgefield and his relationships with other staff from the college.'

The door opened and Ruth Sutcliffe came in carrying a tray containing a glass jug of coffee, a jug of milk, a basin of Demerara sugar, three mugs and a plate of biscuits. Imogen followed closely behind, peeping nervously out from behind her mother's legs at the strange guests.

'I brought you coffee,' Ruth said, unnecessarily, putting the tray down on the desk in front of her husband, 'because that's what we usually have, but if you'd prefer something else – tea or water, perhaps – it'd be no bother …'

'Coffee will be delightful,' Jonah assured her, while Bernie got up and poured milk and coffee into Jonah's plastic cup, which she had brought with them in her bag, and fastened it into the bracket which was attached to his wheelchair for the purpose. Imogen stared, wide-eyed, at the sight of a grown-up drinking from a lidded cup rather similar to her own, and her parents watched the proceedings with interest while pretending not to.

Ruth poured coffee for Bernie and Simon. Then she turned to go, but Jonah called her back.

'Mrs Sutcliffe! Before you leave us, I'd be grateful if you could tell me something.'

'Of course. What do you want to know?'

'It has been suggested that Mr Bridgefield may have made inappropriate advances towards you. Is there any truth in those allegations?'

Ruth sighed and looked towards her husband. Then she walked across the room and sat down in the other easy chair, next to Bernie. Imogen hurried after her and stood leaning against the arm of the chair, still keeping a watchful eye on Jonah.

'I suppose I'd better tell you the whole story,' she said with a sigh, 'or else you'll hear some garbled version from other people.'

'Pour yourself some coffee,' Jonah suggested, inclining his head towards the tray, which still held one unused mug.

'Thanks.'

Ruth nodded gratefully and got up to pour it for herself. Jonah looked at Imogen and smiled at her.

'I was wondering, Imogen,' he said gently, 'if you would do something for me?'

She looked back without speaking.

'I can't ask any of the grown-ups,' he went on conspiratorially, 'because I'm not really allowed biscuits, but I rather fancy those pink ones on the plate there. Do you think you could get one for me?'

Imogen nodded. Then she came out from behind the arm of the chair, walked over to the desk and picked up one of the pink wafer biscuits that were lying on the plate. She came held it towards Jonah, still maintaining a safe distance from his intimidating wheelchair.

'I'm sorry; I can't reach it. Can you bring it a bit closer?'

She stepped tentatively forward and tried to put it into his right hand, which lay lifelessly in his lap.

'I need you to put it right in my mouth,' Jonah explained patiently. 'Can you do that, d'you think?'

Imogen came alongside the fearsome chair and held on to it with her left hand to steady herself as she reached up to hold the biscuit to Jonah's lips. He bit off a piece and chewed it with evident enjoyment.

'Thank you very much. I knew I could rely on you.'

Imogen held up the remainder of the biscuit and Jonah took a second bite. Then she looked at the small portion remaining in her hand and stuffed it into her own mouth. Jonah smiled at her and winked, but Ruth reproved her.

'Oh Immie! That wasn't your biscuit.'

'Not to worry,' Jonah assured her. 'I really am supposed to keep off the biscuits – I have to watch my weight, not being able to burn it off by exercising – so it's all to the good only letting me have half a one. Would you like to come on my lap?' he asked, looking at Imogen, who was standing next to him holding on to his arm. 'You can watch how Bernie here writes messages to me on this screen.'

Imogen nodded and smiled. Then she permitted Bernie to lift her up and arrange her carefully on Jonah's lap with her head resting against his right shoulder, leaving his left hand clear to operate the key pad and joystick on the arm of his chair.

'Right!' Jonah declared, turning towards Ruth. 'Now that we're all comfortable, please could you go on with your story?'

'It was like this,' Ruth resumed. 'We moved here from Nottingham about four years ago. We didn't know anyone here, so we very much depended on people from the college to help us get settled in. Anthony Bridgefield was very attentive and kept inviting us to things and introducing us to people. I thought he was just trying to be friendly and helpful. Then, a few weeks after we came, Simon was away at a conference in Durham so I was alone in the house for the first time. Anthony rang up and asked me if I'd like to go with him to a performance of *The Importance of Being Earnest* that the college drama society was putting on that evening. I didn't particularly want to go with him, but it was supporting the college and he *had* been very nice to us, so I agreed. Afterwards he insisted on driving me home. I'd gone in on the bus, but he didn't like the idea of me going back on my own late at night. When we got back, it seemed only common courtesy to invite him in for a coffee.'

Ruth broke off and took a drink from her mug. Then she exchanged looks with her husband before returning to her account of the events that had taken place.

'After we'd finished our drinks, I tried dropping hints that it was time for him to go, but he didn't take them. Eventually I realised that he was expecting to stay the night to "keep me company". I couldn't believe it at first, but eventually he made it quite clear what he was after. In the end, I had to be very direct with him and I told him if he didn't go I'd call the police. When he finally got the message, he started saying that it was all a mistake and I was jumping to conclusions and he'd never meant anything at all – but I knew that he had. Anyway, he went off and that was it really.'

'Did you tell your husband about what happened?'

'Yes, of course. My first thought was to ring him right away, but when I looked at the time it was past midnight and I knew he'd be in bed, so I decided to wait until the morning.'

'She rang me on my mobile first thing the next day,' Simon confirmed. 'I could hardly believe what she was saying. It's not the sort of thing you expect from a work colleague. Ruth sounded so upset that I skipped the last day of the conference and came home right away.'

'Did you report it to anyone – the college authorities, for example?'

'No,' Simon answered. 'We wondered whether we should, but in the end we decided that it would only make things worse for Ruth – and possibly for me too.'

'We talked it over,' Ruth continued, 'and the more times I went over what happened, the more I started to wonder whether I could have got hold of the wrong end of the stick. And it would always be my word against his, and he was the establishment figure, while I was the newcomer. And then we found out that he was living with Ann and we thought how difficult it might make things for her too.'

'So in the end we let it drop,' Simon finished. 'I wasn't comfortable about it, because I felt I had a duty of care towards any other women he might approach, but I decided that it was better just keeping a watching brief and being ready to step in if he seemed to be trying it on.'

'You didn't see it as your duty, as a man of the cloth, to remonstrate with the bursar and the dean about the poor example they were setting the younger generation?'

'I didn't think that was any of my business. They were both consenting adults. It wasn't up to me to pass judgement on their morals.'

'My father was a Baptist minister,' Jonah remarked unexpectedly. 'I'm sure he would have had no hesitation in denouncing such behaviour from the pulpit.'

'Well, times have changed,' Simon replied, 'and, in the Church of England at any rate, we try not to judge everyone by our own values.'

'I'm sorry. I interrupted you,' Jonah apologised. 'So you decided not to say anything to anyone, but you were keeping a watch on Bridgefield in case he overstepped the mark with anyone else, is that right?'

'Yes, I suppose that about sums it up.'

'And did you become aware of him doing that at all?'

'No. He still flirted publicly in a rather obvious way with any women he came across, which I could see annoyed Ann whenever she was present; but there were no complaints about his behaviour and I got the impression that there were some women who actually enjoyed his attentions.'

'And when he and Ann split up, did she turn to you?'

'No.' Simon hesitated and then continued, 'but, I have pastoral responsibility for all members of the college, including the SCR, so when I heard about it I offered her my support.'

'And did she accept it?'

'Well, we had a long chat about it all.'

'Do you know who initiated the rift?'

'Ann said that she got fed up with his carryings on with other women and chucked him out. *He* took care to let us all know that he had got tired of being tied to her and had decided to leave.'

'And which do *you* think it was?'

'Who can tell?' Simon shrugged. 'A bit of both, I expect. It didn't take him long to shack up with his next conquest, so my guess is he threatened to go off with her and Ann told him she didn't care if he did. Presumably someone's already told you he was living with Penny Green when he died?'

'Yes. I had heard that. Penny's a research assistant working with a Dr Riess, is that right?'

'Yes. She came here in September, nearly two years ago now, from Cambridge. I think Anthony probably got his claws into her almost as soon as she arrived.'

'Now, going back to the events of yesterday, what were you talking about with Ann Lambert at lunch time?'

'Not Anthony Bridgefield, if that's what you were thinking. It was a personal matter.'

Jonah looked at him in silence.

'If you must know,' Simon muttered, eventually, 'I was asking her advice – as a psychologist – about my mother. She's been widowed now for nearly ten years, but she still seems terribly depressed about losing my father. I wanted to know whether it was normal or if I ought to be worried and, if so, whether there was anything I could do for her.'

'Thank you. Now, you and Ann both said that you were together for the whole of the lunch break. Are you absolutely sure about that? You didn't nip out to the Gents for five minutes or anything?'

'No – wait! Hang about! Ann got a call on her mobile and she went outside to take it in private.'

'You mean outside the main entrance?'

'No. She went through the doors into that little corridor that leads to the toilets and the stairs.'

'Can you remember what time that was?'

'Well, we'd been talking for a few minutes after we got to the reception area,' Simon said slowly, 'so it must have been at least quarter past one. She was gone a few minutes, I think, and she came back just as Bev and Charles were coming in from the gardens.'

'Which was about twenty-five past one,' Jonah said helpfully. 'So she might have been away for up to ten minutes between fifteen minutes past one and twenty-five minutes past. Does that sound right to you?'

'I suppose so. I didn't keep looking at my watch, so I can't be sure about times. She definitely wasn't gone long.'

'No, no, of course not. Don't worry, you're being very helpful,' Jonah said reassuringly. 'Now, do you have any idea who it was who called Ann?'

'No. Why don't you ask her?'

'Yes, of course. I'll do that. Now, I just have one final question for you, Mr Sutcliffe. Yesterday, when you asked about whether the next-of-kin had been informed, I got the impression that you thought that there was someone else who also needed to know. Who was that?'

'Penny Green, of course,' Simon said promptly. 'I thought she'd be worried when he didn't come home that evening and I was afraid it might get on the news – which would have been an awful way for her to find out. But then I decided not to say anything in case it made her look like ... well, I don't know. I just thought it wasn't the sort of thing to say publicly. So I waited until we were all allowed to go and then went round and told her myself.'

'I see. So you went to see Bridgefield's mistress, girlfriend or whatever you call her, and told her that he'd been killed? How did she take the news?'

'She was shocked, naturally. I stayed with her for about an hour, then she said she'd be OK on her own and asked me to go; so I went home.'

'Well, I think that just about wraps up my questions. You've both been very helpful.' Jonah directed his gaze towards Ruth, 'Thank you very much for the coffee and biscuit – and for your daughter's company.'

'Thank you for being so good with her.' Ruth got up and picked up Imogen from Jonah's lap. 'She doesn't usually take to strangers.'

Jonah smiled complacently at Bernie as she strapped him into the car for the journey back to Lichfield College.

'Don't say it. Don't say it,' she groaned, getting out and climbing into the driver's seat. 'You're unbearable when you're right!'

'But I'm always right,' Jonah protested mildly. 'Hadn't you noticed?'

'OK. I admit it: Ann Lambert had ten minutes, in which she could have nipped upstairs, strangled the bursar and come back down to meet Simon, Charles and Beverley in the reception area. *And* she lied about being with the reverend the whole time, which is, of course, suspicious.'

'I'm glad you admit my theory has some merit in it.'

'Bu-ut,' Bernie went on, 'Ann's alibi was also Simon's alibi. *He* could have gone up in the lift, which, as I'm sure you recall, is in the reception area, while Ann was on the phone. *He* could have killed Anthony and come back down in the lift, all while Ann was out in the corridor by the stairs. Moreover, we now know that he had at least as good a motive as Ann does. OK, he *says* he believes that Ruth repelled Anthony's advances, but does he secretly suspect that more went on than she's admitting to? Or maybe she's admitted more to him than she did to us. And, even if nothing happened on that occasion, might he be worried Anthony might be more successful another time? If you think about it, a jealous husband is much more likely to want him out of the way than one of his conquests, who can only hope to gain the rather dubious satisfaction of revenge.'

'What about "hell hath no fury" and all that?'

'Hmmph!' Bernie snorted. 'Protecting your family from a predatory male makes a whole lot more sense to me – insofar as committing murder ever makes sense. And – oh! I've just thought! Ruth said they moved to Oxford four years ago, didn't she? And how old do you reckon Imogen is?'

'About three.'

'Exactly!' Bernie declared triumphantly. 'What if Imogen's father is really Anthony Bridgefield?'

'That's an outrageous suggestion, with absolutely no evidence to support it.'

'And you have no evidence to support your fixation with Ann Lambert. You find her irritating (as I do too) and, being a son of the manse, you are naturally reluctant to think ill of the clergy. I, on the other hand, was brought up to be deeply suspicious of protestant so-called priests, and thus have no difficulty at all in suspecting a married Anglican clergyman of any kind of depravity!'

'You talk as if you want it to be the Reverend Simon. What've you got against him?'

'Nothing. And I don't *want* it to be any of them. I'd far rather believe that Simon and Ruth are the happily married couple that they appear to be; and Beverley Greenhalgh is completely innocent of any sort of fraud, let alone murder; and Jessica is the helpful, efficient secretary that she seems and all the others are just ordinary academics with nothing to hide. The more I hear about Anthony Bridgefield, the more I think that, whoever murdered him, it's likely to have been someone a whole lot more likeable than he was. I'm just pointing out that, just because Ann Lambert apparently lied about being with Simon throughout the time when the deed was done, she isn't necessarily guilty of any more than forgetfulness. I'm trying to make sure you keep an open mind, that's all.'

'Open enough to keep your friend Tom Carrington in the frame?'

'Of course, although (a) he isn't particularly my friend

and (b) he doesn't have a motive as far as we know.'

'But he could easily have sneaked out of the bar and upstairs without anyone noticing him go – as could Damien Ogden.'

'The marketing man? Now there's a thought! If only he had a reason for wanting Anthony dead. I'd much rather it was him than one of the dons. But he didn't go to lunch with everyone else, so how would he even have known that the bursar had gone back to the room?'

They pulled up in a disabled bay in the small yard that served as a car park for Lichfield College. Bernie got into the back of the car to help Jonah out.

'Of course,' she resumed, 'if we can get hold of whoever it was that Ann was talking to on the phone, we may be able to rule her out completely. She could hardly have committed murder at the same time.'

'She could have carried the phone upstairs with her while she talked,' Jonah pointed out, 'but I agree with you, she would have had to end the conversation before entering the meeting room. Her mobile phone records will tell us how long the call lasted. We'd better bring her back and ask her about the call and check it out.'

He steered his chair down the ramp and set off towards the entrance to the college. Bernie packed up the ramp, locked the car and followed him. She smiled to herself, pleased to see the energy and enthusiasm with which he addressed his work. His wife's death had been a big setback. It was good to see the old indefatigable Jonah emerging again.

13 THE MASTER

Bernie caught up with Jonah in the quad and hurried on ahead to open the door for him to return to the seminar room.

'The Master is expecting to see you in five minutes,' she said as she hurriedly got everything set up ready for the next interview.

'See if you can get hold of Ann Lambert first. Try ringing her mobile number. We need to know what she was *really* doing during those ten minutes when she wasn't with Simon.'

Bernie obediently found the number on their list of contacts and tapped it into her own phone. It went straight to voicemail, so she left a message asking Ann to ring back. A knock on the door announced the arrival of Dr Featherstone Grainger, Master of Lichfield College. He was a short, rotund man in his late fifties with white hair very thin on top and pale blue eyes behind half-moon glasses. Despite this unprepossessing appearance, he had a bearing of authority and spoke with confidence.

'I saw you arrive back,' he explained. 'I have to leave at three, so I thought if we could do my interview now …?'

'Yes, of course,' Jonah greeted him. 'Please, sit down.'

The Master took the seat opposite Jonah, and Bernie poured him a glass of water.

'Have you made any progress?' he asked. 'As you can imagine, it's very difficult for us to have this hanging over us all like this. Do you have any idea who killed Anthony?'

'I'm afraid we're still in the very early stages of our investigation,' Jonah replied impassively, watching the Master's face closely. 'We've had confirmation that he was strangled – probably by one of the computer cables that were lying around the room – but we're keeping an open mind as to who might have done it.'

'But I suppose you must be working on the hypothesis that it was one of us? That is to say, one of the Lichfield members who was attending the Awayday? You're not looking for anyone else?'

'As you have evidently deduced for yourself, that *is* the most likely scenario. The time window is very limited, so whoever it was would have had to know that he – or she – would find Mr Bridgefield alone in the room, which does narrow it down to members of your party, I'm afraid. Do you have any idea why any of them might have wanted to do away with him?'

'No – no idea at all.' The Master paused for a moment, before going on in a tentative way, as if he did not like what he was saying. 'I have to admit that he was not well-liked among the academic staff. I can't say I particularly liked him myself. But I can't think of anything that could possibly justify murder.'

'There is never any justification for murder, but could one of your colleagues have been driven to it – to protect themselves from being exposed as having committed some lesser crime, for example?'

'Blackmail? I would never have thought so.'

'Mr Bridgefield knew all about the financial side of the college,' Jonah persisted. 'Could he have turned up some sort of fraud and be threatening to expose the perpetrator?'

'I really don't think that's likely. Whatever his other faults, Anthony was very loyal to the college. He was an Oxford man himself, you know and he'd been at Lichfield for many, many years. I wouldn't like to think him capable of blackmail in any case, but certainly I would have expected him to put the well-being of the college first and so expose any fraud against it through the proper channels.'

'But suppose it wasn't fraud directed against the college? Suppose perhaps the college had even benefitted from it …'

'For example,' Bernie added helpfully, 'one of the academics might have indulged in a spot of creative accounting regarding a research grant, which could have meant that the college got more than it was entitled to.'

'Then Mr Bridgefield might have thought it was in the college's interest not to report it, but could still have used it against the person concerned for his own ends,' Jonah finished.

'I think that's all very far-fetched,' the Master declared. 'Do you have any evidence for such an accusation?'

'Not yet, but there have been some indications.'

'What, exactly?' Grainger asked sharply.

'I'm afraid I'm not at liberty to divulge that. As I said, we don't yet have any hard evidence,' Jonah replied smoothly. 'Now, turning to another aspect of our enquiries, Mr Bridgefield appears to have had rather interesting relationships with some of the women of the college. What do you know about that?'

'So long as he confined his activities to consenting adult staff members, I considered it was none of my business. I thought it was odd that he and his wife should both remain at the college after the divorce, but so long as it didn't affect the way they did their jobs, I had no reason to intervene.'

'I'm sorry?' Jonah said, puzzled. 'Do you really mean his wife? I thought Ann Lambert and he were-'

'No, not Ann. I mean his ex-wife, Amanda. She's in charge of housekeeping and conferences.'

'Was it an amicable divorce?'

'I don't know anything about it. They've both been at the college since before I was appointed. I arrived two or three years after the divorce. It was a few months before I realised that they'd been married.'

'Do they have any children?'

'One – a boy. He was at secondary school when I came here. I think Amanda said he'd got a job and moved away now, but I may be wrong about that.'

'And, if we wanted to speak to Mrs Bridgefield, where would we find her?'

'She has an office next to the porters' lodge. Jessica will fetch her for you if you ask her.'

'Thank you. Now perhaps we could talk about yesterday at the hotel. You told Sergeant Lepage that you went to see Mr Bridgefield, in the room where he was later found dead, at about one o'clock?'

'That's right.'

'What was it you wanted with him?'

'Oh, just some small matters of college business,' the Master replied evasively.

'What, precisely?'

'Just one or two points from the annual accounts,' Grainger said vaguely. 'Some things that hadn't been quite clear when he showed them to me.'

'But he was about to give a presentation of the accounts. Wouldn't it all have become clear then?'

'That's just it! I wanted to make sure I'd understood what was in the accounts before he presented them to the rest of the group.'

'I see. And you were there with him for about ten minutes. Is that right?'

'About that, yes. Certainly no more than ten minutes.'

'And he was alive and well when you left him?'

'Yes, of course,' the Master said testily. 'If you don't

believe me, why don't you ask the chap from the hotel?'

'What chap from the hotel?'

'The IT chap: the one who set up the computer equipment and the phone – youngish fellow with dark curly hair and glasses. He was coming back into the room as I left.'

'Alright,' Jonah said slowly. 'Let me get this straight. At about ten past one, or maybe a bit earlier, you came out of the room and one of the hotel staff went in?'

'That's right.'

'Thank you. That's very helpful. So you went out of the room – to where?'

'Back downstairs to the dining room. They had coffee laid out there for us.'

'Did you use the lift or go down the stairs?'

'The stairs.'

'So you went along the first floor corridor, past the lift, down the stairs, along the ground floor corridor, past the toilets, across the lobby and into the dining room?'

'That's right.'

'Did you meet anyone – anyone you knew, I mean?'

'I don't think so,' Grainger said slowly. 'Oh yes! Maybe I did. Yes, I'm pretty sure Graham Weldon was coming through the doors from the lobby as I was going the other way.'

'Good. And did you see any of the Lichfield party in the lobby when you went through? There are some easy chairs where people can sit and wait.'

'No. I didn't notice anyone, but I wasn't looking, so I could easily have missed them if they were there.'

'Of course. And what about the dining room? Were any of them still there when you got back?'

'Jessica was there, eating her lunch. She came down late, because she wanted to get the room ready for the afternoon session first. I don't remember seeing any of the others. Look – I'm sure I told your sergeant all this yesterday.'

'Yes sir. I'm sorry to have to ask so many questions, but, as you saw, people sometimes remember things later that they forgot about initially. What you've just told me about the IT guy going into the room after you narrows down the time of death, which is very helpful indeed. I won't keep you much longer. I'd just like to go back to Mr Bridgefield's relationships with his wife and with Dr Lambert for a moment. How did the two women get on? It must have been awkward for them both to be working here.'

'I suppose it may have been, but they didn't come into contact a great deal. Ann Lambert was a senior academic and Amanda was essentially just the Head Scout.'

'Wouldn't they have both been involved when there were issues around ... I don't know ... students damaging their rooms, for example?' Bernie suggested. 'I mean, as Dean, Dr Lambert was responsible for undergraduate discipline and, as Head of Housekeeping, Mrs Bridgefield was responsible for keeping the rooms clean and tidy and so on.'

'Yes. I suppose they would have to deal with that sort of thing together,' Grainger conceded. 'And as far as I know they did it in a thoroughly professional way; but, I'm sure you will appreciate that I don't get involved in that sort of day-to-day business directly.'

'So you never saw any sign of antagonism between them?'

'Not at all.'

'There's been some suggestion that Mr Bridgefield sometimes made unwanted advances on other women. Did any of them ever complain to you about it?'

'No. I know that some of the female dons disapproved of the way he treated them, but I think a lot of the women he came into contact with enjoyed his attentions. It wasn't sexual harassment, just old-fashioned courtesy: assisting them into their seats, helping them off with their coats, that sort of thing.'

Bernie forced herself to refrain from pointing out that many women would feel patronised by the suggestion that they were incapable of sitting down or taking off their coats without the aid of a male assistant. Jonah remained silent for just long enough for it to become obvious that he was doubtful about the Master's assessment of the bursar's behaviour. Then he continued brightly.

'Well, I think that's all. Thank you for your time. If you think of anything else that might be of assistance to our enquiries, please ring me.'

Bernie handed Grainger a business card and, slightly ostentatiously, opened the door for him to leave.

'Well!' Bernie expostulated after the door closed behind him. 'If we're ranking them in order of which we'd most like to be the murderer, he's gone shooting right up to the top of my list! Unfortunately, assuming that he's telling the truth about the IT guy, it can't very well be him.'

'You're right. We must find out whether anyone from the hotel really did go into the room after one o'clock. If they did, then the window of opportunity for the murderer is becoming almost impossibly narrow.'

'But there are still lots of people who could have done it: Beverley (sneaking in from the garden), Ann (while she was on the phone), Graham (now that we know he didn't stay in the dining room), Damien, Simon and Tom – that makes six,' Bernie said, counting them off on her fingers. 'In other words, everyone except Jessica and her boss, who were in the dining room together during those crucial few minutes. I don't like to sound negative, but we don't really seem much further forward than when we started!'

'It's early days yet. Let's call in Professor Weldon and ask him where he was going at one fifteen. He told Andy that he didn't leave the dining room, so maybe he's got something to hide.'

14 THE CHEMISTRY PROFESSOR

Professor Graham Weldon was a large man with a shock of dark hair, which fell over his face. He kept pushing it back with this left hand, while his right hand fiddled with items in his trouser pocket. He had dark brown eyes, which darted round the room avoiding eye contact with either Jonah or Bernie. He seemed impatient to go and snapped out the answers to Jonah's questions in a jerky staccato.

'I just want to get clear exactly who was where during the lunch break yesterday,' Jonah explained. 'Now, you told Sergeant Lepage that you stayed in the dining room after lunch and had a cup of coffee there, but Dr Grainger says he saw you coming out into the reception area sometime between, say, ten past and twenty past one. Can you tell me where you were going when you left the dining room?'

'I did go to the toilet,' Professor Weldon agreed. 'It must have been about the time you say the Master saw me. I can't say I noticed him.'

'And after that?'

'I went back into the dining room and had coffee, as I

told you.'

'And when you finished your coffee?'

'It was time to go back, so I went up to the meeting room.'

'Where you found the others standing around at the door,' Jonah said, reading from Andy's notes, which he had displayed on the screen in front of him.

'That's right. We all went in and there were Tom and Beverley holding Bridgefield's body, trying to get it to stay in the chair. After they disturbed it, it looked as if it was going to fall on the floor.'

'Did you see anyone when you went out from the lobby into the corridor where the toilets are? Anyone on their way upstairs, for example?'

'Not that I remember.'

'Alright. Now, I'd like to talk about Dr Bridgefield. Do you have any idea why anyone might want to kill him?'

'Plenty of people threatened to kill him – in the way you do, without meaning anything. I probably said it myself a couple of times. He was very arrogant and didn't listen to reason.'

'Can you give me an example?'

'Student accommodation. That's what I was there for yesterday. I'm the tutor responsible. We keep getting complaints about the quality of the rooms and I'd got a programme of refurbishment all drawn up, but Bridgefield says we can't afford it. I told him we can't afford *not* to do it when all the other colleges have upgraded theirs. I very likely did say that I'd kill him, after the last committee meeting when the plan was turned down.'

'Dr Bridgefield's presentation, which he didn't get to show you,' Bernie put in, getting out a printed copy of the slides, 'shows expenditure of four hundred thousand on new undergraduate accommodation in the last financial year and sixty thousand on upgrading old rooms to having en suite bathrooms.'

'Sixty thousand! That must be wrong. Give me those.'

Weldon snatched the papers out of Bernie's hands and looked at the figures. 'There's something wrong here,' he repeated. 'We only managed to finish three rooms, before I was told we'd run out of money.'

'Building work is expensive,' Bernie suggested, 'especially in historic buildings like Lichfield.'

'This wasn't anything elaborate,' Weldon insisted. 'Just a few partition walls and some plumbing. It can't have cost twenty K a throw. We had quotations. I'm sure it was nothing like that. I was told we could refurbish the whole of Overton Quad. In fact, I thought it had been done, but then I discovered that the estates manager had been told the money was all used up and he'd stopped the work after the first three rooms were finished. Can I keep these? I want to take this up with the Master.'

'You'd better ask Jessica Stevens for a copy,' Jonah told him. It's not our business to give you information about your internal college business.'

Weldon looked dissatisfied, but handed the papers back to Bernie.

'Can I go now? I've told you everything I know. I want to get this sorted. If Bridgefield has been syphoning off funds from the accommodation budget, I want to know where it's gone to.'

'Yes. That's all for now. Thank you for your time. Dr Fazakerley will give you the number to ring if you think of anything else that might help us in our enquiries.'

Bernie dutifully handed over one of Jonah's business cards and opened the door for Professor Weldon to leave.

'Do you think there's anything in what he said about money going missing?' Jonah asked when the door had closed behind the Chemistry professor.

'Well, I think it's completely possible that putting an en suite bathroom in a college room *could* cost twenty thousand, but if it did, it probably wasn't worth doing. It'd be better to try to make a feature of the rooms being just as they were when the college was founded back in the year dot. Or else, make those rooms into tutors' rooms, seminar rooms or whatever, and build some more modern accommodation for the students elsewhere. Lichfield has plots of land all over Oxford. The only problem would be getting planning permission.'

'How d'you know all that?' Jonah asked curiously.

'They did an audit of college land a few years back. I saw the map they drew up. You know the saying about how you can walk from St John's Oxford to St John's Cambridge without ever leaving St John's land? Well that certainly isn't true, but some of the Oxford colleges do own a surprising amount of real estate. I'm pretty sure Lichfield had several sizeable chunks.'

'Then how come they were having a financial crisis? Couldn't they just sell some of the land?'

'It's all relative. My old college was only founded in the nineteenth century and owns next to nothing. They'd probably give their eye teeth to enjoy the sort of financial crisis that Lichfield thinks it's in.'

'The question is, did someone use college funds for something other than what they were supposed to be for and if so, who? If it was Bridgefield, as Weldon seems to think, then I can't see why killing him benefitted anyone. On the other hand, if it was someone else and Bridgefield got wind of it ...'

'That opens up the possibility of blackmail,' Bernie finished for him.

'Why don't you pop across to the ever-helpful Jessica and ask her to give us copies of the college accounts for the last three years? And then, wheel in Mr Damien Ogden, marketing officer. I want to know exactly what he was doing all that time he was supposed to have been hanging round in the bar, conveniently hidden around a corner from everyone else.'

15 THE MARKETING MANAGER

Damien Ogden was a small man with sharp brown eyes and a neatly trimmed black beard. He was wearing a navy blue pinstriped suit and a Lichfield College tie. He sat down and looked expectantly across the table at Jonah.

'According to my sergeant's notes, Mr Ogden, you spent the entire lunch period in the bar attending a teleconference on your mobile phone,' Jonah opened.

'That's correct. The conference call was due to start at twelve thirty, so I left the meeting at about twelve twenty-five and went down to the bar. I was on the phone till gone half past one and didn't get back upstairs until everyone else was already there. I can give you the names of the other people at the teleconference if you want to check up on me.'

Bernie silently handed him a sheet of paper and a pen.

'Thank you,' Jonah said. 'Please write down their names and a telephone number or email address so we can do that.'

He waited while Ogden wrote out a list of five people on the paper.

'I've given you the number and email of the chair and the administrator who organised it,' he said, pushing it back towards Bernie, 'but I can't remember the others off the top of my head.'

'Perhaps you could check when you get back to your office and email them to us?' Bernie suggested, providing him with one of Jonah's business cards. 'And please check these email addresses too: they look to be the same as the ones you gave to Sergeant Lepage yesterday and they bounced back.'

'Really? I was sure I'd got them right. What about the telephone number?'

'Only voicemail so far, but we'll keep trying.'

'Dr Carrington says that he went and sat in the bar after lunch,' Jonah resumed. 'Did you see him at all?'

'No. I found a quiet corner, well away from the door and I was concentrating on my meeting. I didn't notice anyone come in.'

'So you can't confirm when he entered or when he left or even that he was there at all?'

'No. Is he a suspect? Is it because Tony stole his girlfriend?' demanded Ogden, apparently relishing the thought that a murderer might be about to be unmasked.

'What d'you mean?' Jonah asked sharply.

'Penny Green. She was going out with Tom for the whole of last Trinity term; then sometime during the summer break, she switched her allegiance to Tony B. Before we knew where we were, he'd upped and left Annie Lambert – you *do* know he was living with her before, I presume – and shacked up with Penny.'

'But isn't Tom Carrington married?' Bernie burst in, regardless of the fact that she was not supposed to intervene in interviews.

'Divorced years ago.'

'How many years?' Jonah asked.

'Well, it was before my time, but I gather it must have been at least ten, maybe fifteen.'

'And his children?' Bernie asked anxiously. 'He had twin boys.'

'Gone off to New Zealand with their mother, I gather. But you ought to ask him; I only know what I hear on the grapevine.'

'And what does the grapevine say about how Dr Lambert felt about Mr Bridgefield's relationship with Dr Green?' Jonah asked.

'I'd say opinions are divided between those who think she's well shot of him and those who think she deserved better from him after all those years they'd been together.'

'Not much sympathy for Dr Bridgefield then,' Jonah observed, 'but you didn't really answer my question. 'How d'you think Ann Lambert actually felt about it? I mean, was she glad to see the back of him? Or was she hankering to get him back? Or did she harbour resentment against him?'

'You'd have to ask her that.'

'Very well. Now, what about the other people who were there yesterday? We've established that both Dr Carrington and Dr Lambert may have had reasons to feel a degree of resentment against Dr Bridgefield. Are you aware of anyone else who might have borne him a grudge?'

Ogden shook his head.

'What about Dr Greenhalgh?' Jonah suggested.

'Bev?' Ogden burst out laughing. 'She never cared a fig for him! She always made it quite clear she couldn't stand the sight of the man. There's no way *she*'s going to be harbouring jealous thoughts about him.'

'I wasn't intending to imply that she might have been an ex-lover or anything of that sort,' Jonah explained patiently. 'There could be all sorts of reasons for someone to dislike Dr Bridgefield. I've heard, for example, that he made a habit of finding out secrets about people and blackmailing them to *keep* them secret. Do *you* have any guilty secrets, Mr Ogden?'

'I'm sorry to disappoint you,' Ogden laughed again, a little nervously this time. 'I don't have anything that a blackmailer might be interested in. Pure as the driven snow – that's me!'

'I doubt that,' Jonah said drily. 'In my experience there are very few people who can claim to be completely devoid of anything that they would prefer other people not to know about them.'

'Of course, in your line of work you must get to see people at their worst. I can assure you that Lichfield College is not staffed by murderers, muggers or thieves.'

'Well, not exclusively,' Bernie observed, 'but you have to admit that it looks very much as if it must have at least *one* murderer on the payroll at present.'

'And talking of murderers,' Jonah went on, 'it's often their better feelings that prompt them: defending a loved-one or their loved-one's reputation, for example. So, do you think Dr Bridgefield could have been blackmailing any of the staff who were on the Awayday?'

'I really couldn't say.'

'Are you happy with the college marketing budget?' Jonah asked, suddenly changing tack.

'No, but I wouldn't be, would I? You could always do more with more money, but I couldn't legitimately complain. And if you're trying to suggest that I did away with the bursar because he didn't give enough funding to marketing then you also need to be investigating Graham Weldon, who was making a big deal out of a shortfall in the allocation for student room refurbishment, and Tom Carrington, who wanted a new open access computer lab with special mathematical software on it, and Bev Greenhalgh, who thought there ought to be more bursaries for overseas students, and Simon Sutcliffe who wanted to redevelop the chapel, and ... well, I should imagine you could find a motive for any one of us! But what would be the point? The bursar doesn't actually hold the purse strings; he just administers the money. So killing him wouldn't get any more for the murderer's pet project, because it would still have to get through the finance committee.'

'What if some funds had gone astray somehow? Would it be difficult to hide that from the bursar?'

'Someone's hand in the till, you mean?'

'Something like that.'

'I suppose he might be the most likely person to spot what was going on. Are you suggesting that someone was embezzling college funds and Tony might have been threatening to reveal all, so they did him in?'

'We're looking at every possibility. We have a completely open mind at present – which is why we need you to tell us if you can think of any reason why someone would want him dead.'

'I'm sorry I can't oblige; but, although I doubt if anyone is particularly sorry to see the back of him, I can't think of anyone who had enough to lose for them to risk wringing his neck.'

'OK. We'll leave it there then. Don't forget to ring me if anything new occurs to you.

Ogden left the room, closing the door behind him. Jonah and Bernie looked at each other.

'I gather all that about Dr Carrington and your toy boy's post doc was all new to you? Jonah said.

'Martin will love the idea of being a toy boy,' Bernie giggled. 'But yes – I had no idea that Tom's marriage had broken down, still less that he would contemplate a relationship with a woman who must be getting on for twenty year his junior. Not that a twenty year age difference is necessarily a recipe for disaster,' she added hurriedly, remembering that her own first husband had been nineteen years older than herself. 'I only really worked closely with him for the three and a half years it took Gerard to finish his DPhil. The twins were born during that time, so I suppose they'd be sixteen or seventeen by now. If Ogden's estimate is right, they will still have been quite small when the divorce happened.'

'And it will have been while you were otherwise

occupied with losing your husband, giving birth and looking after old Peter when his wife was killed. No wonder you didn't manage to keep up with all the maths department gossip as well!'

'Anyway, this definitely moves Tom up the rankings as far as being a murder suspect is concerned. He now has a much more convincing motive, as well as being the first on the scene when the body was found. On the face of it, he could easily have killed him, and then, when Beverley came in, claimed to have found the body a few minutes earlier.

'Which makes it imperative that we find the IT guy who came in after Grainger left, to make absolutely sure that he was still alive then.'

'Surely if he wasn't, the guy would have told someone?' Bernie queried.

'You'd be surprised the sorts of things people do when they find something like that. He may have been scared that he'd be accused of strangling the man, or he may not have wanted to get involved with the police, or he may just have gone into a blind panic and shut the door and run away.'

I'm sure I wouldn't do any of those things. Surely the most sure-fire way of making people suspect you of involvement in a murder is running away and not telling anyone?'

'Ah! But you are assuming that people always behave rationally.'

'Well, I think I do. I'm a mathematician – what do you expect?'

'I'll have to try planting a dead body somewhere for you to find and seeing how you react – purely as a scientific experiment, you understand.'

'If you do, I bet I call the police and the ambulance right away – and I won't go into hysterics and start screaming the way women in detective stories on the television do, either! But, to get back to the matter in hand: who do you want to see next? Tom, I suppose? Or what about Amanda Bridgefield?'

'I think we'll leave Amanda until tomorrow. She's not really a suspect.'

'How do we know that? If she knew about the Awayday, she could have come over specially to do in her wayward ex-husband somewhere where nobody would suspect her.'

'But how would she know he was going to be alone for long enough for her to do the dreadful deed?'

'Maybe she didn't plan to kill him – just to have it out with him about leaving yet another woman in the lurch and seducing yet another vulnerable member of staff.'

'Or maybe she wasn't there at all,' Jonah said decisively. 'If she just wanted to talk to him she could have done it at college any day of the week. So go and find your friend Tom Carrington and let me grill him about his relationship with Penny Green and why he didn't see fit to mention it to me before. Oh – and don't let on to him what it's all about. Just treat him like all the rest: we just want to clarify the times etc. etc.'

'OK. I won't tip him the wink!' Bernie said, smiling as she got up to go. Then she stopped in her tracks. 'Of course, all that about Tom and Penny Green could have been a smokescreen that Ogden's putting up to throw us off the scent – if he happened to be the killer himself.'

'Nice try – but he doesn't have even a whiff of a motive.'

'If I ever commit murder, I'll make sure I don't appear to have a motive either. Ogden strikes me as a very efficient sort of person. I bet he'd be a whole lot better at covering up his motives than the absent-minded professors that make up the SCR! OK, OK, I'm going!' she added, seeing Jonah's reproachful expression.

16 THE DIVORCEE

As he had said he would, Jonah started the interview with Tom Carrington by confirming the times of his movements the previous day. He focussed particularly on the fact that the don was unable to corroborate what the others had said about the period from twelve fifty, when he found the meeting room locked and presumably empty, to just before one thirty, when he found the dead body of the bursar. Tom remained insistent that he had stayed in the bar alone and seen nobody else from the Lichfield College group.

Jonah moved on to the question of who might have wanted the bursar dead – and why. Tom admitted to having been annoyed when his plan for a new computer lab for Lichfield mathematics students was knocked back, but he argued convincingly that this did not provide a motive for murder.

'If you think it's to do with money,' he declared, 'you ought to be looking towards the Master. He and the bursar were always arguing over the finances.'

'Any aspect of them in particular?'

'Not really. I don't think so. I didn't take much interest to be honest. I just got the impression that they each thought the other wasn't being quite straightforward about things. The Master could be quite secretive sometimes. He liked to be able to play the part of the magician pulling a rabbit out of a hat at the last minute, just before a crisis struck.'

'Can you give me an example?'

'Let's see ... well, last year he upstaged the marketing department by getting some celebrity to open the library extension through his own personal connections. Damien was pretty pissed off about it at the time. And before that, I remember we had trouble over planning permission for building the extension in the first place and, again, he suddenly announced that it was all sorted, at a meeting of the Lichfield Society, so as to get maximum personal publicity for it. I know the estates manager, who had worked his socks off over the planning application, was far from amused at the Master taking all the credit. He liked people to see him as Mr Fixit, but I can't see him fixing the bursar by murdering him!' He gave a nervous laugh.

'So what, in your opinion, might drive someone to kill?' Jonah asked mildly.

'I'm a mathematician, not a psychologist,' Tom protested, 'but I suppose, given Anthony's reputation, you'd expect this to be a crime of passion.'

'Did you have anyone in mind?'

'Not really. It's hard to believe that any of us could do a thing like that. I suppose the obvious person would be Ann Lambert. She certainly had a right to feel aggrieved with Anthony for the way he treated her; but then again ...,' he shrugged and looked round with an expression of bewilderment, 'I really can't picture little Ann coming up behind Anthony and ringing his neck!'

'I've had it suggested to me that *you* might have cause to resent Dr Bridgefield moving in with Dr Green,' Jonah suggested. 'Is there any truth in the rumour that you and she were in a relationship?'

'Who told you that?' Tom asked sharply, glancing at

Bernie to try to size up what she thought of this suggestion.

'*I'm* asking the questions. Was there anything between the two of you?'

'We both enjoy chamber music. We went to a few concerts together.'

'And that was all?' Jonah sounded sceptical.

'She was struggling with some of the mathematics behind the computer simulations that she was running for her project and didn't want to admit it to her supervisor. I gave her some help.'

He looked across at Bernie, who grinned back but said nothing.

'Was that the only thing you helped her with?' Jonah pressed him.

'Yes. Well, no. Well, you know.'

'No, I don't know. Tell me about it.'

'Well, one thing led to another,' Tom admitted, studiously avoiding catching Bernie's eye. 'After my wife left me I hadn't so much as taken a woman on a date. With Penny, it all seemed so easy. Anyway, we neither of us made any commitment and after a while she started seeing Anthony and that was that.'

'Didn't you resent the way he took her away from you?'

'No. The relationship had run its course. We never expected it to last.'

'Didn't you? Are you sure?'

'Yes. I'd been married before and it didn't work out, so I'd given up on long-term relationships.'

'Nevertheless, it must have been galling having Dr Bridgefield stealing her from under your nose. After all, he already had Ann Lambert; why should he have your Penny as well?'

'I keep telling you: she wasn't *my* Penny; we were just ships that pass in the night'

'And that's what Penny would say too, is it?' Jonah asked. 'If I were to ask her?'

'Yes,' Tom asserted forcefully. Then he went on with less certainty in his voice, 'yes, I'm sure she would.'

'Can I ask what happened between you and Debbie?' Bernie asked.

'I wish I knew!' Tom sounded genuinely puzzled. 'Everything seemed to be going so well when the twins were born. And after Debbie went back to work, after her maternity leave, I took on my share of the childcare and everything. But then, not long after that, she got this offer of a job in Aberdeen – and she expected me to leave my job and go up there with her! She said it was her big opportunity to take her career forward. I said, "what about *my* career?" And she said that she'd dropped her job to go to Oxford to further my career and now it was my turn. It went on for a long time, but the upshot was that she took the boys up there with her and then after a while she asked for a divorce. It turned out she wanted to make a clean break so that she'd be free to move on to a new post in New Zealand, which is where she is now.'

'I'm sorry, Tom. It must be hard for you not seeing your sons growing up.'

'Yes, well,' he mumbled, looking embarrassed and staring down at the table.

'All right, Dr Carrington,' Jonah brought the interview to an end. 'If you do think of anything else, let me know.'

Tom left and Bernie and Jonah looked at one another.

'What d'you think?' Jonah asked. 'You know the man. D'you think he believed he'd found love again at last and killed his rival when his girlfriend deserted him?'

'I don't know. And it's all very well you saying I know him, but it's been a long time since we worked together and it sounds, from what he says, as if I completely failed to pick up any signs there may have been of his marriage being on the rocks. I always assumed that they wouldn't be starting a family if there was anything wrong.'

'It's surprising how often having kids is what finishes a marriage,' Jonah observed. 'Too many assumptions from both parties about how it's going to be.'

'Mmm!' Bernie agreed. 'I wonder what he considered to be his share of the work. I'd take a bet it wasn't fifty percent. His wife evidently didn't think it was sufficiently valuable to her to keep her from taking the job in Aberdeen.'

'Maybe she had family up there who could provide childcare,' Jonah suggested.

'Well, she didn't sound Aberdonian when I met her,' Bernie declared emphatically. 'She came into the maths department to show off the twins. 'Now that's a sign of how equal things were in the Carrington household: if he'd been a woman, he'd have brought the babies in himself to show to his colleagues. I don't think he was such a New Man as he thought he was. He probably thought he was being ultra-generous changing a few nappies and hoovering the floor occasionally. I've heard any number of women in full-time jobs complaining about how their husbands expect to be congratulated on "helping" around the house, as if it went without saying that it was the wife's responsibility.'

'At least you can't complain about Peter like that!' Jonah observed, surprised at this sudden outburst. Bernie was not usually a particularly outspoken advocate of women's rights, probably because she thought that to argue about them was to admit that they could not be assumed to be self-evident. 'What about before: when you were married to Richard? Did he do his fair share?'

'It was his house,' Bernie laughed. 'He kept it to the standards his grandmother set when he was a boy. I only touched it with permission!'

'He must be turning in his grave to see the state we've got it into, since you took me in!'

'Anyway, getting back to the present,' Bernie said firmly, looking at her watch. 'Are we done here? If you're still planning to leave Amanda Bridgefield for tomorrow we could get an early finish for once – to make up for the early start.'

'Not quite: you're forgetting that I'm terribly anxious to meet Martin Riess. Quite apart from his evidence as a witness in this case, I want to vet him for suitability to associate with you and Lucy!'

17 THE GEOLOGIST

'Come in Dr Riess – or may I call you Martin? I've been waiting to meet you for a long time!'

Martin Riess entered the room in response to a call from Bernie on his mobile phone. He was quite unlike the big, confident German that Jonah had imagined he would be. He was small and wiry with straw-coloured hair and pale blue eyes masked by metal-framed glasses. He held out his hand by way of greeting and then snatched it back when he realised that Jonah was unable to reciprocate.

'We'll take the handshake as read, shall we?' Jonah said brightly. 'Sit down and we'll get on. I'll try not to keep you too long.'

Martin sat down opposite Jonah and looked across the table enquiringly.

'As I'm sure you are aware,' Jonah went on, 'Bernie is acting as my assistant and she'll be taking notes of what you say. You're here as a witness to the murder of Dr Anthony Bridgefield yesterday. There's nothing to worry about; we just want to get a clear idea of what happened at the Awayday and some background on the relationships between those people who were there. Do you understand?'

'It was definitely murder then?'

'It's difficult to see how it could have been anything else. Did you have a particular reason for asking that?'

'No. it just seems so, well *unreal*. You know – not the sort of thing that happens, except to other people.'

'Well, based on the assumption that it *has* happened, we need to know exactly what went on yesterday before and during the lunch break. You weren't present, but attended by telephone – is that right?'

'Yes. I was with a group of students on a field trip. Actually, I fixed the date of the trip *after* I got the Master's invite. I was hoping to get away with skipping it altogether; but he started leaning on me rather heavily, so I agreed to dial in. We were down in a quarry looking at sedimentary rock formations, so I had every hope that there wouldn't be any mobile phone signal, but it turned out they'd put a mast up on the hill, right above where we were, so I had no excuse.'

'How frustrating for you,' Jonah observed drily. 'Now, according to the minutes, you dialled in at about ten-thirty and gave your piece about Schools' Liaison. Is that right?'

'Yes. I was planning to dial out again as soon as that was done, but in the end I stayed until the lunch break.'

'Why was that?'

'Well, things got a bit interesting shortly after that.'

'Could you elaborate on that?'

'Well, the next item was about increasing our research income. The Master asked me to stay on the line, because I was one of the few dons who actually have a Research Council grant. Anthony raised the issue of Research Assistant salaries, which he thought weren't high enough to attract the best people. That set the cat among the pigeons because (a) it's no business of his to be saying that we don't attract the right people for research, which is something he knows nothing about, (b) we don't have any choice about how much we pay, because there are salary scales and so on that we have to use, and (c) everyone jumped to the conclusion that he was simply arguing for a raise for his latest girlfriend, who happens also to be my RA.'

'Penny Green?'

'Presumably someone will already have told you that she'd gone off with Anthony Bridgefield? I was most disappointed in her. I thought she had more sense.'

'I gather this wasn't the first time she'd had a liaison with an older man,' Jonah suggested.

'What makes you think that? It's the first I've heard of it.' Martin sounded combative, as if he was perhaps wondering if he was being accused himself.

'Someone told me that she had what used to be called a "fling" with Dr Carrington, before changing allegiance to Mr Bridgefield.'

'Well whoever it was they were talking through their hat. I don't believe a word of it.'

'Tom more or less admitted it,' Bernie put in quietly. 'Although naturally he's playing down the significance'

Martin looked from Bernie to Jonah and back again.

'Well!' he said at last. 'It looks as if I've completely misjudged Penny. Who would have thought it? And Tom too! Fancy him having his head turned by young Penny!'

'You weren't tempted yourself in that direction at all then?'

'No. My relationship with Penny was strictly work-related,' Martin said calmly. Then he looked towards Bernie and a smile gradually worked its way up his face from his mouth to his eyes.

'After all,' he went on, forcing his face back into a deadpan seriousness and looking Jonah straight in the eye, 'I can't let anything distract me from my mission to seduce Our Bernie. They've told you, I assume, that I'm determined to win her heart and sweep her away with me?'

'Bernie did mention something of the sort,' Jonah admitted, succeeding with difficulty in keeping a straight face. 'Of course, you do realise that I have a vested interest in ensuring that you fail?'

'Hmm! Yes, I do see the difficulty,' Martin mused. 'Tell you what,' he went on cheerfully after a few seconds, 'how about if I win her heart and sweep her away just at weekends and return her to Peter during the week so that you can carry on living with them Monday to Friday?'

'If you can achieve that,' Jonah agreed, still speaking as if in all seriousness, 'then I would be forced to withdraw my objections.'

'Excellent!' Martin declared triumphantly. 'So can I rely on you backing my efforts?'

'I will watch from the side-lines with eager anticipation,' Jonah promised. 'However,' he went on, 'I'm afraid I do have to drag you back to the events of yesterday. You were telling me about the reaction when Mr Bridgefield started talking about Research Assistant salaries and everyone assumed he meant that Penny deserved to be paid more. There's nothing about all that in the notes that Miss Stevens took of the meeting.'

'No, there wouldn't be. Once things started to get personal, the Master made it clear that the discussion was not to be minuted.'

'Alright. So tell me about the discussion. Who started it, for instance?'

'I'm not sure. You have to remember that I was only listening in on the phone, so it wasn't always easy to know who was speaking. I think it was probably Simon, the chaplain, who started accusing him of self-interest. And Tom, or it might have been Graham, suggested that he wasn't really interested in RA salaries at all: he was just trying to find a way of boasting about his new girlfriend. And I seem to remember Bev Greenhalgh saying something about how it wasn't the salaries that were the problem as much as the insecurity and how much more difficult it was for women who wanted an academic career because they still essentially had to choose between that and having a family.'

'Tom's wife seems to have managed both,' Bernie commented. 'Except that she appears to have found it necessary to jettison her husband on the way.'

'I'm just repeating what Bev said. After that, the Master called the meeting to order and said there was to be no more on this subject because it wasn't what we were there for.'

'Did anything else "interesting" happen while you were on the call?' Jonah asked. 'Especially anything that will have escaped the minutes.'

'I don't think so. The Master took me to task over falling numbers of working class applicants from north of Birmingham, which was tiresome for me personally, but …'

'Yes,' Bernie broke in, 'Jessica gave us your paper with the figures in. I'd noticed numbers were down. Of course it's all your fault,' she added turning to Jonah with an accusing look on her face.

'Me! Where do I come in?' he protested, realising that this outrageous accusation was part of the strange, almost surreal, relationship that Bernie had with Martin.

'For the last five – or is it six? – years Martin and I have blitzed THE NORTH for the whole of September with our famous double-act, drawing in the crowds from inner-city comprehensives, inspiring them to aspire to greatness and fill in their UCAS forms. By last September – which is when this year's applicants would have been targeted – I'd given up the day job to look after you, and Martin had to go it alone. Now numbers are down. So clearly you are to blame.'

'I repent in dust and ashes,' Jonah declared sombrely. 'However, I do think you might do well to consider whether there's any possibility that you might be jumping to conclusions here. I don't have the benefit of a university education, but I do remember something about post hoc not being the same as propter hoc …'

'Or, as we ignorant scientists would put it,' Martin

agreed, 'a statistical association is not the same as a causal link.'

'Beside the fact that one year's figures can't be assumed to represent a trend,' added Bernie. 'So, what did you tell the Master?'

'Just the usual stuff about how we were working to build links with state schools. Tom chipped in with a plea for more cash for his summer school and Bev said there ought to be more effort being put in to get girls to consider Oxford.'

'Our Bev has got a bit of a bee in her bonnet about women being disadvantaged,' observed Bernie. 'Any idea what the bursar thought of her? He doesn't strike me as your archetypal feminist?'

'Hardly!' Martin laughed. 'But I don't think they were on sufficiently bad terms for her to strangle him for being a male chauvinist pig, if that's what you're getting at.'

'There has been some suggestion,' Jonah said cautiously, 'that the bursar might have been blackmailing Dr Greenhalgh over some sort of irregularity with visas for overseas students. Had you heard any rumours about that?'

'Oh dear!' Martin suddenly looked serious. 'What have you been told?'

'Just what I told you now. I take it that you know more?'

'Have you asked Bev about it? What did she tell you?'

'She simply denied it all categorically.'

'Then I really don't think I ought to say anything,' Martin looked uncomfortably from Jonah to Bernie.

'If you insist on saying nothing,' Jonah explained patiently, 'we shall have to draw our own conclusions. My sergeant is already in touch with the Border Agency, but we are not working for them. All I want is to know whether Dr Greenhalgh might have had a motive for killing Mr Bridgefield. At the moment, we know that several people thought that he might be exerting pressure on her and we also know that she could have got into the room and killed him and then got away again before Dr Carrington came in and discovered the body. So, please, tell me what you know and save us the time and bother of finding it out by more laborious methods.'

'OK. I suppose you've got to know, but I'm sure it's got nothing to do with Anthony's death and it may hurt someone else – and not just Bev.'

'Go on. We won't tell anyone else unless we need to.'

'I have a DPhil student from Pakistan. Well, actually, he's being jointly supervised by me and Bev. She's a plant scientist and his project is all about improving crop yields in mountainous areas of the third world, using techniques drawn from both plant and earth science. He came over first to do a Masters and then stayed on for his DPhil. Bev has a remit to provide pastoral care for all the overseas students, so she knew him quite well. He went to her, just when he was completing all the paperwork for the DPhil and he told her that he wanted to apply to bring his younger sister over to live with him in Oxford for the three years while he did his doctorate. He told Bev that their mother was dead and their grandmother, who was in charge of the household, was determined to arrange a marriage for the girl, even though she was only fifteen. He thought the only way of preventing this was to bring her to England.

'The rules allow students to bring dependants with them, but a sister wouldn't count. However, it so happened that my student's name is the same as his father's, so he proposed that he filled in the forms as if he were the father, and Bev went along with it. Please don't blow the whistle on them. The girl's just done her A' levels this term and has applied for a place to study medicine, and if Kamran is sent back now, he won't get his DPhil and won't be able to carry on working to improve farming methods.'

'So, you're saying that this was just one isolated case?' Jonah asked. 'You're sure it was just one student?'

'Yes. Of course. Bev felt sorry for the girl and was just trying to help her.'

'There's no possibility that Dr Greenhalgh was running any sort of racket? She wasn't selling student visas in any sense?'

'No! Who's been telling you that?' Martin sounded indignant. 'Bev never made any money out of it. In fact, it was quite the reverse. She transferred her own money into Kamran's bank account so that he had the amount you need in order to demonstrate that you can support yourself and your dependants. The Pakistan government was paying for him, but he didn't have enough for his sister too, so Bev gave him the money. He's paying her back in board and lodgings for his sister, who's living with Bev. She's sort of unofficially adopted her.'

Martin looked round anxiously at Bernie and Jonah, trying to gauge their reactions.

'You won't have to tell on them, will you? I mean, it didn't do any harm did it?'

'Well, you could argue that your student's sister benefitted from free state education to which she was not entitled,' Jonah pointed out. He sat for a few moments, watching Martin's face carefully. Martin continued to look pleadingly back.

'Thank you for telling me anyway,' Jonah said at last. 'I'll see what I can do. Now, moving on, there have also been suggestions that several of the Awayday attendees had grudges against the bursar for the way he limited their budgets for various schemes and even possibly that he might have been embezzling funds. Have you heard anything along those lines?'

'No.' Martin shook his head emphatically.

'What about student accommodation?' Jonah prompted him. 'Did you ever hear Professor Weldon complaining about how there didn't seem to be as much in the kitty as he'd been led to believe?'

'Oh Graham was always complaining about that!'

Martin said dismissively. 'If you ask me it was all in his imagination. He told me about it a few weeks ago, but it wasn't the bursar that he suspected – not then at any rate – it was the Master. And I don't think he thought it was embezzling, as such, more just moving money around to different pots within the college so as to keep promising everyone what they asked for, only to be told later that there wasn't enough cash after all.'

'Alright. I think that's probably all for now,' Jonah concluded the interview. 'Let me know if you think of anything else.'

Bernie handed Martin one of Jonah's cards. He got up to go, but Jonah called him back.

'Just one more thing: I'd better speak to Penny Green about all this, where will I find her? I imagine she's taking some time off work. Do you have her home address?'

'I do, but you'd do better to meet her at the lab. She's working as usual today. To be honest, I don't think she's that bothered about Anthony's death – except perhaps in respect of who's going to pay the rent on their flat.'

'Now that's a very interesting remark you've made. Are you suggesting that she'd lost interest in him?'

'You'd better ask her, but I really never got the impression she was that interested in him in the first place. She's very dedicated to her career and her subject. I would never have expected her to be this sort of femme fatale that you're painting her as. She shares an office in the Earth Sciences building and does most of her work in the Biogeochemistry lab. Bernie will be able to show you: her office isn't far from mine.'

'It's a modern building,' Bernie assured him, 'with accessible rooms. Why don't we pencil in a meeting with Penny first thing tomorrow morning? What time does she usually get in?' she asked, turning to Martin.

'Early – seven-thirty, eight, something like that – like I said, she's keen.'

'Tell her to expect us around nine,' Bernie said,

jumping in before Jonah could propose an early start or even a visit there and then. 'And, if she shares an office, is there anywhere we could meet with her privately?'

'You can use my room,' Martin suggested. 'I can go off and get a coffee downstairs while you talk.'

'Thank you. We'll be there at nine prompt,' Jonah said authoritatively. 'And now I think that really is all, so you're free to go.'

'And you will do what you can to avoid dropping Bev and Kamran in it?' Martin asked, looking pleadingly at Jonah.

'I can't promise anything.'

Bernie got up and opened the door for him to leave. As he passed her, she put her hand on his shoulder and said something into his ear that Jonah was unable to catch. He saw their heads together and noted that, although Bernie was no more than medium height, Martin stood only two or three inches taller. His slight build gave the impression that he was younger than his actual age. Jonah reflected that, viewed from behind as they were there, they could easily pass for mother and son.

After Martin had left, Bernie and Jonah looked at one another.

'And what sweet nothings were you whispering into young Martin's shell-like ear?'

'If I'd intended you to know, I wouldn't have been whispering, would I? But, since you ask, I was only reassuring him that you would do the right thing as far as Bev Greenhalgh and the fraudulent visa application is concerned. The trouble is, I rather fancy that's what he's afraid of. Will you have to report them?'

'We'll see. If Bridgefield *was* blackmailing her about it and she killed him for it then it will all have to come out in court. If she had nothing to do with his death then … well, like I said: we'll have to see.'

'OK. Well, that's the last interview over with; time for us to go.'

Bernie started collecting their things together and packing up ready to leave.

'This Ms Green interests me strangely,' Jonah mused as he watched her.

'*Dr* Green,' Bernie corrected him. 'You can't be a post doc without being a doc first.'

'She appears to be all things to all people,' Jonah continued, ignoring the interruption. 'To Martin here, she's a hard-working scientist determined to further her career and her work. To Ann Lambert, she's a victim who's fallen prey to Anthony's lust. To Jessica, she's an enigma with a distinctly weird taste in men-'

'You mean because Jessica so clearly sees you as more fancy-able than Anthony?' teased Bernie.

'Reverend Simon says she's grieving for her dead lover, but Martin says she's carrying on with "business as usual". According to Tom Carrington, she went in for casual relationships without commitment, but then she sets up home with a man old enough to be her father in a way that has every appearance of permanence.'

'Well, I wouldn't give much weight to Martin's opinion myself,' Bernie observed. 'He can be pretty single-minded over work, himself. He probably didn't notice how she was behaving, so long as she turned up regularly and got on with the project.'

'Is that why he's remained single?' asked Jonah, interested to know more about this friend, who so obviously featured significantly in Bernie's life.

'No. You know why he's still single: he's besotted with me!'

'Joking apart; and he must have had plenty of opportunities before he met you, anyway. When was that, incidentally?'

'It rather depends what you mean. We were first in the same room together roughly fifteen years ago – just after Richard died – but it must have been seven or eight years before we actually spoke to one another. We were both members of a particularly tedious university committee and used to meet monthly in that context – if you can call it meeting. But then, I'd known his mother for years before that, because she was an old friend of Richard's. Martin went off to America on a Fulbright scholarship after he got his PhD and then he worked at some American university for several years. He'd only just got back to his post in Oxford when Richard died and, what with one thing and another, I didn't keep up with his mother and, well it took a while before Martin and I got to know one another properly. And now,' she said firmly, bringing this unusually long speech to a close, 'it's time we were getting home. It's been a long day and Andy's coming to tea, remember.'

18 THE DOCUMENTS

'Andy not here yet then?' Jonah called out as he steered his chair into the hall of the house in Headington.

'No. He rang to ask what time to get here and I told him half six, to give you time for your physio before he arrives.' Peter answered, coming out of the kitchen.

'Good work, Peter,' Bernie said approvingly. 'I assume Lucy's already gone off to Samantha's, so I'm afraid you'll have to manage with me today,' she added to Jonah, leading the way through his study into the bedroom beyond.

'Couldn't we give it a miss, just this once,' Jonah pleaded. 'I want to go through all the notes of today's interviews so I'm properly on the ball when Andy gets here.'

'Absolutely not! The whole point of Andy coming over is to allow you to put maximum time into working on the case without disrupting your routine. If I'd thought you'd use it as an excuse to-'

'Oh, alright, I know when I'm beaten,' Jonah sighed, suddenly remembering the conversation that morning and forcing himself to accept he had a responsibility not to put enthusiasm for his work ahead of caring for his own health. 'Let's get on with it.'

Bernie smiled, knowing how much it cost Jonah to admit that he couldn't any longer throw himself into an investigation with careless abandon, forgetting such insignificant things as mealtimes and sleep until he had solved the crime or else established that there were no further avenues to explore. She tried to think of a way of making this enforced time out more bearable for him.

'Tell you what,' she said as she started the process of taking off his work clothes and preparing him for his therapy session. 'While you do your workout, I'll take you through the notes that Jessica made of the Awayday meeting, together with the presentation slides, so you can get a feel for exactly what went on and how the off-the-record discussion that Martin told us about fits in with it.'

'No, I've got a better idea. You tell me all about this Martin Reiss character and his background and how old Richard came to know his mother. I haven't forgotten what you said about him having taken a shine to Lucy. If he's a rival for her affections, I need to know all I can about him!'

'OK. What do you want to know?'

'Oh just his life history will do,' Jonah said carelessly.

'Well, let me see …' Bernie carefully used a mechanical hoist to move Jonah into position in a piece of equipment that enabled his paralysed legs to perform cycling movements through electrical stimulation of the muscles. 'He was born in Halle, in East Germany. His father was a physicist – a professor at Halle-Wittenberg University – and his mother was a concert pianist.'

'Wittenberg?' Jonah interrupted. 'Isn't that where Martin Luther nailed his ninety-five theses to the church door?'

'That's right,' Bernie confirmed. 'I imagine Martin is a pretty common name in those parts. But, to get back to *our* Martin's parents, they both had western sympathies but they kept their heads down and avoided open opposition to the communist regime. When Martin was eight, his mother managed to get permission to go on a concert tour outside the eastern bloc – she was a concert pianist, you see – and, almost unbelievably, she was allowed to take Martin with her – or maybe she smuggled him out somehow, I'm not sure. *Anyway*, while they were abroad they got the news that his father had been arrested and accused of giving scientific secrets to the Americans. His mother applied for asylum in Britain, on the grounds that they would be in danger of being arrested as well if they were to go back to East Germany.

'A retired Music professor living in Oxford supported their application and Richard got involved as a representative of the local police. I'm not sure about the details, but I think there was some suggestion that they might need protection from a possible attempt on their lives even over here. Anyway, that's how Richard met them and somehow he and Martin's mother hit it off. Then a few months later they heard that his father had died and that finished any possibility that they might ever go back. Even when the Berlin wall came down, they didn't try to pick up with any of their family or friends.

'I don't know whether there was any truth in the accusation that Martin's father had betrayed his country. Martin's mother thought it was just a pretext invented by the Stasi for getting rid of him, because they thought he was having a bad influence on younger scientists who worked with him. Martin had the rather bizarre theory that his father had made up the story that he was working for the Americans in order to get himself arrested, as a way of persuading his mother to apply for asylum and make a better life for herself and Martin. It made him feel that he was responsible for his father's death, which was a bit weird, but typical Martin. He broods on things and blames himself whenever he imagines he could have done things better.'

'Like some other people I could mention,' Jonah

murmured. He had several times taken Bernie herself to task for blaming herself about things that were beyond her control.

Bernie disconnected Jonah from his exercise machine. She continued talking as she transferred him on to his bed and started making a detailed examination of his body, applying cream to areas of skin that were suffering from chafing or pressure and gently massaging it in.

'Martin's mother got a job as a piano teacher in Oxford and Martin applied to do his degree here so as not to leave her on her own. Afterwards, he went to Cambridge for his doctorate and then got a Fulbright scholarship to go to America. He taught at a university over there for a while before landing a fellowship back here at Lichfield, which is where he is still, as you know.'

'And Lucy said he's eight years younger than you, which makes him forty-seven. That's a bit long in the tooth to still be a bachelor with no attachments.'

'There was a girlfriend from his Cambridge days apparently, who was supposed to be waiting for him to come back from America, but I gather he stayed away too long and she got fed up with waiting.'

'Which is why he decided to throw himself at *your* feet I suppose?'

Bernie laughed.

'What makes you think any other explanation beyond my extreme charisma is required?'

The doorbell rang.

'That must be Andy,' Jonah said. 'Hurry up and get me dressed.'

'There's no rush,' Bernie answered smoothly. 'He's a few minutes early. You'll be ready in time for tea, don't worry.'

Nevertheless, she put away the moisturising cream and started to dress Jonah in some comfortable jogging trousers, which he was in the habit of wearing during the evenings. They heard voices in the hall, which confirmed that his sergeant had indeed arrived.

'Not those,' Jonah complained. 'The suit – I'm still working.'

'No you're not,' Bernie argued, continuing to work the trousers gently on to his legs. 'You don't need your smart clothes just for Andy. The main thing is to have something soft that won't rub, and this weather I don't know how you can bear wearing a tight collar and a tie.'

'It's for my own good, I suppose,' Jonah grumbled.

'That's right.'

The trousers on, Bernie brought the versatile wheelchair over to the bed and pressed buttons to make it recline so that she could roll Jonah gently on to it. Then she raised it into a sitting position before leaning him slightly forward in order to put on a polo shirt. Jonah felt her hands on his shoulders as she smoothed out the fabric so that there would be no wrinkles between his back and the chair. She sat him back and checked that the headrest was properly adjusted. Their eyes met as she fastened the buttons of his shirt, leaving the top one undone in the interests of comfort.

'I'm sorry,' Jonah said humbly. 'I don't know what's got into me today. I'm not usually such a grouse – or am I and I hadn't noticed?'

Bernie blinked back tears, finding herself unable to answer in the joking style that she would normally have adopted in this sort of situation, where emotions seemed liable to be displayed openly. Since his wife died, Jonah's usually even temper had become more irascible and he had seemed more discontented and frustrated with his paralysed state. The mere fact that he had noticed it and regretted the impact it was making on those who were caring for him made her feel suddenly all the more fond of him. She leaned forward and hugged him round the shoulders, burying her face in his neck.

'No,' she said softly, 'you're not usually a grouse, but you'd better stop acting like one or it'll become a habit.

Now let's go and see if Peter's got the tea ready for the workers.'

'... and so far, unless Jonah has any news from the interviews this afternoon, we haven't been able to eliminate any of them,' Andy was saying as they entered the kitchen. Seeing Jonah come in, he turned to him and went on, 'I've just been bringing Peter up to speed on all the suspects, sir.'

'You can drop the "sir". Our Bernie tells me we're not really on duty. So now Peter, what d'you think? Too many "possibles" and not enough "probables" in my opinion.'

'I think I need more to go on,' Peter answered cautiously.

'Typical Peter!' Jonah smiled, 'you were never a one to stick your neck out.'

'I've always thought it was only asking to have your head cut off. So I prefer to wait until I have all the evidence before trying to draw conclusions. Now, sit down Andy, the food's all ready.'

Bernie went over to the sink and washed her hands carefully, while Peter starting dishing up the meal. Andy sat down in the chair that Peter had indicated to him on one side of the long wooden table. Jonah positioned his wheelchair at the end of the table next to Andy. Bernie came and sat down opposite Andy, next to Jonah on the other side. Peter left the pans soaking in the sink and sat down at Bernie's other side.

'Now Andy,' Jonah said, while Bernie attached a white bib around his neck. 'Peter wants more evidence so we'd better give him some. I'll be in trouble if I try to talk and eat at the same time, so let's start off by you telling us about what you've found out from nosing round the records. Have any of our suspects got form?'

'No. The worst I managed to find on any of them was riding a bicycle without lights. There were a couple of parking offences and Ann Lambert has been sent on the speed awareness course after hitting thirty-seven on the Botley Road.'

'Nothing to help us there then,' Jonah commented. Bernie's hand holding a forkful of spaghetti Bolognese en route to his mouth stopped in mid-air while she waited for him to finish speaking. 'So what else do you have for us?'

'Well, I contacted the Border Agency, as you suggested. I've got a list of overseas students studying at Lichfield who were granted visas in the last five years. I can't see anything fishy about them – but then presumably if there was anything obviously wrong, the agency would have picked up on it themselves.'

'I wouldn't bank on it,' Jonah mumbled through a mouthful of spaghetti.

'Was there one called Kamran Desai?' Bernie asked.

'Hang on, I'll check.'

Andy got out his notebook and thumbed through the pages.

'There's a Muhammad Kamran Desai here,' he said at last, 'from Pakistan, aged thirty-one. He applied three years ago for a visa to continue his studies after completing an MSc in Earth Sciences.'

'That'll be the one,' Jonah said excitedly. 'Did he have any dependants listed on his application?'

'Yes – a daughter, Nafisa. That's odd: she's down as age fifteen, which means he was only sixteen when she was born. But maybe that's normal in Pakistan?'

'According to Martin Reiss, she was really his sister,' Jonah explained. 'And, also according to him, that was the sum total of Beverley Greenhalgh's involvement in fraudulent visa applications. Apparently the girl was being pressurised by an overbearing grandmother to get married and her brother brought her over here to escape.'

'Beverley's contribution,' Bernie added, 'wasn't so much falsifying the application as providing the cash that Kamran had to have to prove that he could support his sister while she was here.'

'But all this was illegal,' Peter pointed out. 'So, if Bridgefield knew about it, he may have been blackmailing Greenhalgh and, if she's really determined to help the girl and couldn't see any other way of keeping him quiet, she might have killed him.'

'Yes,' Bernie agreed. 'It'd be much easier to justify murder in defence of someone you cared about than just for your own sake. Remember: Martin said the sister was living with her. Over nearly three years, she could have built up quite a bond with her and be willing to do anything to stop her being sent home.'

'She'll have to go when her brother finishes his degree,' Andy commented.

'Not if she can get the university place that she's after,' Bernie argued. 'Didn't Martin say she'd just done her A' levels? If she got a place at a British university and someone to pay her fees and living expenses, she could apply for a student visa in her own right.'

'And do you think Dr Greenhalgh was planning to do all that?' Andy asked. 'Why would she?'

'Why not?' Bernie shrugged. 'She's got no other family that we know of, never married, no kids. She's probably enjoyed playing mother to this girl who's so keen to study and become a doctor. OK, the overseas fees are pretty high, but if Bev is as single-minded about her work as everyone seems to think, she won't have had time to fritter away her salary on leisure activities and she's probably got plenty of cash stashed away in the bank.'

'You can almost see yourself doing it, can't you?' said Jonah, remembering how many years Bernie had spent as an unmarried tutor with no family before her belated marriage.

'And you can almost see your Margaret doing it,' Bernie replied so quietly that Andy could hardly catch what she said. 'But I hope we would neither of us have gone on to kill – but, I don't know, in the heat of the moment, if Bridgefield was being really obnoxious ...'

'And she'd see herself as saving both Kamran and his sister from having their lives wasted,' Jonah continued, 'because if they were sent back, then neither of them would get their degrees.'

'OK,' Peter intervened. 'Suppose for the time being we assume Beverley Greenhalgh is our murderer. How do the timings work out? Can you go through them again for me, Andy?'

'We've got the Master leaving the room at about ten past one. Then at about half past, Dr Carrington finds him dead.'

'And for the whole of that time,' Bernie observed, 'Bev Greenhalgh was supposedly walking in the gardens, from which she could have slipped in by the side entrance and got up the stairs without anyone seeing her.'

'But the Master claims that he met an IT guy from the hotel going into the rooms as he was coming out,' Jonah interjected. 'We don't know how long he was in there, but it must cut down the time available for the murderer to get in and out by a few minutes at least.'

'Well, assuming it's true, at least that makes it almost certain that the Master can't be the murderer,' Peter pointed out, 'because the technician fellow will be able to confirm that Bridgefield was alive after the Master left the room.'

'One down, eight to go,' Bernie declared. 'Can we eliminate anyone else?'

'Hold on, not so fast,' Jonah cautioned. 'First we need to get hold of the IT guy and check that the Master's story isn't made up.'

'I can do that tomorrow,' Andy volunteered. 'I think I interviewed the man yesterday – if it was the same one as set up the room in the first place. He's been there for about four years, he said, and the manager says he's very reliable and conscientious; so I should think he'll remember if he really *did* go into the room.'

'Right, you do that. Now carry on. Have you managed

to turn up any other interesting facts for us?'

'I've seen a copy of Bridgefield's will,' Andy reported casually. He was rather proud of himself for having thought of this without having been told to do so and hoped that his initiative might gain some sign of recognition.

'Good,' Jonah said, stopping short of actual praise, despite being both impressed by Andy's enterprise and annoyed at not having thought of it himself. 'I can see you're dying to tell us all about it so go ahead and amaze us!'

'It's a very simple will,' Andy began, prolonging the account with the aim of increasing the drama. 'He left his entire estate to Lichfield College.'

'Nothing for Ann Lambert or his ex-wife or his son?' Peter queried in surprise.

'It looks as if he thought he'd given them enough during his lifetime,' Andy replied.

'Hmmph!' Bernie snorted. 'As far as I can see, he gave them precious little. His wife was working while they were married and the family home belonged to the college and she was turned out of it at the divorce; Ann took him into *her* house and also continued to work; and I wouldn't mind betting that Penny goes shares on the flat – that is assuming she isn't paying *all* the rent. Anthony's contribution appears to be restricted to his own company and a few compliments and presents!'

'Not your sort of guy,' observed Peter, 'but obviously some women liked it.'

'And when was this will made?' Jonah asked sharply. 'Before or after he broke up with Ann.

'Before. About five years ago, which means it was well after the divorce and well before any sign that the arrangement with Ann wasn't permanent. According to his solicitor, he considered that he had nobody that he owed anything to and he wanted to leave a permanent legacy for himself so that he would be remembered by future students and staff. There was a stipulation that a part of the money was to be used to erect a sundial in the main quadrangle in his memory with an inscription recognising his contribution to the college.'

'A sundial?' Jonah and Peter chorused.

'I think maybe I can offer a possible explanation for that choice,' Bernie ventured. 'The Master said Bridgefield was an Oxford graduate, so I looked him up and he was a Corpuscle.'

'A what?' Andy, Peter and Jonah all demanded to know.

'He went to Corpus Christi College,' Bernie explained. 'They call themselves Corpuscles. Anyway, one of the things that Corpus is famous for is its pelican sundial; so I'm guessing that was what inspired Bridgefield to choose to have something similar erected as his memorial. Did he specify anything in particular about the design of the sundial?'

Andy shook his head.

'No, it just said that it had to be carved stone and erected in the centre of the main quad.'

'Based on what we know of him,' Bernie suggested, 'I'd say a tom cat would be an appropriate substitute for the pelican.'

'The main thing is that, assuming that he was open about how he was planning to leave his money, there's nobody who stands to gain financially from his death,' observed the practical Peter.

'In particular, my private theory that Ann might have wanted to do away with him in order to inherit before he had a chance to will everything away to his new girlfriend doesn't hold water,' Jonah admitted ruefully. 'And talking of Ann, we'd better arrange to see her again and quiz her about that telephone call which she didn't bother to tell us about before. Unless whoever was on the other end of the line can give her an alibi, she's another person who could have sneaked up the stairs between when the IT guy left the bursar in the meeting room and when Tom Carrington found him dead.'

'Or she could have seen one of the others going past her to get to the stairs,' Bernie said, remembering that Ann was supposedly standing in the passage between the lobby and the stairs while she took her phone call. 'Tom or Damien, for example.'

'Right,' Jonah agreed. 'So tomorrow we need to talk to Penny Green, Ann Lambert and the IT guy – anyone else?'

'Bridgefield's ex-wife,' suggested Peter. 'She's the person who's most likely to be able to give you a picture of what he was really like. And she may know things from his background that would be useful.'

'Brampton,' added Andy. 'He rang the incident room this afternoon wanting to know what was happening and whether there'd been an arrest yet. He seemed a bit put out, apparently, that no one had interviewed him yet. I get the impression he heard you'd been talking to some of the others and he sees it as some sort of insult that he wasn't top of the list!'

'You interviewed him yesterday,' Jonah said cautiously,' d'you really think he's got anything else to tell us?'

'Probably not much,' Andy shrugged. 'There is just one thing though: you remember we asked everyone to leave the room exactly as it was when they went down for lunch?'

'Yes?'

'Well, Brampton left a little electronic organiser on the table – basically just a diary. I've had a look through it. Nothing much there – except that it seems interesting that he has regular meetings every couple of weeks with Ann Lambert in her room in college.'

'You're right,' Jonah agreed,' that *is* interesting. OK then. Tomorrow you take the organiser back to Brampton and see what you can get out of him. He may know all sorts of gossip about the college, which could be helpful to us. I'm meeting Penny Green at nine, why don't you come with us and see what you make of her? And then, after that, we'll split up: you can go over to Brampton's and we'll tackle Ann Lambert again. Then let's meet up at Lichfield College and interview Amanda Bridgefield together.'

'What about the IT guy?'

'We'll leave him to last. I can't see him having anything very startling to tell us. We just need to get him to corroborate Grainger's story that Bridgefield was alive at ten past one.'

19 THE RETIRED POLICEMAN

When the meal was over, they adjourned to the living room. Jonah led the way, opening the electronically controlled doors with an authoritative 'open sesame!'

'Don't mind him,' Bernie said to Andy in a stage whisper, 'he's only showing off the voice-activation. Normally he makes them open using a wireless signal from his chair, but commanding the doors to do his bidding is more dramatic, for the benefit of guests.'

Andy said nothing. His immediate thought was that the adaptations that Peter and Bernie had made to their house in order to accommodate Jonah must have required considerable expense. Who had paid? He followed Jonah into the large room and stood staring round at somewhat shabby furnishings. There was a settee and an assortment of easy chairs, all rather the worse for wear. Opposite the door was an old-fashioned marble mantelpiece over a large fireplace, which was hidden behind a screen embroidered with a peacock design on a black background. The room was dominated by an enormous Welsh dresser, on which were displayed calendar plates for the years 1958 to 1976. The rest of the walls were lined with bookcases, except at one end where there was an upright piano with a pile of sheet music on top of it.

Peter had never invited him home during the time when they had worked together. This house was much larger and grander than Andy had imagined. On the other hand, the fading curtains and stained seat covers were exactly what he would have expected from Bernie, who never seemed to care for outward appearances. He wondered how the immaculately turned out Jonah would get on living permanently in a household where chips in the paintwork were not immediately covered up and where tell-tale rings on the surface of the coffee table testified that hot drinks had been put down without any concern for protecting the varnish.

Peter brought in a tray bearing mugs and a coffee jug and set it down on the dresser. Bernie motioned to Andy to sit down in one of the easy chairs. Jonah manoeuvred his chair into the space between Andy's chair and the settee. Bernie set up a whiteboard on an easel then sat down on the settee at the end next to Jonah's chair. Peter poured coffee for them all and handed it round before joining Bernie on the settee.

'Right,' said Jonah, taking charge, 'Let's just check we've looked at all the evidence we've got so far. Bernie: where are those accounts that you got from the ever-obliging Jessica?'

'Here.' Bernie placed a manila folder on the coffee table in front of them. 'I gave them a cursory read and there's nothing immediately obviously wrong, but then you wouldn't expect it. If one of the dons was embezzling college funds, they'd surely be clever enough to cover their tracks well enough to fool an amateur like me. Last year's accounts have got the name of the auditors on them. Would it be worth asking them if they ever had any doubts about the accounts?'

'No. They wouldn't say if they did,' Jonah opined. 'If they had doubts they ought to have raised them and investigated at the time. Andy – get one of our tame accountants to go over these with a toothcomb looking for any potential irregularities, especially relating to the student accommodation budget and anything to do with international students. Now what's next? Oh yes – Bernie, you've had a look at the bursar's presentation. Did you spot anything that any of the others might have wanted to stop him showing to the world?'

'No,' Bernie shook her head. 'you can have a look for yourself if you like, I've loaded it on to your computer, but it's basically just a list of figures and graphs showing how income has been declining and expenditure rising over the last five years. There's nothing controversial.'

'Apart from the expenditure on accommodation being a whole lot more than Professor Weldon believed it could actually have been,' Jonah pointed out. 'I wonder whether there were any other figures which members of the audience would have been likely to have questioned if he'd gone ahead with his talk.'

'You mean he could have been killed to stop him giving his talk?' Andy asked. 'Who by?'

'Whoever purloined the money that had been earmarked for student accommodation, perhaps.'

'Hang on,' Peter objected. 'That won't wash. Preventing the bursar giving his presentation wouldn't stop it getting out. We're looking at a copy of it ourselves. The murderer couldn't possibly count on it never being seen.'

'But it would buy him time,' Jonah replied. 'Perhaps he'd only borrowed the money and was going to pay it back.'

'Or he could have been wanting to avoid the figures being discussed publicly,' Bernie suggested. 'I mean *we* wouldn't have spotted anything fishy in the amount spent on accommodation; it was only because Graham Weldon knew how little had actually been done that he questioned it.'

'I'm still not convinced,' Peter remained sceptical. 'Did

you have anyone specific in mind as the embezzler?'

'The two people who have been named in that context are Bridgefield himself and the Master, Featherstone Grainger,' Jonah told him.

'The Master?' Andy queried. 'That might work. Apart from the IT guy – and we only have the Master's own word for it that there *was* any IT guy – he was the last person to see Bridgefield alive. What if Bridgefield had discovered that Grainger had squirrelled away some of the accommodation budget and was threatening to expose him? Grainger goes along to the room to persuade him to change his mind, and when Bridgefield refuses, he snatches up a computer cable and strangles him with it.'

'Yes,' Jonah mused, 'that would work – provided the IT guy either didn't really go into the room or didn't notice that the bursar was dead or was too frightened to say that he'd found a dead body. Grainger didn't mention him when he spoke to you yesterday. He only remembered when I asked him about his movements. Maybe it occurred to him that he needed to establish that he'd left the bursar alive and he hoped that so long as he sounded confident enough we wouldn't check his story.'

'OK,' Bernie got up and wrote on the whiteboard, 'we've got two definite suspects: Bev Greenhalgh, to stop him getting her protégé sent back to Pakistan; and Featherstone Grainger, to conceal his embezzlement of college funds. Anyone else?'

'Ann Lambert,' Jonah said promptly. 'She still strikes me as the one with the most motive. 'Remember, she's given about fifteen years of her life to this guy, including ignoring his numerous infidelities, and now he's thrown her over for some slip of a girl who doesn't even seem to be that bothered about him, judging by the way she switched so rapidly between him and Carrington.'

'OK,' Bernie added the name to the board, 'although I'm still sceptical about whether she had the strength to do it. Strangling someone isn't easy.'

'You would know I suppose,' Peter said. 'I'll make a point of steering clear of you if I see you with a rope in your hand, seeing as you clearly consider yourself an expert in the field.'

'You should worry!' Jonah joked. 'What about me? If she takes agin me I'm literally a sitting target.'

'I thought Ann had an alibi,' Andy said, unsure how to react to this levity. 'Wasn't she with the chaplain for the whole time?'

'No,' Jonah reminded him, 'he now remembers that she went out of the room to take a phone call – *and* she went into the corridor leading to the stairs which could have taken her up to the meeting room where Bridgefield was.'

'Or,' Bernie put in, writing *Rev Simon Sutcliffe* on the whiteboard, 'the chaplain could have gone up in the lift while she was out of the room, killed Bridgefield and come down again before she got back.'

'Why would he want to do that?' Peter asked.

'Revenge for Bridgefield attempting – or even succeeding – in seducing his wife,' Bernie replied promptly. 'Or else, he could have been working together with Ann to pay Bridgefield back for his behaviour towards her or towards womankind (or morality) generally.'

'I think,' Peter said, decidedly, 'that you need to find out who Ann was speaking to.'

'Which is precisely why we have her on the list to interview again tomorrow morning,' Jonah said a little shortly. 'OK who else had a motive to kill Bridgefield?'

'His ex-wife,' Peter suggested.

'Except that she wasn't there,' Andy pointed out.

'Can we be sure about that?' Jonah asked, suddenly excited at the suggestion. 'She worked at the college, so she might have known about the Awayday and gone over during her lunch hour to – I don't know – to demand more support for her or their son or to berate him for deserting yet another woman and going off with Penny.

They argued and she grabbed one of the cables that was lying around and strangled him.'

Bernie silently added *Amanda Bridgefield* to the list.

'If we include Mrs Bridgefield, shouldn't we also have Penny Green?' Andy asked. 'I mean, she probably knew about the Awayday from Bridgefield himself and she might have wanted to do away with him just as much as any of the other women. Everyone agrees that one woman at a time was never enough for him, so she may have found out that he was being unfaithful to her, or maybe she believed that he'd made a will in her favour and didn't want to have to wait for the money.'

'Good thinking, Andy,' Jonah agreed. 'We'll explore that possibility when we interview her tomorrow.'

Bernie stepped forward and added *Penny Green* to the list on the whiteboard.

'Brampton and Ogden could both have done it,' Jonah mused, 'but we don't have any convincing reason why they would want to.'

'The same goes for Carrington and Weldon,' Andy suggested tentatively. 'Only Jessica doesn't have either a motive or any opportunity. She was eating her lunch in full view of the staff in the dining room when the murder must have taken place.'

'Don't forget those meetings that Brampton had with Ann Lambert,' Peter reminded them. 'If he's got some sort of relationship going on with her, then that might give him a reason for disliking Bridgefield.'

'Don't worry, I'll find out about that tomorrow,' promised Andy, pleased to feel that he was being given an opportunity to do more than simply pacify the Old Boy by undertaking a routine interview.

'Ogden doesn't have any obvious motive,' Jonah mused, 'but he does seem a bit over-anxious about establishing his alibi. He's sent us through half a dozen email addresses of other participants on the teleconference.'

'But do they check out?' Andy asked. 'The ones he gave me were duds.'

'That's another little job for you tomorrow. I've forwarded the email to you. He's given us new versions of the email addresses that he gave you: a character or two out in both cases. My guess is they'll work this time. Either he isn't very good at remembering that sort of thing – especially when he's stressed out by having just found a dead body lying around – or he deliberately gave you non-existent addresses so that he'd have time to contact the people concerned and brief them to confirm that he was on the call for the whole hour.'

'If it's OK with you, I'll do that first thing tomorrow morning,' suggested Andy, 'instead of coming with you to see Penny. Then I'll be able to update you when we meet back at Lichfield to interview Mrs Bridgefield.'

'Of course,' put in the ever-cautious Peter, 'Even if he did slip out of the teleconference that wouldn't necessarily mean it was in order to kill the bursar. He might just have wanted a fag or something.'

'We'll see,' said Jonah. 'Now, I disagree with your assessment that Carrington doesn't have a motive. He *says* that his relationship with Penny Green was just a transient aberration, but what if it was more than that – on his side anyway? He might have thought that killing Bridgefield would enable him to get her back.'

Bernie added *Tom Carrington* to the list on the whiteboard. They all sat for a few minutes looking at it.

'Well,' Peter said at length, 'I'm glad I'm not the investigating officer. It looks as if you still have practically all your original suspects still in the frame and some additional ones as well.'

'I reckon it was the IT Guy wot dunnit,' Bernie declared wildly. 'We've got the time window down so small now that he's the only one left who's still definitely got the opportunity to have done it.'

'For what reason?' Jonah asked, smiling at the facetious

suggestion.

'Oh I don't know – maybe Anthony criticised the way he set up the computer and he took it personally and lost his temper.'

'Or maybe he fell madly in love at first sight when he met Jessica that morning and was trying to protect her from the predatory male,' Peter suggested with a grin.

Andy looked at him in surprise. In all the time he had worked with Peter, he had never known him to take this light-hearted approach to a case. In many ways he was a quite different person when he was at home with his wife and the ex-colleague who was clearly also a close friend.

A soft beeping noise announced that the urine bag attached to Jonah's leg beneath his trousers needed to be emptied. He and Peter went to his bathroom to deal with it while Bernie collected together the empty coffee mugs and carried them back to the kitchen. When she came back into the living room, she saw Andy standing in front of the large mantelpiece looking at one of the photographs that stood there. It was a portrait of a black woman about fifty years of age. Her hair, which was braided tightly across her head, was peppered with grey. There were laughter lines around her eyes. She smiled cheerfully at the camera, her chin held high.

'That's Peter's wife, Angie,' Bernie said. Then, seeing the confusion on Andy's face as he turned at the sound of her voice, she added hastily, 'I mean Angie was Peter's *first* wife. I keep forgetting. I'll always think of them as "Angie and Peter" but of course technically *I'm* Peter's wife now. Not that that makes any difference: Angie will always be the One as far as Peter's concerned.'

'Well, if that's the way he makes you feel-' Andy began hotly. He liked Bernie, although he was slightly in awe of her and often found it hard to know what to make of her. He did not like to think of her locked in a loveless marriage to a man who did not appreciate her.

'No,' she cut in sharply, 'that is *not* how he makes me

feel. That's how *I* make me feel. Angie and Peter were married for twenty-five years. I knew them for most of that time. Angie was my very best friend – the best friend anyone could have. It's impossible for me to think of them as anything other than a couple. Peter's still in love with Angie, and I don't want that ever to change. He and I are a sort of mutual support association, that's all.'

'I'm sorry. I didn't mean to …' Andy didn't know what to say to this unexpected outburst.

'No, of course you didn't. I'm sorry. I didn't mean to shout at you.'

They stood in silence, contemplating Angie's portrait.

'She's very beautiful, isn't she?' Peter said, coming in and seeing them both by the mantelpiece. 'That was taken at our daughter's twenty-second birthday, about nine months before she died.'

'I never knew you married a black woman,' Andy commented, unsure what to say.

'I didn't. I married Angie.'

Peter spoke calmly, but there was a slight edge to his voice. He was used to people expressing surprise at his mixed marriage, but he hadn't expected to hear it coming from Andy. During the period when they had worked together, Andy had never volunteered any information about his family background and Peter had never asked, but he assumed that, like his own children, Andy would have ticked the 'Black British' box on the Equal Opportunities Monitoring Form.

'I would have thought that you, of all people, would appreciate that nobody is defined by the colour of their skin. I married *Angie*,' he repeated emphatically. 'The fact that she happened to be a black Jamaican is completely irrelevant. I didn't decide to marry a black woman any more than she chose to marry a white man. We're all the same underneath. It makes no difference what colour we are on the outside. I would have thought you'd have known that.'

Andy felt stung. First Bernie, and now Peter, appeared to have taken offence at his innocent attempts to make conversation; and now here was Peter, lecturing him on racial discrimination!

'And what makes you think you can tell what I think?' he responded angrily, catching a glimpse of Jonah watching him intently from the doorway, but unable to stop himself. 'It's all very well for you to talk about us all being the same underneath. That's the sort of thing my mum thought when she started going out with a black man eight years older than she was. But she realised she'd got it wrong when she got pregnant and he buggered off back to Nigeria to the two wives he already had out there.'

Andy paused for breath and Peter opened his mouth to say something but, before he could work out what he wanted to say, Andy went on, speaking very fast and avoiding eye contact.

'It's all very well for you to talk about it making no difference what we look like outside, but you never saw how my mum felt when people saw us together and assumed I must be adopted. You weren't the kid in the Primary School who always had to be the one holding the teacher's hand in the crocodile because nobody else liked the idea of touching you. You weren't different from everyone else in your family. You-'

'I think it's time for you to go home now, Andy,' Jonah broke into the tirade, speaking calmly and firmly. 'We need to make another early start tomorrow.'

Andy turned to see the stern look on his commanding officer's face. He opened his mouth to say something and then changed his mind.

'Goodnight then,' he muttered as he strode across the room towards the door.

'No, wait!' Peter said urgently. 'Don't go yet. I need to know – I mean I'd like to ask you-'

'Sorry, Peter,' Jonah interrupted, 'it really is getting late. And Lucy'll be back any minute, so we mustn't carry on talking shop.'

'I'll see you to the door,' Bernie offered, following Andy out into the hall.

'You really don't have the faintest idea what you've done, do you?' she said in a low, weary voice, as she opened the front door and ushered him out of the house.

'I don't understand what you mean,' Andy said, genuinely bemused by what was happening.

'I know: that's what's so terrifically sad,' Bernie sighed. 'Don't worry; we'll work something out.'

She put out her hand and placed it lightly on his shoulder as he stood hesitating part way down the ramp that led up to the front door from the drive. Then she became aware of voices in the road and, looking past him, she saw Lucy running down the drive towards them.

'Hi Mam! I'm sorry I'm late.'

'Lucy, let me introduce Detective Sergeant Andy Lepage.'

Andy turned to see a slim teenage girl with curly blond hair and blue eyes. She smiled up at him and put out her hand.

'I'm very pleased to meet you,' she said in a formal way that was unexpected in a girl of her age. 'I've heard a lot about you. You used to work with Peter as well didn't you?'

'Yes. He took me on when I was promoted to DS. He taught me a lot.'

'He always said you had great potential. I know he was dead chuffed when he found out Jonah had got you.'

'Yes, well,' Andy felt awkward, 'I'd better be going. Goodnight.'

'What's eating him?' Lucy asked, as she and her mother watched his car drive off.

'It's nothing,' Bernie replied dismissively, 'just some silly argument he had with Peter. It'll blow over.'

That night, in bed, Peter returned to the subject of

mixed marriages.

'Bernie,' he began tentatively, 'you got pretty close to Eddie when he was young: did he ever let on to you that he was unhappy about being mixed race?'

'Oh Peter! You mustn't let what Andy said get to you. His situation was quite different from Eddie and Hannah; and anyway, everyone's different. You can't assume that-'

'You haven't answered my question,' Peter interrupted. 'Did you and Eddie ever discuss it? Did he ever tell you he was being bullied at school, for example?'

'I think he did sometimes feel a bit out of it,' Bernie said cautiously, wanting to be honest but also wanting to avoid giving Peter any excuse for feeling guilty, 'being neither one thing nor the other; but it was just a passing phase. All teenagers go through that sort of thing. They all get ideas of why they aren't like everyone else and worry about not being how they think they ought to be. If it hadn't been that, he'd have found some other reason for being dissatisfied with himself. I mean – you're always telling us about how you were bullied at school for having ginger hair. I got stick at school for playing in the Salvation Army Band – and in the Army there were people who thought it was dead strange that I was at a convent school and went to confession every Saturday. Kids are just like that – they want to be just the same as everyone else and at the same time to be something special!'

'Still I ought to have realised …'

'And been watching out all the time for any sign that Hannah and Eddie were being picked on, ready to wade in and embarrass them? Don't be daft!' Bernie said scornfully, adopting shock tactics in the hope of heading Peter away from the train of thought that he was following. 'You and Angie were great parents, and Hannah and Eddie were great kids. You've got nothing to be ashamed of about how you brought them up.'

'I ought to have realised,' Peter repeated. 'I ought to have given them more support,'

'No you shouldn't,' Bernie said firmly, leaning over and putting her arms round Peter beneath the sheets and hugging him hard. 'No kids like to have over-protective parents. I used to get students sometimes who went through agonies because Mum and Dad insisted on visiting almost every weekend and making complaints on their behalf about the accommodation or the tuition or the cost of the washing machines in the college laundry room! Benevolent neglect is the key to successful parenthood, you mark my word.'

'That's all very well ...' Peter muttered, still dissatisfied.

'Oh Peter!' Bernie groaned, deciding to try a different approach. 'Whatever you did or didn't do wrong in the past, it's too late to worry about that now. Hannah and Eddie have turned out well enough, haven't they? They've both got good jobs and they're both married and they both appear to be as perfectly happy as anyone ever is – not to mention Hannah having presented you with two adorable grandchildren. Emily has even inherited your red hair! What more do you want?'

'I suppose I want to know for certain that they don't either of them think that it was all a big mistake Angie marrying me.'

'Oh Peter! How could you ever think that? You and Angie were the closest couple I ever knew. You were made for each other. You can't possibly imagine that either Hannah or Eddie would have wanted you to have done anything different.'

'Eddie went back to Jamaica so he wouldn't stand out like a sore thumb any more,' Peter argued, apparently determined to find a reason to feel guilty.

'No: he went there to find his roots, which is something different altogether. And he stayed because he met Crystal, and because he had a job he was enjoying, and because he can help Angie's family, who need him more than we do. He married a black woman and Hannah married a white man – so what does that tell you? I'd say they are both very well adjusted individuals who can make up their own minds about things and don't need you worrying over them. Now, how about trying to get some sleep?'

20 THE RESEARCH ASSISTANT

The following morning, Bernie and Jonah arrived promptly at the Earth Sciences building. Martin Riess opened the door of his office at the sound of Bernie's knock and held it open for Jonah's wheelchair to enter.

'I've cleared off my desk so that you can use that,' he said. 'I think the wheelchair will fit behind it.'

'Yes, that will be fine,' Jonah answered, making his way carefully round the desk to avoid knocking over a pile of books that lay on the floor. Bernie drew up a chair and sat down next to him, before getting out her computer ready to take notes.

'Penny's room is just down the corridor; shall I go and ask her to come in?'

'Yes please.'

'Right,' Martin hesitated at the door. 'I'll send her along and then go down to the coffee shop on the ground floor. Ask her to let me know when you've finished with my room, will you?'

'Yes, of course,' Bernie assured him.

He left. A few minutes later, there was a knock on the door and a young woman entered. She had dark curly hair tied back with black elastic, brown eyes and a tanned complexion. She was wearing a white lab coat, which hung open to reveal tight jeans and a brown tee shirt bearing the words 'Geology: making the Earth Move'.

'I'm Penny Green,' she introduced herself. 'Martin said you wanted to see me.'

'Indeed we do,' said Jonah genially. 'Let me introduce myself. I'm Detective Chief Inspector Jonah Porter, the officer leading the investigation into the death of Mr Anthony Bridgefield on Wednesday, the day before yesterday. This is Dr Bernadette Fazakerley. She's my right-hand man and looks after my every need. She'll be taking notes of our conversation because I have a memory like a sieve. I won't take long: I just want to ask you a few routine questions to fill in some of the background to Mr Bridgefield. Now, do you have any questions about the procedure before I start?'

'No, not really,' Penny hesitated, 'except I would like to know: am I under suspicion?'

'Not at the moment. *Should* we suspect you of something?' Jonah asked innocently.

'No, of course not. I just thought, I mean I wondered what people had told you about me.'

'I'm here to give you the chance to tell me the truth. Perhaps you could start by telling me exactly what your relationship was with Mr Bridgefield?'

Penny laughed.

'I suppose Ann told you I'd stolen him away from her? And Tom probably told you that Tony stole me away from him! The truth is, as far as I was concerned it was purely business. He was bored with Ann and wanted someone younger and more *adventurous* – if you know what I mean. I wanted somewhere better to live than the crappy old college room I'd been given, but I didn't fancy paying the sort of prices that flats cost in Oxford. He paid for the flat and I paid him ...' she trailed off, giving Jonah a meaningful look.

'I see. And how long did you expect this convenient arrangement to last?'

'My project's funded for another year and a bit, to the end of August next year.'

'So you're saying that in just over a year you would have expected to move on?'

'Unless I found something better in the meantime. It's tough getting on in the academic world – especially if you're female. I'd have kept my eyes open for the main chance and taken it if and when it came along.'

'Meaning?'

'Well obviously, if there was a research fellowship or something going I might need to make myself available to whoever was in charge of appointing to it.'

Jonah glanced at Bernie, who maintained a stony silence in the face of this suggestion that the bedroom was the best route for female academics to rise in their profession.

'And now that Bridgefield's dead,' Jonah asked bluntly, abandoning any attempt to treat the woman in front of him as a bereaved party, 'what will you do?'

'The rent on the flat's paid up until the end of August, so that gives me nearly eight weeks to find alternative arrangements. I'm sure something will turn up. There are a few likely targets working here in the labs. I'm spoiled for choice really.'

'Can you think of anyone who would want to kill Mr Bridgefield? Did he have any enemies?'

'I wouldn't have thought so,' Penny pursed her lips as she considered the matter. 'I mean, Ann went absolutely ballistic when she found out, but she'd have been more likely to murder *me* than him. She sent me a whole lot of hate mail – using her college email address. I bet I could have got her the sack if I could have been bothered. You know, I think she must have been really in love with the guy – the poor cow!'

'Could you show me any of the emails? Did you keep

them?'

'Course I kept them! You never know when that sort of thing might come in handy, do you? What d' you want me to do? Shall I forward them to you?'

'Yes please.'

Bernie silently handed over one of Jonah's business cards, indicating with her finger where the email address could be found.

'So in your opinion, Ann wanted Bridgefield to stay with her?' Jonah asked. 'She didn't tell him to get out of her house after she found out about you?'

'No way! He had to sneak out to get away from her; and after we moved into the flat she came round and tried to persuade him to go back to her.'

'Did Bridgefield ever discuss his will with you?'

'No. Why would he?'

'He might have wanted to leave you something.'

'Why would he want to do that?'

'As some sort of recognition of what you meant to him – or to spite his ex-wife and ex-mistress.'

'He never said a word. *Did* he leave me anything then?'

'No.'

'So why d'you ask?'

'I have to cover all bases. If someone – Ann, for example – had *thought* that they stood to gain financially from his death then that would have been a motive for killing him, even if it turned out not to be true. So I wanted to know what he'd said to people about it.'

'I see.'

There was a long pause while Jonah decided which of his lines of enquiry to tackle next.

'Before you moved in with Mr Bridgefield,' he began at last, 'you went out with Tom Carrington, I gather?'

'Yes – going out is about right! He took me to these dead boring concerts with violins and cellos and whatever. It took weeks before he would even come in for a nightcap after he'd taken me back to my room. And when eventually he invited me to his house, he spent the whole time talking about his ex-wife and how much he misses her now she's in Australia-'

'New Zealand,' interjected Bernie, unable to resist the temptation to correct Penny's statement.

'New Zealand then – it's the same difference. The whole house is full of pictures of her with their two kids. He even had a photo of her beside his bed – which he turned face down before we made love! It was just too weird! After that, I knew I was never going to get anywhere with him, so I looked around for someone who didn't have so many hang-ups.'

'And were Carrington and Bridgefield the only men you tried to ensnare during your time in Oxford?' Jonah asked, trying to avoid sounding judgemental, while strongly disapproving of this young woman's attitude to personal relationships.

'Well, of course I started with Martin, my supervisor. He was one of the reasons I applied for the RA post. I researched him before I applied. He's forty-seven and single. I was expecting to be able to work on him to get me a permanent post here in the department or at least to name me on his next grant. But he just doesn't seem interested. He was a great disappointment, but maybe now I'll have another go. I began to think he must be gay, but there's a rumour going round that he's having an affair with some older female don at another college. I must be more attractive than her, so maybe it's worth working on him again.'

Bernie and Jonah studiously avoided looking at each other, conscious that it would be impossible to keep a straight face if they were to catch one another's eye.

'I suppose you find this shocking?' Penny asked, misinterpreting the long pause as discomfiture on Jonah's part.

'My working day is filled with murder, rape and other atrocities,' he replied calmly. 'What makes you think I would find your antics shocking?'

'What about you?' Penny asked, turning to Bernie, apparently determined to show the older generation that she had rejected their standards of morality. 'I don't suppose my behaviour is quite what you'd want for a daughter of yours.'

'In view of the fact that my daughter is only fourteen,' Bernie replied drily, 'I naturally hope that she is not engaged in attempting to seduce your supervisor. You on the other hand are an adult, as is he, so it's not my place to pass judgement.'

'How did you find out about Mr Bridgefield's death?' Jonah asked, remembering that the chaplain had told him that he had broken the news to Penny.

'Simon Sutcliffe came round. He made out that he was concerned about me, but I think he just wanted to see whether I was going to break down and go into hysterics or something.'

'He told me that you seemed upset at the news.'

'Well, of course I had to put on a bit of a show or it would have looked as if I'd just been taking Tony for a ride.'

'Which, of course, you were,' Jonah could not help remarking.

'He got what he wanted from me and I got what I wanted from him – it was a perfectly fair arrangement. Anyway, it wasn't all an act: I *was* a bit shocked. I mean, now I've got to find somewhere else to live, apart from anything else!'

'Finally,' Jonah said, keeping the amusement out of his voice with difficulty, 'just for the record, where were you on Wednesday between, say, eleven in the morning and one thirty in the afternoon?'

'I was here, working in the lab,' Penny replied promptly. 'You can ask the lab technicians. I got here at eight and worked through to one. Then I went down to the coffee bar and had lunch and got back to the lab again about half past I should think.'

'I see. And did you make or receive any telephone calls during that time?'

'Not that I can think of,' Penny said, frowning in thought. 'No, I'm quite sure I didn't.'

'In that case, I'll just thank you for your time and we'll be off.'

'OK, I'll get back to the lab then,' Penny turned to go, then hesitated and turned back, looking doubtfully at Jonah's wheelchair. 'Will you be alright? You don't need any help getting out of the building or anything?'

'We'll manage,' Jonah assured her. 'As I told you, Our Bernie takes care of my every need.'

Penny left and Jonah and Bernie made their way downstairs to the coffee bar to let Martin know that his room was free again. It was not until they were in the car and heading for Ann Lambert's house in the Oxford district of Jericho that they permitted themselves to speak about what Penny had told them.

'I don't know whether to laugh or cry,' Bernie said. 'Poor Martin! We'll have to warn him that Penny's after both his body and his research grants!'

'What I want to know is who you slept with in order to get your fellowship at St Luke's!'

'I'll pretend I didn't hear that.'

'Tell me Bernie - you're closer to the younger generation than I am – am I totally out of touch? Is Penny Green's attitude towards men typical of young women today?'

'Oddly enough, the pros and cons of furthering one's career by offering sexual favours to people in positions of power in your employer's organisation wasn't something that came up very frequently in tutorials.'

'Maybe not, but your students are the sort of people who go on to become the likes of Penny Green. D'you think they all see sex as just a commodity to be bought and sold?'

'Well, I'm sure that's not how our Eddie and our Hannah see it – nor your two boys either. They've all found partners of their own sort of age who aren't in a position to help them up the greasy pole.' Bernie thought for a moment. 'But it's well-known that some of the female students resort to prostitution of the more conventional kind as a more lucrative sort of part time job than stacking shelves. I think in a way, selling themselves for sex makes them feel empowered: they're exploiting the men whose physical urges force them to pay for something that the girls can provide at no expense to themselves.'

'It makes you wonder,' Jonah mused,' what would happen if Penny Green ever found someone she really cared for.'

'You mean: would she ditch all the men she was stringing along for what they could do for her and her career?'

'Or would she expect to carry on using them while expecting the new boyfriend – or girlfriend – to tolerate it for the sake of what she, stroke they, could get out of it?'

'Maybe the IT guy's Penny's secret boyfriend and he killed Bridgefield out of jealousy!' Bernie suggested facetiously.

'Stranger things have happened,' Jonah smiled. 'Well, at least we have two lab technicians who back up Penny's story that she was there all day on Wednesday, so she can't have gone out to the hotel personally and strangled her lover.'

'Unless she persuaded the technicians to lie for her – they were both mere men, after all!'

21 THE MISTRESS

They pulled up outside a terraced house in Jericho. Jonah had telephoned Ann Lambert the previous evening to arrange the meeting and she was waiting for them when they arrived. She came out and watched as Bernie set up the portable ramp to enable Jonah to drive his wheelchair in through the front door.

'Take the door on the right,' she called after him, as he headed down the hall.

Ann followed Jonah into the house while Bernie packed up the ramp and stowed it away in the car. Then she went inside, closing the front door behind her, and looked around. A door on the right of the passage was open so she went in and found Jonah already in conversation with Ann.

'Sit down,' Jonah instructed. 'I've just been telling Dr Lambert about the interesting conversation we had with the Reverend Simon yesterday.'

Bernie deposited herself in a sagging easy chair and got out her computer to take notes. Jonah turned back to Ann.

'As I was saying, the chaplain told me that you had a phone call during the time that you and he were sitting together in the foyer. Do you mind telling me who it was from?'

'Well yes, I do rather – it was personal.' Ann looked pleadingly into Jonah's eyes. 'I'd really much rather not say.'

'If it has nothing to do with the murder of Anthony Bridgefield then it wouldn't go any further than this room,' Jonah assured her. 'But we do really need to know how long you were on the phone, because that would tell us whether or not you had time to go up to the meeting room where Mr Bridgefield was while Simon thought you were still on the phone. Am I making myself clear?' There was a definite menace in Jonah's voice now.

'Oh, I see.' Ann flushed red and looked disconcerted. Then she looked round at both Bernie and Jonah, apparently gathering her thoughts.

'Very well,' she said at last, 'I'll tell you. It was Amanda Bridgefield – Anthony's ex.'

'I see. And what was the subject of your conversation with her?'

'It was private.'

'Bearing in mind that we have an appointment to meet with Mrs Bridgefield later this morning, I think it would be better if you told me. As I said, if it doesn't have any bearing on the case, I won't need to pass the information on to anyone else.'

'She rang to tell me …,' Ann began. She got up and walked around the room, twisting her hands together in agitation. 'She told me … she said that Penny was having Anthony's baby!'

In the stunned silence that followed, Bernie and Jonah could hear Ann's breathing coming in jerky sobs. Then she flung herself back into her chair and put her face in her hands. Her hair fell forward and she pushed it back with one hand revealing the tears, which were now flowing freely. Bernie reached into the top pocket of Jonah's jacket and pulled out a neatly folded white handkerchief, which she pushed into Ann's hands. Then she went out of the room, leaving Jonah watching the distraught don.

Jonah sat in silence. He disliked it intensely when witnesses became emotional. At least, he reflected, his condition meant that he was spared the predicament of having to decide whether offering the proverbial shoulder to cry on would be seen as a sympathetic gesture or sexual harassment. He decided that the best course of action was simply to wait until she indicated in some way that she was ready to answer more questions.

A few minutes later, Bernie returned carrying a tray containing two mugs, a stainless steel teapot, a small jug and a sugar basin.

'I made us all a brew,' she announced, putting the tray down on a small table in the bay window and pouring milk and tea into one of the mugs. 'I thought you could do with one,' she added, handing the mug to Ann, who took it in both hands, dropping the handkerchief into her lap as she did so. She nodded briefly, but seemed still unable to speak.

'Sugar? Bernie enquired, holding out the basin towards Ann. 'My mam always said sweet tea was the best pick-me-up there is.'

'No – thanks,' Ann shook her head. She put the mug down on the floor next to her chair while she wiped her face with the handkerchief. She looked down at it and gave a little gasp. Then she looked directly at Jonah. 'Oh dear! I've got mascara all over your hankie!'

Jonah inclined his head slightly in a gesture that indicated that she was not to be concerned about the damage to his property, while Bernie reclaimed the handkerchief and handed Ann a box of tissues, which she had found in the kitchen. Ann blew her nose and wiped her eyes again. Then she picked up her mug and sat cradling it between her hands and looking nervously towards Jonah.

While Ann was composing herself, Bernie poured tea

for herself and Jonah, carefully positioning his cup so that he could reach the straw easily but without it obscuring his view of Ann. He continued to watch her closely. Eventually he decided that she was in a fit state to face more questions.

'I take it that the news came as a surprise to you?' he asked gently.

'Yes! A complete shock. It was so unfair! After all those years when I kept asking Anthony to let us start a family, I just couldn't believe that he'd allowed it to happen with that girl.'

'Let me get this straight,' Jonah said carefully, hoping that he could find out what he wanted to know without provoking more tears. 'You had been hoping that you and Anthony would have children, but he was against the idea?'

'That's right. He said that one kid was enough trouble and he didn't want to start all that again. But it isn't as if he ever had anything to do with the child. I know Mandy used to pester him for money sometimes – for school uniform, that sort of thing – but I'm sure he never gave her much and he absolutely never went round to see him or to take him out or anything. And I could have kept working, so it needn't have cost him anything, but he said it wasn't just the expense it was the commitment he didn't want.'

'You must have felt very upset and angry when you heard he was going to be a father with someone else,' Jonah suggested. 'Nobody would blame you if you went and found him right away so you could have it out with him there and then?'

'What could I have said to him?' Ann wailed. 'It was too late, wasn't it? I mean, he *had* to stay with Penny after that.'

'So did you go back to the reception area straight away after the phone call?'

'No. I couldn't face meeting anyone, so I went and sat on the stairs for a while trying to get my head round what I'd just heard. Then I realised people would be going back to the room soon, so I went back and sat down with Simon again.'

'Did you tell Simon what Mrs Bridgefield had just told you?'

'No. I suppose I was trying to pretend it wasn't true. If I'd told someone it would have seemed more real somehow.' She turned and looked at Bernie. 'Do you know what it's like to want children so badly?'

'Well,' Bernie began, considering the matter, 'I think I can probably imagine what it might be like, but if you mean did I ever wish for children when I couldn't have them, well no – not really. It never occurred to me that I might have them until it happened, so I didn't think about it.'

Seeing Ann's look of puzzlement, she went on.

'I didn't get married until I was thirty-eight and I assumed it was too late for children. As it turned out I was wrong.'

'But before that,' Ann insisted, 'didn't you ever yearn for a child of your own?'

'No, I really can't say I did,' Bernie shook her head. 'I don't think I could ever want children in the abstract like that. It would have been different if there'd been someone who I might have wanted to be the father of my children, but there wasn't – or at least not until I thought it was too late.'

'Dr Lambert,' Jonah intervened, 'can you tell me a bit more about what happened when you and Mr Bridgefield parted company? Earlier, you said that you told him he had to go, but I gather from speaking to other people that he put it about that he had left you.'

'It was like this,' Ann replied, turning wide, sad eyes on Jonah, 'Anthony proposed that Penny Green should come to live with us. He meant that he wanted her to live here rent free!'

'You mean he was suggesting a sort of ménage à trois?' Jonah asked.

'That's right. I told him it was a ridiculous idea and if he wanted her so much he had better go and set up home with her somewhere else. I thought ...,' Ann swallowed hard and blinked rapidly, apparently fighting back a return of her tears, 'I thought he'd see sense and stay with me like he did with all the rest of them, but of course I didn't know about the baby. That must have been why he thought he ought to give her a home. He must have felt responsible for seeing she was OK.'

'So essentially you told him that he had to choose between you and Penny and he chose to go off with Penny? That must have been very hurtful for you after so many years.'

'Yes – no, well I'm not sure. At first all I could think about was *how dare she try to take him away from me after all these years?* But then after the initial shock it was almost a relief in a way.'

Jonah looked at Ann interrogatively, encouraging her to go on, with what he hoped was a sympathetic smile.

'Ever since I turned forty,' she resumed after a short pause, 'I'd been wondering what the point of it all was. I came to realise that it was only the hope of having children that made me stick with Anthony for so long. I started wondering why I put up with him living here in my house when it pleased him to do so, and going off with any woman that took his fancy whenever he got the opportunity. I started to feel he was just using me. But now ... oh I just don't know!'

'We've been talking to Penny Green this morning. She claims that you sent her some rather unpleasant emails recently. Is that true?'

'Well, I did tell her what I thought of her,' Ann admitted, 'and I tried to warn her that she needn't expect Anthony to be exactly a loyal companion to her. She's so young, she probably has all sorts of illusions about how he was desperately in love with her and was going to devote his life to her – all the sorts of things I thought fifteen years ago,' she added bitterly.

'And then, after you heard about the baby, did you try to contact Penny again?'

'Does she say that I did?'

'I'm asking you.'

'Yes. I emailed her again on Wednesday night and on Thursday,' Ann admitted, opening her eyes wide and looking pleadingly into Jonah's face. 'I think I probably accused her of causing Anthony's death. I didn't mean anything by it – after all, she wasn't there, so she couldn't have done it, could she? But I somehow thought that if she hadn't tricked him into getting her pregnant, none of this would have happened. I was upset. I probably said all sorts of silly things.'

'So you consider that Penny deliberately arranged to become pregnant in order to persuade Mr Bridgefield to leave you and set up home with him? You don't think it could have just been an accident?'

'She isn't the sort of girl who has accidents. And if she had, I don't doubt she'd have got rid of it. No, I'm sure she did it deliberately. I only wish I'd had the courage to do it myself years ago.' Ann dabbed her eyes with a tissue and blew her nose again. 'All that time I kept telling myself it wouldn't be fair on Anthony. I thought about it lots of times. Sometimes I almost decided to do it – I told myself that he'd be pleased about it in the end. But then I thought about how he'd left Mandy and Matthew and I thought that maybe Matthew had been Mandy's idea and Anthony hadn't wanted him. So I decided that I'd be honest with him and just try to persuade him to agree, but he never did. And now I can't help wondering whether if I had just stopped taking the pill without telling him we might have had children and he might even have been pleased about it. It just seems so unfair!'

Jonah and Bernie looked at each other as Ann broke down into sobs again. Jonah waited for the weeping to subside before posing his next question.

'Do you have any idea what Penny will do now?'

'No.' Ann shook her head. 'It must be too late for an abortion by now. So she'll have to go ahead with having the baby; but I wouldn't be surprised if she has it adopted – unless, unless she really cared for Anthony after all and wants to keep his child.'

Bernie reflected to herself that this was probably correct: the calm, calculating Penny did not seem likely to allow a child to get in the way of her career. On the other hand, it might be the one thing that could win over Tom Carrington – assuming that Penny was still interested in using him as her stepping-stone to security of both housing and employment. Would he perhaps find Penny's baby a substitute for the twin sons whom he had somehow allowed to slip away to the antipodes?

'Going back to yesterday,' Jonah interrupted her thoughts, 'did anyone pass you while you were sitting on the stairs?'

'No – at least, I don't think so.'

'And while you were in the corridor on the phone, did you see anyone?'

'Graham came out of the Gents just as I came through from the lobby. I remember holding the door open for him.'

'So could he have overheard any of your conversation?'

'I shouldn't think so. The door closed on him and I walked further down the corridor before I'd said more than "hello".'

'So, as far as you know, the only people who knew about Penny's pregnancy were you, Penny and Mr and Mrs Bridgefield?'

'Yes, but once Mandy knew she might have told anyone.'

'Alright. I think that covers all my questions,' Jonah concluded, feeling relieved that this trying interview was almost over, 'unless you have anything else that you'd like to tell me?'

Ann shook her head vigorously as she got up to see them out.

'No. Thank you: you've been very kind and understanding.'

Bernie packed away her computer and Jonah's cup. They followed Ann to the front door and then Jonah and Ann had to wait while Bernie went out to the car to retrieve the ramp to enable Jonah to descend to the pavement.

'Do you think you'll ever find out who did it?' Ann asked.

'I certainly intend to do my best. It's early days yet. We're still collecting the pieces of the jigsaw. It'll be a little while before we're ready to start putting them together and working out what the picture is that we're looking at.'

When they were back in the car, Bernie gave a low whistle of relief.

'I'm glad to get out of there,' she declared decisively. 'I don't like the way she keeps trying to play on people's emotions. All that "you should sympathise with me, we're all women together" rubbish!'

'So are you coming round to my opinion that she's the most likely murderer?'

'You bet I am! In fact, for a moment I thought she was working up towards a confession: maybe throwing herself on the mercy of the court with a plea of manslaughter on the grounds of extreme provocation. Or she might even go for diminished responsibility. Presumably, as a psychologist, she could well have friends in the mental health field who would testify to her state of mind at the time of the killing.'

'I have to admit,' Jonah said gloomily, 'that unless she *does* confess there's not much chance of us getting a conviction. All she has to do is to hold her nerve and keep saying that she never went near him during the lunch hour and there's nothing we can do. Forensic evidence won't help us because there's no dispute that they were all there in the room. And they could all have touched the computer cables for perfectly innocent reasons. Unless someone saw her going into the room between when the Master came out and when Tom Carrington went in, we're completely scuppered.'

'What about the IT guy? Maybe he would have seen her.'

'Let's hope so. That's another reason why we've just *got* to talk to him today.'

'Don't worry! It's pencilled into our itinerary – for this afternoon. First it's back to Lichfield to meet Mrs Amanda Bridgefield.'

'Do we have time to call on young Penny again?' Jonah asked. 'I'd like to find out why she didn't tell us about her pregnancy.'

'If she really is pregnant!' Bernie said rather scornfully. 'It wouldn't surprise me if she made it all up to force Bridgefield to provide a flat for her. In answer to your question – no, we agreed to meet Andy at Lichfield at eleven and it's five to now.'

They pulled up in the Lichfield College car park and Bernie started the process of getting Jonah out of the car.

'Do you really think Penny was lying to Bridgefield about the baby?'

'Absolutely, I do. She's a self-centred little madam who's only interested in anyone for what she can get out of them. She'd never want to burden herself with a child. If she *was* ever pregnant, which I doubt, she'd have got rid of it without a second thought. No – my bet is she just wanted to apply pressure to dear Tony's chivalrous streak and get him to do his version of the decent thing, by housing her for nothing. That would fit in completely with wanting her to live with him and Ann. He may even have anticipated that Ann would enjoy the idea of looking after the baby!'

'You don't like Penny, do you?'

'No. I can't say that I do.'

'It hasn't occurred to you that she might be a frightened young woman who's trying to put a brave face on things so as not to admit that she's made a mess of her life?'

'Is that what *you* think?'

'I don't know – I merely offer the possibility for your consideration.'

'Well, I've considered it and I'm not convinced. For a start, she doesn't *look* pregnant – which she would if we accept Ann's assumption that it was her telling Bridgefield that he was going to be a father which prompted him to set up home with her. By all accounts he left Ann about six months ago.'

'Well not strictly, no. That's what Jessica said, but Beverley Greenhalgh said "a couple of months" so we don't really know.'

'When it comes to accurate date and times, I'd put more reliance on an efficient secretary than a scatter-brained academic,' Bernie said decisively. 'And "a couple" is a very elastic sort of term. Anyway, Ann clearly thought that Penny must be beyond the limit for a termination, which means twenty-four weeks these days, doesn't it?'

'Of course that's all assuming that Ann's right and that's what precipitated Anthony's decision to set up home with Penny,' Jonah pointed out. It could have happened more recently than that.'

'I suppose so,' Bernie conceded reluctantly. 'Anyway, for Martin's sake I hope she *isn't* pregnant: maternity leave wreaks absolute havoc with a research grant! You have to pay them maternity pay, which means there isn't enough left in the kitty to pay for a replacement – and in any case, because you have to keep the job open for them to come back, you can't offer a long enough contract to attract anyone decent – so the work doesn't get done, and then you have to argue with the funder over an extension, but by then all the other people employed on the grant have finished their contracts and disappeared off over the horizon. It's an absolute nightmare. It can really put you off taking on female RAs!'

'It sounds as if you have personal experience.'

'Yes. Been there, done that, got the tee-shirt! It was a project with Martin as it happens – a big one involving mathematical modelling of some geological phenomena. The RA in question was supposed to be collecting the data on which the models were going to be based, so my part of the team was kept waiting around while she wasn't producing the numbers they needed to go into their simulation programs to test them and modify them. It was a complete shambles! Though, of course, that wasn't what we put in our end of project report to the Research Council,' she added hurriedly.

They turned into the Lichfield College car park and pulled up in a disabled bay. Bernie got out and came round to release Jonah.

'But what's more worrying,' she said, as she bent over him to undo the straps which held his chair in place, 'is the thought that, if Penny *is* about to become a single mother, poor Martin might feel sorry for her and decide he needed to look after her somehow. You heard what she said about having another go at entrapping him. I could well imagine her turning the waterworks on if she thought it'd impress him and he might fall for the story of the poor innocent girl seduced by an older man and left facing a cruel world all alone.'

'You really like Martin, don't you?'

'Yes. I don't mind admitting it. He's a really nice guy – and rather vulnerable in his own way. In fact, if Angie hadn't been killed so that I ended up marrying Peter, it's not beyond the bounds of possibility that I might have accepted Martin's offer in the end.'

'Does he know that?'

'Do you mean Martin or Peter?'

'Either – or both. I'm just intrigued by this strange triangle you seem to be in.'

'I think it's probably more like a tetrahedron than a triangle,' Bernie remarked obscurely, 'but to answer your question: I did tell Martin. He was feeling very low at the time and needed a pick-me-up. And, when I tell you what he said about it, you'll understand what I mean about him being a really nice man. He said that he wished Angie hadn't died so that he'd have been in with a chance with me, but that given that she did, he was glad that he'd been so slow about making his advances, because he wouldn't have wanted Peter to have been left on his own when Angie died. That's what he's like: he really does put other people before himself – which is why I don't want him thinking he ought to help young Penny out of whatever mess she may have got herself into. She doesn't deserve him.'

'Or is it that you want to keep him for yourself?'

'No, I just don't want him getting hurt, that's all.'

22 THE OLD BOY

Andy Lepage pulled up outside the address that Charles Brampton had given him in Chipping Norton. It was a modern bungalow, but built out of concrete blocks the colour of Cotswold stone, presumably in an attempt to blend into its surroundings. He looked at his watch: seven minutes late, compared with the time he had agreed with Brampton on the phone. That was down to his having got lost in the maze of intersecting roads that made up the housing estate where Brampton lived. He hoped the Old Boy was not a stickler for punctuality.

Before getting out of the car, he checked his notebook carefully to make sure he knew exactly what questions he needed to ask. He wanted to have some useful evidence to share with Jonah when they compared notes later. Then he straightened his tie before getting out and locking the car.

He walked up to the front door, looked for a bell but didn't find one, so knocked as hard as he could, using the lion's head knocker attached to the solid oak front door. He listened for any sign of life within and he was soon rewarded by the sound of footsteps in the hall. A moment later, the door opened to reveal Charles Brampton. He was more casually dressed than on the previous occasion when they had met: he had swapped the black two-piece suit, which he had evidently considered necessary when attending an official college event, for corduroy trousers, an open-necked shirt and a cardigan. He looked disappointed when he saw that Andy was alone.

'Your boss not with you then?' he asked abruptly, as he shepherded Andy through into the small living room and waved at him to sit down.

'No. He has other business to attend to – other witnesses to interview.'

'I see,' Brampton said, in a tone which suggested that he considered it strange that the senior officer had not felt the need to come in person to interview such an important witness as Charles Brampton, President of the Lichfield Society. 'Well I suppose you'd better get on with it.'

'Yes. Thank you sir,' Andy tried to gather his thoughts. He could not help thinking that Brampton resented being interviewed by what he would probably have termed 'a coloured boy'.

'Well – get on with it!'

'Before I begin,' Andy said, playing for time, 'I have an item of your property to return to you.'

He handed over the electronic organiser, which Brampton had left in the meeting room. Brampton took it from him and briefly checked that it was still working.

'Thank you. Now, what did you want to know?'

'First sir,' Andy began, 'I'd like to go through the statement you made on Wednesday, just to check the times and so on, now that we've had time to compare with what everyone else said. We want to be absolutely sure we know where everyone was at the time of the murder.'

'So it definitely *was* murder?' Brampton asked eagerly.

'It would appear that way, sir. So if we could just recap on what you said? The meeting was scheduled to start at ten and you arrived in good time – probably at about nine-forty-five, is that correct?'

'That's right. I believe in being punctual,' Brampton said pointedly, removing any doubt from Andy's mind that he had noticed his late arrival.

'When you got there, Miss Stevens, Dr Carrington and Dr Greenhalgh were already in the room, but Mr Bridgefield hadn't arrived yet?'

'That's correct. I told you all that before.'

'Yes, but now we've also got other people's statements and I want to be sure that they are all consistent,' Andy explained patiently. 'It's important to know who Mr Bridgefield might have spoken to that morning, in case something was said that could have precipitated the murder. One of the others thought that Mr Bridgefield arrived just *before* you did. Do you think that's possible?'

'No. I'm quite certain I was first. When I got there, there was a young chap fiddling with the computer, and the Master's secretary was standing next to him holding one of those pen drive things and Tom and Beverley were pouring coffee for themselves. I went and sat down and Jessica – the secretary – asked me if I'd like a drink and *then* Anthony Bridgefield came in. I remember, because Jessica already had the coffee pot in her hand and she poured him a cup as well before she brought me mine.'

'Thank you. That clears that up. It's very useful to have a witness who remembers those little details,' Andy said, hoping to mollify the old gentleman with some mild flattery and to encourage him to volunteer any additional information that he might think of. 'And then the Master came in a few minutes after that and then everyone apart from the chaplain, who arrived late. Have I got that all correct?'

'Yes. That's how I remember it.'

'Now, going back to the young man who was setting up the computer – did he speak to anyone else apart from Miss Stevens?'

'As far as I remember, only the Master. He arrived just after I did, and he had his presentation on a pen drive. The young man helped him to load it into the computer.'

'Mr Bridgefield was also giving a presentation. Did he give it to the young man to load too?'

'No. Jessica already had his slides. He must have given them to her earlier.'

'So the young man and the bursar didn't speak to one another at all?'

'That's correct.'

'I see. Now, moving on to lunch time: Mr Ogden left early because he had a teleconference and Miss Stevens stayed behind to set up the room for the afternoon, but did the rest of you all go down to the dining room together?'

'That's right. We all went down in the lift.'

'And you ate together on the same table?'

'Yes.'

'Now, everyone agrees that Dr Greenhalgh, Dr Carrington and Mr Bridgefield all left the dining room at about ten to one, but it's important for us to know exactly what order they left in and who knew that Dr Bridgefield was going back up to the meeting room. Can you remember what he said before he left?'

'Yes. I remember perfectly. He said, "I won't bother with coffee, because I want to go up and run through my presentation before everyone gets back from lunch." Then Carrington said he wouldn't stay either because he needed to check his emails and Beverley said she wanted to get a breath of fresh air.'

'So they were both still in the dining room when Dr Bridgefield announced that he was going back up to the meeting room?'

'Yes, I'm sure of it.'

'That's extremely useful information. What about you? Did you have coffee in the dining room?'

'Yes. I'd finished my food before some of the others, so I had some coffee and then I went outside for a smoke before the afternoon session started.'

'Where exactly did you go?'

'Just outside the main entrance. There was a notice asking people not to smoke in front of the doors, so I went a little way down the path that goes along the side of the building to the left. I found a bench to sit on down there.'

'Did you see anyone else outside while you were there? A gardener, perhaps? Or security guards or new guests arriving?'

'No. I don't remember anyone – until Beverley Greenhalgh came back at about twenty-five past one.'

'Which direction did she come from?'

'Along the path. As she passed my bench, she told me it was time to get back. She seemed a bit out of breath, as if she'd been running. I didn't think anything of it at the time, but now, I can't help wondering …'

'Did you know of any reason that she might hold a grudge against Bridgefield?'

'Not in particular, but she made it very obvious that she didn't like him – perhaps a bit too obvious. It did cross my mind that it might be a case of "the lady doth protest too much". After all, she is a woman of a certain age – if you get my meaning.'

'Can you think of anyone else who might have wanted to kill Mr Bridgefield?'

'Ah now, there you're asking,' Brampton thought for a few moments. 'He was rather a nasty piece of work in my opinion. If it had been up to me, I'd never have appointed him as bursar. He may have been an Oxford graduate, but he really didn't fit in – of course, you can't be expected to understand what it means to be a real Oxford man. I don't suppose your people have any experience of what it means to go to a good university.'

'Perhaps you might try to explain,' Andy, who had a first class degree in criminology from the University of Leicester, suggested mildly, biting back the urge to demand to know what exactly Brampton meant by 'your people', which he strongly suspected was a reference to the colour of his skin.

'He saw everything in terms of money – no idea of the importance of scholarship for its own sake. He'd been to a comprehensive school in Hemel Hempstead and you could tell that he'd never picked up proper manners.'

'Someone told me that he had rather old fashioned manners when it came to the way he treated women,' Andy suggested tentatively. 'Would you disagree with that?'

'On the surface, perhaps,' Brampton conceded, 'but it was all superficial; there was no substance to it. No gentleman would have resorted to the sort of innuendo that he used. I know a lot of women were very uncomfortable in his presence.'

'So I've heard. Do you think that could have provided a motive for killing him?'

'I don't know about that, but I certainly think there must be a good many women who won't be sorry to hear that he won't be troubling them again. Take Ann, for example …'

'Dr Lambert?'

'Yes. I've known her since she was a baby. Her father was my old college tutor you know – back in the sixties before the college went co-ed. Maxwell Lambert taught me Greek. Now he was a *real* Oxford gentleman, not like the dons you get these days. He used to live in college in my day, but then he married and moved out to Summertown. His wife always made his old students welcome when we visited him there after he retired. Ann was their only child. They married late you see.'

'So is that why you have regular meetings with Dr Lambert?' Andy asked.

'What do you mean? Who told you that?' barked Brampton.

'There were appointments in your diary-,' Andy began.

'And who gave you permission to look in my private

diary?'

'It was left on the table in the meeting room. It isn't password-protected so anyone could have looked in it during the lunch break on Wednesday. If you considered it to be private, why didn't you take it with you to the dining room? It was part of the evidence in a murder enquiry and we felt obliged to check that there was nothing in it of relevance to the case. I can assure you that anything we found there will be kept completely confidential – unless it turns out to be needed as evidence in a prosecution.'

Brampton continued to look affronted, but Andy pressed on regardless.

'Now perhaps you could answer my question. You are in the habit of meeting with Dr Lambert every two weeks or so. Can you tell me what those meetings are about?'

'Since her father died she's come to rely on me for advice. Her mother has dementia, poor woman and had to go into a home. She's a great worry to Ann, who already had enough on her plate with Bridgefield hanging around her. He, incidentally, was no use at all at helping with her mother – he was worse than useless. Ann always seemed to feel she was letting him down whenever she spent time with her mother instead of dancing attendance on him; but of course, if he felt like staying out all night with some floozy, she wasn't to complain about *that* – it was his right to do as he chose!' Brampton snorted. 'The best thing that ever happened to little Ann was when he walked out on her – not that she'll ever see it that way. In her mind he could do no wrong.'

'That's interesting. So you think she still entertained romantic feelings towards him? You don't think she might have wanted to punish him for the way he behaved?'

'I certainly wouldn't have blamed her if she *had* killed him. It would have given me great pleasure to do it myself. He got what was coming to him, in my opinion. But Ann was so kind-hearted and gentle – and physically not very strong. I don't see how she could have strangled a man with her bare hands.'

He looked down at his owns hands as he spoke and Andy followed his gaze. They were blue-veined and gnarled with arthritis. Andy felt certain that these could not be the hands that had placed a cable around a man's neck and pulled it tight enough to squeeze the life out of him.

'Can you think of anyone else who might have born Bridgefield a grudge? Did anyone appear unusually antagonistic towards him on Wednesday – as if they had had an argument? Your evidence is particularly useful to us,' Andy went on, hoping to encourage Brampton to open up by playing on his self-importance, 'because, as an outsider, you may see things that wouldn't be obvious to the college staff.'

Brampton thought for a while before answering.

'There was a lot of talk about that girl that he'd run off with,' he said at last. 'I thought it was rather indelicate considering that Ann was present. I think several of the others thought he was out of order this time, because she was in such a junior position. They thought he was exploiting her.'

'Did anyone in particular voice this opinion? Who said it first?'

'I think it was probably the chaplain. And quite right too – he ought to be doing something to safeguard the morals of the college members.'

'Do you have any idea what he thought about Dr Lambert's relationship with Bridgefield? I mean, that wasn't strictly according to the rules of the Church of England was it?'

'I dare say he felt obliged to disapprove, but I think he didn't really blame Ann. They always got on very well together.'

'Do you think,' Andy asked cautiously, 'that the chaplain could have gone to remonstrate with Bridgefield about his behaviour during the lunch break? I mean, do you think he felt strongly enough about it?'

'Are you suggesting that he could be the murderer?'

'No, I'm just asking how strong you think his feelings were about Bridgefield's behaviour.'

'I think he felt sorry for Ann and disapproved of Bridgefield's attitude towards her, but he was too easy-going in my opinion – no real moral fibre. I doubt he'd even have the courage to tell Bridgefield what he thought of him, never mind killing him.'

'Someone must have done it,' Andy pointed out. 'Do you have any hunch who it might have been? A man of your experience must have some ideas ...'

'I wouldn't like to point the finger at anyone, but if I had to pick one person out of the lot of them, I suppose it would be Beverley Greenhalgh.'

'And why would that be?'

'She's a fanatic about women's rights. The most dangerous people in society are the ones that believe in a cause. I could well imagine she could have killed Bridgefield and thought she was striking a blow for freedom against male tyranny.'

'Thank you. That's a very interesting point.' Andy looked up from his notes and smiled at Brampton. 'Well, I think that's all. If you do think of anything else that might help us, don't hesitate to give us a call.'

23 THE WIFE

When Jonah and Bernie entered the archway that led into Lichfield College, they found Andy waiting for them.

'I've got the room all set up ready for you,' he greeted them. 'Jessica says she's booked it out all day again for us.'

As they followed him into the seminar room, a ringing sound announced that someone was trying to contact Jonah by telephone. A few movements of his left index finger allowed him to answer the call.

'Hi Dad,' came a voice through the loudspeaker. 'Are you OK to talk?'

'Go ahead Nathan. You just caught us in time before we start interviewing our next witness.'

'Good,' there was a pause and then the voice went on, 'I'm really sorry Dad. I could really do with staying in London this weekend. Do you think Bernie and Peter could put you up for a few more days, just this once? You see, I've been invited – well they've invited us both, that is me and Georgia too – to this prestigious legal dinner on Saturday night. I was going to say "no" but our head of chambers is really keen that we should go. Do you think Bernie will mind?'

'Don't worry, Nathan,' Bernie broke in, anxious to put the lad out of his misery. 'We'll cope. In fact, we'll enjoy it. You go ahead and tell your boss you'll be there at your posh dinner do.'

'Thank you,' Nathan said gratefully. 'I won't make a habit of it I promise.'

'You'd better not,' his father growled. Although secretly pleased at the prospect of spending the weekend with his friends instead of returning to his old marital home to be looked after by his willing, but often inept, son, he felt obliged to make it clear that Nathan had no right to expect to be able to hand over his responsibilities in this way.

'Indeed you mustn't,' Bernie chipped in cheerfully. 'If you keep letting us have him all week like this, one day we may decide we're not handing him back at all!'

'Well thanks anyway,' Nathan replied, not quite sure how to respond to this. 'I'd better let you get on. Bye!'

The call ended and Jonah looked up at Bernie with an expression of disapproval on his face.

'I don't know what that boy thinks he's playing at,' he declared. 'He might at least have given you some notice. What if you'd been planning to go away for the weekend?'

'Well we're not, so it doesn't matter.'

'No, I suppose not,' Jonah grumbled, more annoyed than Bernie was because he felt that this inconsiderate behaviour reflected badly on his son's upbringing. 'OK. We'd better get started. Bernie, could you go and fetch Mrs Bridgefield?'

Bernie nodded and got up to go. Jonah watched her as she went out and closed the door behind her. Then he turned his chair so that he was facing his sergeant.

'Now Andy, before Our Bernie gets back, tell me what on earth got into you when you were talking to Peter yesterday.'

'I don't understand,' Andy blustered. 'Why is everyone making such a big deal out of it? All I said was-'

'You really don't understand, do you?' Jonah broke in, shaking his head in disbelief. 'You really don't see what you've done to poor Peter. Alright, let's start again. Let me tell you a few things about old Peter that you may not have heard about. Did anyone tell you how his wife died?'

'No. When we were working together, he never even mentioned he'd been married before. It was only when you introduced me to Bernie that I realised she wasn't the first Mrs Johns.'

'Angela Johns was stabbed to death in a vicious attack in her own kitchen.'

'How dreadful for him!' Andy exclaimed, shocked. 'I never knew. What happened? Was it racially-motivated?'

'Sort of, but it was more complicated than just that. At first, everyone assumed it must have been white racists, killing her as some sort of ethnic cleansing; but we were wrong: it turned out to be a gang of black youths who didn't approve of a black woman marrying a police officer. You can imagine how that makes Peter feel.'

Andy sat in silence, not knowing what to say.

'Peter has two kids,' Jonah resumed, 'Hannah and Eddie. They both consider themselves to be black, so Peter has always been the ethnic minority in his family.'

'But he must have had parents,' Andy objected, starting to feel that Jonah was being unreasonably harsh in his criticism, 'and brothers and sisters. It's not the same as being the *only* one.'

'No. Peter was brought up in a children's home, so his wife and kids were the only family he ever had,' Jonah went on remorselessly. 'Eddie went off to Jamaica to live with his relatives over there after his mother died. What d'you think that does for Peter's self-esteem as a father? Do you think he needs you to tell him that being a mixed-race kid isn't easy?'

'I told you: I didn't know,' Andy muttered angrily, staring at the floor. 'How was I to know?'

The door opened and Bernie ushered in a woman in

her early fifties wearing a floral pattern dress. She looked round nervously at the two police officers.

'This is Mrs Amanda Bridgefield,' Bernie introduced her.

'Mrs Bridgefield, thank you for coming,' Jonah took over. 'I'm Detective Chief Inspector Jonah Porter and this is Detective Sergeant Andrew Lepage. We're investigating the death of your ex-husband, Anthony Bridgefield, and we have some questions about him that we think you may be able to answer for us. Please, sit down.'

Amanda Bridgefield sat down opposite Jonah. Her eyes continued to dart nervously around the room. Bernie poured her a glass of water before resuming her own seat on Jonah's left.

'Mrs Bridgefield,' Jonah began again.

'Mandy, please. Everyone calls me Mandy.'

'Whatever you prefer. Mandy, in order to find out what happened, we need to get the best possible picture of what your hus- that is, Mr Bridgefield, was like. I'm afraid we may have to ask you some quite personal questions about your marriage and so on, but you can be confident that we'll keep your answers confidential. Do you understand?'

'Of course,' Mandy nodded, appearing to relax a little, 'not that I'm likely to tell you anything that isn't common knowledge around the college. Anthony seemed to take pride in flaunting his affairs in front of everyone.'

'That must have made things difficult for you. Did you ever think of finding another job after the divorce – to get away from him?'

'No. Why should *I* leave?' Mandy's nervousness seemed to have subsided and she sounded combative. 'Everyone knew that he was the guilty party. Besides, I was here first. If anyone ought to have left it was him.'

'I see. Well now, perhaps the simplest thing would be if you started from the beginning. You married in 1989, is that correct?'

'Yes, in June of that year.'

'And your son was born in October of the same year?' Jonah asked, glancing down at the information that Andy had provided for him from the register of births, marriages and deaths.

'Yes. And, yes, you're right in deducing that it may well be that it was only the imminent arrival of our son which persuaded Anthony to get married at all. The Master of the day was very particular about that sort of thing and made it abundantly clear what was expected of us. To be fair to him, he arranged for Anthony to be given a college house for us to live in. That hadn't been part of the deal when he was appointed. I think that, underneath, he felt rather sorry for us and wanted to make things as easy as possible.'

'But you think that if it hadn't been that his employer expected it of him, he would probably not have wanted to marry you?'

'No. Monogamy didn't suit him at all. Even before our son was born I was quite aware that he was playing away on a regular basis.'

'And how did that make you feel?'

'Pretty fed up, if you must know, but I had the baby to think of, and I told myself that Anthony was still very young and things would calm down as he got older.'

'But they didn't?'

'No. If anything, they got worse. About ten years into our marriage, I think he had a sort of premature mid-life crisis and felt he had to prove to himself that he was still attractive to women. That's when his affair with Ann Lambert started.'

'Ah yes – that seems to have been a bit different. D'you have any idea why he decided to move in with her, rather than just treating her as a bit on the side, like all the others?'

'I think she probably made it clear to him that she wasn't interested in anything less. People get the wrong idea about Ann,' she went on, seeing Jonah's look of mild surprise. 'She looks tiny and pretty and vulnerable, but she's really quite a strong character. She wouldn't have been made Dean if she didn't know how to deal with students who step out of line. She has a very intimidating line in quiet reasonableness which reduces even members of the rugger club to wobbly heaps of jelly.'

'So you think she was expecting him to leave you and become faithful to her?'

'Yes, I really think she thought he would do that. I think she thought he ran around after other women because he was somehow dissatisfied with what I had to offer and that, once he had her, he wouldn't need to do it any more.'

'So he moved into Ann's house and then, a couple of years later, you were divorced?'

'Yes, that's right.'

'And that meant both of you giving up the college house. Where did you go?'

'Fortunately I'd had the sense to keep our finances separate, so I'd managed to save up quite a decent deposit in my own name to put on a house. I carried on working after Matthew was born, you see. Anthony was ordered to pay some maintenance for Matthew, which helped to pay the mortgage. The Master was very generous and let us stay in the house for a few months while we got ourselves sorted out.'

'That was the old Master – the one who persuaded you to get married – not Grainger?'

'No, it wasn't either of them. Sir Marcus Titherington retired a few years after we were married – he was in his nineties so it was a wonder he hadn't gone before – and he was succeeded by Dr Samuel Arbuthnot. Featherstone Grainger wasn't appointed until after we got divorced.'

'I see. Now, tell me, what sort of relationship did Matthew have with his father? Were they close?'

'Matthew had no time for his father and Anthony had no time for anyone except himself! No, they weren't close.

After he left us, Anthony didn't even so much as send Matthew a card on his birthday. He had no interest in being a father.'

'What about before he left?' Jonah persisted. 'While Anthony was still living with you, did they get on?'

'Like I said, Anthony never showed any interest in Matthew. Right from when he was a baby, as far as Anthony was concerned Matthew was my responsibility.'

'Do you think Matthew resented that?'

'Well, he'd never known anything different, had he?'

'Alright. So, what about when Anthony left home. How did Matthew feel about that?'

'You'd better ask him, hadn't you?'

'But you're his mother: you must have worried about how he'd take it. You must have some idea how it was affecting him. For example, was he angry with his father for deserting you? Or was he pleased at not having to share your affections with anyone else any more?'

'I'd never really thought about it much,' Mrs Bridgefield answered, looking rather perplexed. 'I suppose probably there was a bit of both. He did go through a phase of being very protective of me. I remember thinking that it was a good thing I didn't have any plans for finding a new partner, because I couldn't see Matthew accepting another man in the house.'

'Does Matthew still live with you?'

'Yes. He's saving up to buy himself a place of his own, but property prices in Oxford are just ridiculous! In the end I even tried asking Anthony to give him something towards a deposit – or even to lend it to him – but he wasn't having any of it.'

'When was that?'

'Just this week: Tuesday, I suppose.'

'I see. Now can we go back a bit? You split up with your husband and then got divorced. He was living with Ann Lambert in her house and you were all three working here at Lichfield College. Wasn't that very awkward, for all three of you?'

'We managed,' Mandy said coldly. 'I wasn't going to let Anthony force me out. Why should I go just because he decided to shack up with one of the tutors? Anthony, I imagine, enjoyed the notoriety. It suited his male ego for everyone to see him working alongside both his ex-wife and his new partner. And Ann had no choice but to put up with it.'

'She could have looked for another job,' Jonah suggested.

'More fool her, if she had! I imagine she rapidly came to realise that she couldn't expect to keep Anthony exclusively to herself. At least if she was working with him she could keep a close eye on who he was chatting up and she could make sure they were aware that he was spoken for.'

'Why d'you think she stayed with him so long – after she realised that he wasn't going to marry her and settle down?'

'You'd have to ask her that, but for what it's worth I think maybe she never quite accepted that he *wouldn't* eventually settle down. Even after he left her, I think she had hopes that he'd come back. I couldn't believe how shocked she sounded on the phone when I told her his latest conquest was pregnant.'

'That was the phone call that you made to her on Wednesday?'

'Yes. She told you about it then?'

'How did you find out that Penny Green was expecting his child?'

'Anthony told me, when I went cap in hand to him to beg for a contribution towards Matthew's house. He said that he'd already paid his dues as far as his first family was concerned and now he had to concentrate on how he was going to support the new baby.'

'Were you surprised to hear the news?'

'Yes and no. I was surprised that Anthony had allowed

it to happen – but then, when I thought about it, I thought probably the girl had arranged it deliberately in order to get him to leave Ann. In many ways, that had been the real surprise. I'd been wondering why he hadn't just strung Penny along the way he usually did. It looked as if she'd been too clever for him and tricked him so that even he felt obliged to "stand by her" as they used to say. I don't imagine for a minute that it would have lasted. Anthony likes his comfort too much. A cramped flat with a girl young enough to be his daughter and a baby keeping them both awake at nights just isn't his style. He'd soon have started missing Ann's home cooking and the way she paid all the bills.'

'Alright. Now you say Ann sounded shocked when you broke the news to her. Do you just mean that she was upset or did she sound angry?'

'She must have been a bit of both, I imagine.'

'And was her anger directed towards Anthony or Penny?'

'You'd better ask her, but again, I'd say a bit of both.'

'Did she say what she was planning to do about it?'

'You mean, did she say she was going straight off to murder him? She'd hardly do that, would she?'

'No, I meant, did she say she was going to confront him? Or perhaps to talk to Penny?'

'No. she didn't say anything. She went very quiet and then thanked me for telling her and rang off.'

'I see. Now, tell me, *why* did you ring her?'

'I thought she ought to know about Penny before it became obvious to the world. After Anthony left her, I felt sorry for Ann. She probably really loved him; although I can't think why, when you consider the way he behaved all the time. I actually thought it might soften the blow a bit for her if she knew he hadn't just got tired of her and gone off with Penny because she was younger.'

Remembering Ann's anguish when she had described to them how much she had longed for a child of her own,

Jonah wondered to himself whether Mandy could really have misjudged her so badly as to think that it would be a comfort to know that Anthony's new girlfriend had achieved what Ann had hoped for in vain for so long. Was she really trying to lessen Ann's pain? Or had she, rather, hoped to turn the knife in the wound?

'Thank you for being so frank about your relationship with your husband. Now, just for the record, I have to ask you where you were on Wednesday between twelve thirty and one thirty.'

'I was here in college.'

'Is there anyone who can confirm that?'

'Let me see … I was with Bernard Malpas, the head porter, from about eleven thirty until twelve forty-five. We were discussing the arrangements for a conference of Japanese businessmen that starts next week. After that, I went to lunch in hall. You can ask the staff who were serving: they all know me, and it was a quiet day with so many of the dons away.'

'Did you know where the Awayday was taking place? I mean, which hotel?'

'Oh yes: I recommended it. It's all part of my job, you see. Conferences play a big part in keeping the college afloat financially. In many ways, the college is like a large hotel. In term time our clients are the students and out of term we cater for businesses and educational establishments who want to put on conferences and training courses in the environment of an Oxford college. The local hotels are in some ways our competitors but they are also useful to us on occasions when we need extra accommodation or facilities or, as in this case, just somewhere off-site. When the Master decided to put on this Awayday he came to me and I recommended the hotel.'

'Now, getting back to your son, what's he doing now? I take it he must have a job?'

'Yes. Actually, he works at the Ivy Tree hotel – where

the Awayday was. The manager's a friend of mine and after Matthew graduated, he was kind enough to give him a trial. He's been there for nearly four years now.'

'Really? What does he do?'

'All sorts. He mans reception sometimes and sometimes waits on in the dining room – whatever's needed really. It's not really a graduate job, but he's doing management training and there's a good chance he'll get promoted.'

'And did you tell him that his father was going to be there on Wednesday?'

'No, I didn't know that he was. I might have said that there was going to be party from the college, but the Master didn't give me a guest list so I had no idea exactly who would be there.'

'If Matthew happened to meet any of the staff from the college while they were there, would they have recognised him? Did they know him at all?'

'I shouldn't think so. Matthew never came to the college. I don't suppose that even Anthony would have known who he was. They hadn't met for years. When Anthony was killed, Matthew didn't realise that it was his father. All they told him was that one of the delegates had died and the police had said no one was to go in the room. He didn't find out who it was until he got home and I told him that the police had been to see me.'

'So you didn't telephone your son to tell him about his father's death?'

'What would have been the point of that? He was going to find out soon enough. He didn't like me phoning him at work.'

'And when you did tell him, how did he take it?'

'Like I expected, he wasn't bothered. Anthony never paid him any attention so he didn't see why he should pretend to care about it when he died. It really didn't make any difference to us. As far as I remember, I told him and he just grunted and then took the dog out for its walk as usual.'

'Did you and Mathew expect to inherit anything in your husband's will?'

'We'd learnt not to *expect* anything, but I suppose I did hope he might leave Matthew something. I think he owed him that much, but I don't suppose he will have thought of it that way.'

'So you weren't worried that his having another child would affect you or Matthew financially?

'How could it?' Mandy shrugged. 'You can't get less than nothing can you?'

'Did you tell Matthew about Penny's baby?'

'No. I couldn't very well tell him without admitting that I'd asked his father for money and he wouldn't have liked that. He didn't want us to be dependent on Anthony in any way. If he *had* given Matthew anything towards the house I'd have had to find a way of dressing it up somehow so that he didn't know where it had come from.'

'And does he know now – about the baby, I mean?'

'Not from me, and I can't think of anyone else who would tell him.'

'What about Ann Lambert? If she happened to meet him at the hotel after you'd broken the news, d'you think she'd have said anything to him?'

'Why should she? Anyway, how would she know he was Anthony's son? They never met as far as I know. After the divorce I kept Matthew strictly away from the college and everyone involved with it – especially Ann, as you can imagine.'

'I see. Now, finally, can you think of anyone who might have wanted Anthony dead?'

'How long have you got?' Mandy chuckled grimly. 'Apart from me and Ann there must be a couple of hundred women who have good reason to bear him a grudge – not to mention all their husbands and boyfriends! He just used people and then discarded them. The trouble was, at the time he was doing it he was so charming and generous that you couldn't help imagining that you were the one for whom it would be different – but of course it never was.'

'I wasn't necessarily thinking of the women with whom he had affairs,' Jonah explained. 'It's been suggested to me that he might not have been above a spot of blackmail – if he found out something that someone else wouldn't want to be made public. Do you think he would do that?'

'I don't know,' Mandy said slowly. 'He did like to feel that people were sort of under his control – but that was more to do with the idea that they were so attracted to him that they would do anything for him. I can't quite picture him extorting money in exchange for keeping quiet about something, if that's what you mean by blackmail. Maybe though, maybe he'd enjoy telling the person that he knew their guilty secret, just for the fun of seeing them squirm.'

'That's interesting. Thank you. I think that's everything, unless you have any questions for Mrs Bridgefield, Andy?'

'I'd like to ask how well you know Beverley Greenhalgh,' Andy said, remembering that Charles Brampton had identified her as the most likely murderer. 'And in particular what you think her opinion was of Mr Bridgefield.'

'She and I have both been at the college for a long time, but we aren't particular friends. She makes no secret of the fact that she despises Anthony and the way he can't – I mean, couldn't – keep his eyes – or his hands – off any pretty woman, well any woman more like. Why do you ask about her particularly?'

'We just have to find out as much as we can about everyone who was there,' Jonah said quickly. 'It's all just routine.'

'Thank you, that's all from me,' Andy added. 'I'll just give you one of our cards in case you think of anything else later.'

Bernie opened the door for Mandy to leave and then closed it firmly behind her.

'Right,' Jonah said in a business-like way. 'Andy, you go and find that head porter and check her alibi. It's nearly lunchtime, so you ought to be able to talk to the staff who serve in the dining hall too. I don't doubt she's telling the truth about being here, but we'd better make sure.'

'Right you are, sir. And then, would it be OK for me to take my lunch break after that? I've got one or two things I need to do.'

'Yes. Go ahead. After that, our next port of call had better be the hotel. We need to re-check whether Ann Lambert could have got up to the room after her telephone conversation with Mandy Bridgefield. And we need to find out whether Matthew Bridgefield was on duty that morning and might have bumped into his father. And we need to talk to the IT guy, who should be able to pinpoint the time of the murder to within about 5 minutes. So ... let's see ... how about if we meet you there at two? Will that give you time to do your errands?'

'Yes sir. That'll be fine. Thanks.'

24 THE TUTOR FOR OVERSEAS STUDENTS

Andy went off in search of the porter. Bernie packed up their things and held the door open for Jonah to go through. They were just emerging into the sunshine outside, when a voice called to them from across the patch of grass in the middle of the quadrangle. It was Beverley Greenhalgh.

'Excuse me,' she called, 'can I have a word?'

'By all means,' Jonah answered. 'Shall we go back inside?'

'No, it's alright, it won't take a moment. I just wanted to tell you ...' Beverley hesitated for a moment and then resumed, 'Martin told me you'd been asking about Nafisa's visa. I wanted to ask, will you really have to tell the Border Agency about them? Couldn't you at least wait until Kamran has got his DPhil and Nafisa's A' Level results are out?'

'Dr Greenhalgh,' Jonah answered, picking his words carefully to avoid committing himself to anything, while still allowing her some hope. 'I'm conducting a murder investigation. Anything that I consider pertinent to it will have to be recorded in the files, but I will not necessarily have time to follow up on everything that I happen to find out if it is not directly relevant. I do, however, have to warn you that more than one person has suggested to me that Mr Bridgefield was suspicious about student visas for which you were responsible and that I am therefore forced to consider the possibility that he could have been blackmailing you. Do you have anything to say on that subject?'

'Alright, I'll explain. You were quite right. Anthony Bridgefield had found out about it and he was being extremely unpleasant, threatening to tell the university authorities and so on. I was hoping I could put him off doing anything at least until Kamran had submitted his thesis, but honestly I didn't kill him to stop him talking.'

'Was he asking for money?'

'No! It was far worse than that,' Beverley stopped, appeared to be thinking, and then went on, speaking rather fast. 'Look, if I were to confess to killing Anthony Bridgefield would you be able to keep the business with Nafisa's visa quiet? I mean, would you be able to overlook it and let her go on to do her degree and become a doctor? You'd have got what you want – a conviction for the murder.'

'I'm sorry, I don't do deals of that sort,' Jonah said coldly. 'If you did murder Anthony Bridgefield then I advise you to make a full and frank confession without conditions. Even if I wanted to, I couldn't promise what you want, because it wouldn't be up to me what the prosecution decided to bring out during the trial. Presumably your motive for killing him was to prevent him from exposing your visa fraud?'

'What if I said it was nothing to do with that? If it was that I was outraged by his behaviour towards young women and wanted to put a stop to it once and for all?'

'Then I'm afraid that I wouldn't believe you, and I don't think the crown prosecution service would either.

Now tell me what you meant by saying that Bridgefield wasn't asking for money but for something far worse.'

'He wanted me to arrange for him to sleep with Nafisa,' Beverley said, speaking in an undertone as if she were ashamed to have to relay this information. 'He said he'd always fancied Asian girls, but he didn't get many opportunities to meet them.'

For a few moments nobody spoke. Jonah and Bernie were both shocked at this revelation, which showed Bridgefield in a quite different light from the charming Casanova, as which he had been portrayed up until now.

'Did you tell her about it?' Jonah asked at last.

'No, of course not. And I told *him* that it was out of the question, but he wouldn't let it drop and I was really afraid that in the end he would tell the authorities and they'd both be sent home in disgrace. It was so unfair! All Kamran wanted was to help his sister to make a career for herself. I didn't know what to do. That's why I went for a walk that lunchtime. I was trying to think of a way of stopping him from ruining both their lives.'

'And your career,' Jonah observed drily.

'Yes, but that wasn't the main thing at all.' Beverley turned to look at Bernie. 'You understand don't you? You understand why I wanted to save Nafisa from an early marriage to a man she hardly knew? You surely appreciate the importance of education for girls like her?'

'Yes,' Bernie sighed, 'I think I do understand. I think I even admire you for being willing to take the risks you did, but I can't help thinking about the girl's father and grandmother, who were probably only doing what they thought best for her; and about the way you allowed her brother to risk his own career and reputation and his relationship with his own family too ...'

'But surely you can see?' Beverley began. 'Why can't you both see?'

'Dr Greenhalgh,' Jonah said firmly. 'I advise you to go away and consider your position. If you did kill Mr

Bridgefield then be sure that I will find the evidence to prove it; so it would be far better if you were to save us all the trouble of continuing to search by giving a clear statement of what happened. On the other hand, if you *did not* do it then please don't waste my time pretending that you did. It may surprise you to know, but what I'm interested in is getting to the truth – not just getting a conviction regardless.'

'Isn't there anything I can do to persuade you to allow Kamran and Nafisa to stay?' Beverley pleaded. 'Whoever else killed Anthony, *they* certainly had nothing to do with it.'

'If, when I discover who the murderer really is, it has nothing to do with your little fraud,' Jonah said wearily, 'then I dare say I might be too busy tidying up the case to remember to inform the Home Office. What I want from you is for you to tell me anything you saw or heard that could have a bearing on Bridgefield's death – the truth mind you, not what you think I'd like to hear. Now for a start, we know you went round the side of the hotel while you were out for your walk. The CC-TV camera on the corner of the building caught you. Were you aware that there's a door into the building on that side?'

'I saw the door when I got round there, yes.'

'Do you know where it leads to?'

'What do you mean?'

'If you'd gone in that way, what part of the hotel would you have got into?'

'I don't know. The kitchens, maybe?'

'After you went round the side of the building, where did you go?'

'I just wandered around.'

'But staying on that side of the hotel?'

'Yes, I suppose so.'

'Did you see anyone else round there? In particular, did you see anyone go in through the side door?'

'No. I didn't see anyone at all. I just walked around

trying to think of a way of preventing Anthony from telling the university about Nafisa. I do wish I could get you to understand how devastating it would be for that poor girl if-'

'Alright, that'll do,' Jonah cut in. 'We'd better be going. If you think of anything else that might help, you know how to contact us.'

Beverley nodded and turned away to walk back across the grass and in through a door on the opposite side of the quad. Jonah and Bernie made their way back to the car.

'What a mess!' Bernie said as she fixed the ramp to the back of the vehicle to allow Jonah to enter. 'Do you think she did do it? That's the best motive we've heard so far.'

'I don't know. You're right about the motive and she certainly *could* have slipped in through the side door and up the stairs, but somehow, I'm just not convinced ...' Jonah paused, while Bernie attended to the straps that secured his chair for the journey. 'There's something else you were right about,' he added, 'I reckon *whoever* did it, it'll be someone a whole lot nicer than Anthony Bridgefield!'

25 THE POLICE SERGEANT

Peter was just winding up the flex of the hoover after cleaning the living room, when there was a ring at the door. He went to answer it and found Andy waiting there, shifting from foot to foot looking most uncomfortable.

'Were you looking for Jonah?'

'No. I – I – I need to talk to you. I want to apologise for last night.'

'You'd better come in.' Peter stepped back to allow Andy into the hall. Then he closed the door again and ushered him into the living room.

They sat down in easy chairs facing one another across the room. Andy twisted his hands together in his lap wondering how to start.

'I suppose Our Bernie's been getting at you,' Peter suggested, trying to help him out.

'No. She didn't say a word. Well,' he corrected himself, 'that's not quite true. She did make a few cryptic remarks as I was leaving yesterday, "more in sorrow than in anger" sort of thing.'

'That's the worst!' Peter said, smiling. 'She's got you in her sights now and once that happens you might as well give in. First off, you'll find that you've suddenly become "our Andy" and then the next thing you know you'll be getting an invitation to High Tea one Saturday. She'll have got you marked down as "family" by now and if you take my advice you'll just accept the inevitable and go with the flow!'

Andy paused for a minute, looking at Peter, trying to work out whether he was supposed to take any of this remotely seriously. He pulled himself together and had another go at explaining what he had come for.

'It was Jonah who sorted me out. He told me about how your first wife died. I'm sorry. I had no idea.'

'There's no reason why you should have.'

'It must have been a dreadful shock for you.'

Peter nodded.

'In some ways, it was even worse for Our Bernie: she was the one who found her.'

'Bernie found your wife when she'd been killed?'

'That's right. They were great friends. Angie took Bernie under her wing shortly after we were married. Bernie had been going through a bit of a bad patch just then – but that's her story not mine – and after that they were pretty well inseparable. Anyway, Bernie found Angie one morning, lying dead in the kitchen in a pool of blood. I'd gone off to work only an hour or two before, leaving everything just a usual. It was the most enormous shock to us all.'

'She was killed in the kitchen? In this kitchen here?'

'No, no. This is Bernie's house, or rather, it belonged to her first husband, Lucy's father. You've probably heard people talking about him. He was my boss: Detective Superintendent Richard Paige. He was killed in the line of duty a few months before Lucy was born. Angie and I had a much more modest terraced place down Cowley Road. Anyway, Bernie called round to take Angie shopping and when she didn't answer the door she let herself in and found – well!' Peter shook his head, picturing the scene in his mind. 'It was pretty horrendous. They'd trashed the kitchen and then stabbed Angie over and over again. I'm just eternally grateful that Bernie had left Lucy in the car, so she didn't have to see it. She was only three – it might have scarred her for life.'

They sat together in silence for a few minutes. Then Andy plucked up courage to speak again.

'And all that stuff about you not understanding what it was like for me and my mum – that was out of order. I'd got no business-'

'But that's just what I wanted to ask you about,' Peter interrupted eagerly. 'My kids would never say anything, but you can tell me what it's really like. I mean-'

'No, but I can't. It's not the same at all. Jonah made me see that. Your kids had two parents. They could see both sides. I mean – they were part of two communities: black *and* white. I only had my mum and she could only show me the white part and I – I – well, because I didn't seem to fit there I suppose I resented being different. Plus, I was so angry all the time with my dad for what he did to her. I've really hated him all my life. I still do. I don't think I can ever stop hating him. Your kids – well I hope they're proud to be black *and* white.'

Peter got up and went across to the large dresser standing against the wall next to the fireplace. Her opened a drawer and got out a photograph album. Then he came back and sat down on the settee, beckoning Andy to join him.

'Come and have a look at the Johns family album and tell me what you think of us.'

Andy watched as Peter turned the pages, giving a commentary on the pictures displayed there.

'This is our honeymoon. We saved up so we could afford to go to Jamaica for me to meet Angie's family. Her youngest sister had never seen anyone with red hair before and she kept wanting to touch it to prove it was real!'

'Here's Hannah, as Mary in the school nativity play. The parents of one of the other girls complained that it wasn't authentic having a black Mary, but the teacher told them that Hannah probably looked more like the real Mary would have done than the little blond girl they'd had the year before.'

'Ah! Now this reminds me,' Peter pointed at a picture of himself, holding a five-year-old dark-skinned boy in his arms. 'I was thinking about what you said about your mum having to keep explaining to people that you weren't adopted. When people see me and Lucy together you'd be surprised how often they tell me that they can see a family likeness. Nobody ever suggested that either of my own children take after me – not in looks at any rate.'

Andy peered closer at the photograph, trying to find something similar in the two faces that were smiling up at him from the album.

'I'm sorry,' he said at last, 'I'm afraid I can't see it either. Perhaps if I looked at a more recent picture of your son?'

'Tell you what,' Peter said, getting up and fetching another album from the drawer. 'Why don't you compare wedding photographs? This is Eddie and his wife Crystal – and this is me and Angie when we were about the same age.'

He held out the two albums, each open at a photograph of a young couple standing in their best clothes on the steps of a church.

Andy was spared the awkwardness of having to admit that he was still unable to detect any resemblance between Peter and his son, by the sound of the front door opening as Bernie and Jonah arrived home, having decided to call there for lunch on the way to the hotel. They were surprised to find Peter and Andy sitting companionably together on the settee.

'Has Andy brought you up to date with the latest developments?' Jonah asked. 'It looks as if we may have another potential suspect.'

'No. We've had more important things to talk about,'

Peter replied, getting up and putting the albums away. 'I suppose you're expecting me to get you lunch now?'

'Tell you what,' Bernie volunteered, 'I'll do it, while Jonah fills you in on the late Anthony Bridgefield's family. Then you can give them the benefit of your vast experience to help them when they go in search of his estranged son. And Jonah – you also need to tell our Andy about the very interesting little chat we had with Beverley Greenhalgh after he'd left.'

'What is it?' Jonah asked, seeing the look of amusement that Peter and Andy exchanged as Bernie left the room.

'No, nothing,' Peter assured him, resuming a straight face with some difficulty. 'Go on: spill the beans. What have you found out this morning?'

Jonah related Mandy Bridgefield's story of her marriage, highlighting especially the fact that their son now worked at the hotel where the Awayday had taken place. Then Andy reported that the head porter had confirmed that Mandy had been with him in the room at the back of the Porters' Lodge until nearly one o'clock on Wednesday and that the staff serving lunch had remembered her buying a chicken salad shortly afterwards.

'So, however she felt towards her ex-husband, she can't have actually done the deed herself,' he concluded, 'but do you think she might have put her son up to it?'

'Difficult to say,' Peter mused. 'Neither of them really have anything to gain from killing him – unless they didn't know about the will and thought that the new baby would do the son out of his inheritance. If Bridgefield had died intestate then the boy would have inherited whatever he had to leave, but that would have changed if he'd acknowledged the new baby as his own. That business of blackmail with Dr Beverley Greenhalgh seems a more likely motive to me – if we can assume that she was lucky enough to just happen to have picked the few minutes left when Bridgefield was alone in the room to sneak in through the side door and attack him.'

'But that's your inbuilt prejudice against the academic community,' Bernie interjected, coming into the room with a tray of sandwiches and a bowl of fruit. 'You don't want it to be the hardworking hotel clerk or his equally hardworking mother. You'd much rather think that a Botany tutor with a first in natural sciences from Cambridge indulged in a little experiment to see how tight you needed to pull a wire round someone's neck in order to squeeze the life out of them – purely in the interests of science, you understand!'

'I'm just looking at the facts,' Peter protested, picking up a sandwich and taking a bite, 'I can't help it if they point towards a kindred spirit of yours.'

'Don't take any notice, Peter,' Jonah advised him, with a smile, 'according to Our Bernie, I'm prejudiced in Beverley's favour because she's a strong woman from Lancashire and I'm hoping to convict Ann Lambert because she irritates me!'

'I think It'd be difficult for Beverley to have done it,' Andy said, breaking into this exchange with what he hoped was a more rational contribution. 'If she came in through the side door, how would she have got past Ann? And if she came in through the front, why didn't Simon or the receptionist notice her?'

'You're right,' Jonah agreed, turning his face away from the sandwich that Bernie was attempting to put into his mouth. 'With Ann hovering around that corridor, the side door theory just doesn't work any more.'

Suddenly Peter remembered what Andy had said to him only a short while earlier: *I was so angry all the time with my dad for what he did to her. I've really hated him all my life. I still do. I don't think I can ever stop hating him.*

'Hang on!' he shouted, 'I reckon Bernie was right – it *is* the IT guy who did it.'

The others all looked at him in surprise.

'But why? Andy asked.'

'Because the IT guy is Bridgefield's son. His mother

told you that he worked at the hotel. Matt the technician is Matthew Bridgefield-'

'Yes!' Bernie exclaimed, 'his mother said he filled in doing all sorts around the hotel. Being one of the younger members of staff he'd be expected to know all about IT, so it wouldn't be surprising if he was the one who looked after that sort of thing.'

'He's angry with his father for leaving his mother to bring him up alone,' Peter resumed. 'Quite by chance he finds himself alone with him. Maybe he asks him for money and Bridgefield refuses, but most likely he's just boiling over with pent-up rage at the man who never seemed to care ...'

'Y'know Peter,' Jonah said, 'you could be right. We've got the timetable pinned down so tight now that it really is just between the IT guy and Tom Carrington. Nobody else had time to slip in and out between when the one left the room and the other went in. And the evidence of motive against Carrington is weak at best.'

'And Matthew Bridgefield might have been brooding for years about what he'd like to do to his father if ever he got him alone,' Andy said quietly. 'I really think you've got it there.'

'Don't count your chickens,' Jonah warned, feeling just a little resentful that his retired colleague might have solved the case for them. 'We don't know for certain that the IT guy really was Matthew. It may just be a figment of Peter's fevered imagination!'

Bernie's mobile rang. She fished it out of her pocket and looked down at the screen.

'It's Martin. I wonder what he wants.'

She switched the phone to loudspeaker, and propped it up in front of Jonah so that the microphone would pick up his voice if he spoke.

'I thought you ought to know,' Martin said, 'Penny Green has handed in her resignation.'

'Why's that?' Bernie asked.

'She's landed herself a junior lectureship at Keele. I suppose I ought to have told you about it before. I knew she'd been shortlisted, but I thought she didn't have enough experience.'

'I suppose it all depends who else applied.'

'Yes. Anyway, she's going as soon as she's served her three months' notice.'

'So you'll have to start looking for a replacement. I suppose at least it's not as bad as if she'd told you she was going on maternity leave!'

'Why do say that?' Martin asked sharply.

'Oh, no reason,' Bernie quickly tried to backtrack realising that she was in danger of having given away confidential information. 'I was just thinking about all the trouble we had with Chloë.'

'It's just, that was the other thing I was going to tell you. There's this strange rumour going round. I rang Jess Stevens to let her know that Penny had resigned and we'd need to be advertising for a new RA and she told me that people were saying that Penny's having a baby in the autumn! I was gobsmacked. She never said a word about it to me. I wonder whether her new employer knows about it.'

'Well,' Bernie said, 'I have to admit that the rumour had reached us, but not until it was too late to ask Penny about it when we saw her this morning.'

'Typical!' Martin complained. 'It looks as if I must be the last one to know. Of course, I'm only her supervisor. There's no need to inform me!'

'I was wondering,' Jonah put in, 'would you be able to bring the conversation round to the subject and try to find out from Penny whether it *is* just a rumour or if there's any truth in it?'

'I'll do my best,' Martin said doubtfully. 'It's not an easy question to ask, you know.'

'As her line manager you have a right to know,' Bernie pointed out. 'Especially with her working in the lab. There might be noxious substances that she's got to steer clear of or something. She ought to have come to you and asked health and safety to do a risk assessment.'

'OK. Like I say, I'll do my best.'

'That's the spirit,' Bernie said encouragingly. 'And remember: a lie can run round the world while the truth's still getting its boots on.

'You mean the rumour may not be true?'

'Precisely,' Jonah declared decisively. 'I have a definite feeling in my bones that Penny has been leading us all a merry dance with this one.'

26 THE PENITENT

'Now Bernie,' Jonah said, as they shared a pot of tea after lunch. 'I've been trying to work out what you meant by this "love tetrahedron" that you said you were in. A tetrahedron is like a triangular pyramid, is that right?'

'Yup –that's the one!' Bernie agreed, grinning broadly and casting a glance in Peter's direction.

'So it has four sides. Is that what you're getting at?'

'Yes – you're getting it,' Bernie nodded

'So presumably we've got you, Peter and Martin as three of the sides. What I want to know is who's the fourth?'

'You, of course, Dumbo,' Peter answered before Bernie had a chance to reply. 'As if you didn't know!'

'Actually I thought it was probably Lucy. She must come in somewhere.'

'I suppose,' Bernie said, thinking quickly, 'Lucy would have to be a sphere inside the tetrahedron touching all four sides. What do you think, Peter?'

'That describes things perfectly,' he agreed.

'Hmm!' Jonah mused, smiling up at Bernie. 'Isn't it a bit arrogant of you to portray yourself as the top of a pyramid with us three men at the base gazing worshipfully up at you?'

'But that's not how I see it at all,' Bernie protested. 'As you said: we're each one of the faces of the tetrahedron, not the vertices. Each face joins on to *all* the others, and it's a regular tetrahedron, which means that it's symmetric – there isn't a top. Of course, the edge that joins you and Martin is a bit weak at the moment, but we'll soon sort that out – especially with you staying here over the weekend – which reminds me,' she turned to Andy, who had been watching this interchange with a mixture of amusement and bewilderment, 'are you doing anything tomorrow? Would you like to come to Saturday tea with us?'

Andy hesitated. He very much liked the idea of joining this strange new 'family', but he was unsure whether it was appropriate for him to accept the invitation. Up to now, he had always tried to keep his work and social life separate. Then he looked up and saw Peter, who was standing behind Bernie, grinning at him. When he saw Andy looking at him, he rolled his eyes expressively and gave an exaggerated shrug, clearly conveying the message *what did I tell you?*

'Thank you,' Andy said, at last, 'I'd like that.'

'Good,' Bernie smiled complacently, 'we'll expect you about five. Now hadn't we better be going?'

Their preparations for departure were interrupted by the arrival of an email in Jonah's inbox. Its subject was *URGENT: re A Bridgefield murder.* The sender was Beverley Greenhalgh.

Peter, Andy and Bernie clustered round Jonah's chair so that they could read it over his shoulder.

'I've decided to tell you everything,' Jonah read out. 'I hope that you will be able to find your way to being discrete about things that are not directly relevant to the death of Anthony Bridgefield so that nobody else need suffer as a result of what I did.'

'Presumably that's her way of asking you not to inform

221

on them about the girl's visa, without actually mentioning it,' Peter commented.

'I killed Anthony Bridgefield,' Jonah read on, nodding at Peter in agreement, 'by strangling him with a strap which I keep in the car for attaching things to the roof rack. When I went out for my walk at lunchtime, I went through the gardens at the side of the hotel to the car park and got the strap. Then I went in through the side door and up the stairs to the meeting room. Anthony was sitting there on his own. I came up behind him and put the strap round his neck and pulled it tight.'

'Would the marks on his neck be compatible with a strap?' Bernie asked. 'Didn't Mike Carson say that the ligature had to be something thin and smooth?'

'It rather depends what this strap was like,' Andy commented. 'We'll have to ask her to give it to us for tests.'

'If the rest of this so-called confession is sufficiently convincing to warrant it,' Jonah agreed sceptically, 'but let's see what else she has to say.'

'Once I was sure he was dead,' Bernie read out, resting her chin on Jonah's shoulder, 'I went back down the stairs and out of the side door and returned the strap to the car. Then I noticed the time and ran back through the gardens to get back to the hotel before the afternoon session started. I met Charles Brampton outside the main entrance and we went in together.'

'Would those timings work?' Peter asked. 'Would she have had time to get to the car park and back between killing Bridgefield and meeting Brampton?'

'It'd have been tight,' Andy said, checking his notes. 'But if we assume the IT guy spent next to no time in the room, she could have got there at, say twelve minutes past one, done the deed, run downstairs and outside *before* Ann Lambert came into the corridor to take her call, raced across to the car park – well, we'd need to have a look to see how far that is – and then got back in time to meet

Brampton at about twenty-five past.'

'Didn't you say Brampton thought she'd been running?' Jonah asked.

'Yes. He said she seemed breathless when she passed him on the bench.' Andy confirmed.

'I killed him,' Bernie continued reading, 'to stop him preying on women. I'd recently heard that a young research assistant whom he'd seduced was pregnant. I was afraid that she would waste her life tying herself to this worthless man in the way that Ann Lambert did. I hoped that, by getting rid of him, I would enable her to break free and make a life for herself and her child. She was just one of a long series of women who had suffered at his hands. I decided that the only thing to do to protect them was to get rid of him permanently. That is the only reason that I decided to kill him.'

'Huh!' Jonah snorted. 'Whatever truth there may be in the rest of this, *that*'s a lie.'

'Yes, but can we really discount this confession altogether?' Peter asked. 'It all depends-'

'On the IT guy,' the others finished with him in chorus.

'Right,' Jonah said decisively, 'we'd better get off to the hotel and interview this elusive IT wallah. I won't reply to this email. We'll leave Dr Greenhalgh to stew in her own juice for a while. Maybe she'll have second thoughts about falling on her sword when she realises that her stated motive still sounds dreadfully weak. After all, she doesn't even claim that it was done in the heat of the moment. There's all that stuff about fetching the murder weapon from the car.'

'Which is the one thing that makes me wonder whether her confession could possibly be true,' Peter said. 'I mean, apart from the motive which we all agree is to do with her Pakistani protégés. She walked around the garden, trying to think of a way of shutting Bridgefield up, and suddenly it comes to her. He's all alone in the meeting room – she's not to know about the Master or the IT guy popping in on him – and she's got a handy strap in the boot of her car that would just do as a garrotte. There's the side door right there, so nobody need see her go in. It all looks foolproof. And, once Bridgefield's out of the way, nobody need ever know that there was anything wrong with the visas.'

'Except,' Bernie took up the narrative, 'what she didn't know then was that Bridgefield had already hinted about irregularities with the student visas, which prompted us to investigate.'

'Alright, I agree it's not impossible that she's the killer,' Jonah admitted. 'But I'll need some forensic evidence from the strap in her car to convince me. Meanwhile, we still have to question the famous IT guy, so let's cut the cackle and get off.'

27 THE IT GUY

'Park round the side,' Jonah ordered as they approached the hotel down its long drive. 'I want to see how far it would have been for Beverley Greenhalgh to get between her car and the side door.'

Bernie obediently turned to the right, through an almost empty section of the car park to a secluded part surrounded by low bushes. There was a cluster of cars in one corner, which Bernie correctly deduced belonged to hotel staff, who had parked close to a narrow path leading to the side entrance. She pulled up next to a green hatchback.

'I hope nobody comes and parks opposite,' she observed a few minutes later, as Jonah descended the ramp at the back of their people carrier, 'or there may not be enough room for you to get back in.'

'Then you'll just have to move the car, won't you?' Jonah answered somewhat impatiently. 'Now get me over this kerb on to the path.'

Bernie carefully tilted the chair so that the front wheels were on the edge of the kerb. Andy stepped forward to help her lift the weight of Jonah and the chair and push it forward so that it was on the path. No sooner had they done so than Jonah was off, heading towards the hotel building at the maximum speed that the chair allowed. It took less than a minute to reach the side door.

'It looks as if Dr Greenhalgh's story could be true,' Andy said as they stood together by the entrance. 'Assuming she'd parked in that section of the car park, it wouldn't have been far at all for her to go to get the strap and then to return it afterwards.'

'But why would she park there instead of nearer the main entrance?' Bernie demanded.

'Perhaps that area was full.'

'At half past nine in the morning? Wasn't our Bev one of the first to arrive?' Bernie objected.

'I'm more interested in why Andy didn't get any pictures from that CC-TV camera,' Jonah broke in, tilting his head up towards a camera on the wall above, positioned to record anyone going in or out of the side entrance. 'I should have come round here before, instead of relying on what the hotel security told us. There's no substitute for checking the crime scene yourself. Did you know about this camera, Andy?'

'No. I asked to see all the CC-TV footage from the day of the murder. They gave me stuff from five cameras: the one at the front, the one on the corner (which caught Dr Greenhalgh), two at the back of the building where there's a sort of delivery yard beyond the kitchens, and one at the bottom of the drive by the entrance from the road. Nobody told me about this camera.'

'Well, I think we'd better ask them now, hadn't we? Let's go in.'

Bernie opened the door and held it while Jonah steered his wheelchair up the concrete slope and into the building. Andy followed and soon they were heading along the corridor past the ladies' and gents' toilets and the stairs. Bernie and Andy went ahead to hold open the double doors leading out into the lobby. The young woman at the reception desk looked up as they came in and recognised

Andy.

'Sergeant Lepage,' she greeted him warmly, 'what can I do for you?'

'We need to speak to a couple of people again, I'm afraid' he answered. 'Just a few questions to help us with our enquiries. First of all, we think Security may have forgotten to give us the recording from one of the CC-TV cameras and we'd like to ask them about it.'

'Just a minute, I'll get someone.'

The woman disappeared through a door behind the desk and reappeared shortly, accompanied by a man in a navy blue uniform with *security* embroidered on the pocket. Andy recognised him as the man who had shown him the recordings from the cameras on the previous occasion that he had visited.

'It's Jim, isn't it?' he said. 'This is my boss, Detective Chief Inspector Porter, and his assistant, Dr Fazakerley. We noticed the camera outside the side entrance and we were wondering why you didn't show me any footage from it the other day.'

'Um, well,' Jim said nervously, looking rather embarrassed, 'that camera has been on the blink for a few weeks now. I suppose I should have got it fixed, but to be honest the staff don't like it. That's the way they all come in, in the morning, and they don't like the idea that I can tell exactly what time they get here.'

'Thank you. That's all we needed to know,' Jonah dismissed him and turned to the receptionist, whose badge indicated to them that her name was Melanie. 'Now, we'd like to speak to the person who set up the computer equipment for the meeting on Wednesday. I think his name was Matthew.'

'Yes, that's right,' Melanie confirmed. 'It was Matt. I'll give him a call. If you'd like to take a seat over there ...'

Bernie and Andy sat down in two of the easy chairs, which Melanie had indicated, and Jonah brought his chair over to join them. Melanie was talking on the phone, presumably summoning Matthew from wherever his duties had taken him.

'It looks as if it wasn't any sort of conspiracy that stopped you seeing the view from that camera by the side door,' Jonah murmured to Andy, 'just that the employees didn't like the management being able to monitor how often they slipped out for a smoke during working hours.'

'It's difficult to see why anyone from the hotel would have wanted to stop you knowing about Beverley Greenhalgh going in that way anyway,' Bernie whispered. 'And any of the staff who took a fancy to a spot of murder wouldn't have needed to use that route.'

A young man in a grey suit and a striped shirt, matching the one that receptionist Melanie was wearing, came up to them. He had dark curly hair and was wearing glasses, which, Jonah recalled, fitted the description given by the Master. The name badge on his lapel said *Matt*.

'Melanie said you wanted to speak to me,' he said, addressing Andy. He stood rather awkwardly with his hands clasped behind his back.

Bernie noted with annoyance that he ignored Jonah's presence, speaking over the top of his wheelchair as if he were not there. She studied the technician's face. He was a good-looking young man, she decided. Apart from his eyes, which were deep brown like his mother's, he could easily have been a slimmer, more youthful version of his father. She began to understand why women might have been attracted to the bursar in his younger days.

'Yes,' Jonah answered, as if Matthew had spoken to him. 'May I introduce myself? I'm Detective Chief Inspector Porter and this is my assistant, Dr Bernadette Fazakerley. You already know Sergeant Lepage, I understand. I wanted to ask you about your movements on Wednesday, in connection with the death of Mr Anthony Bridgefield, who I believe was your father – is that correct?'

'What did you want to know?' Matt asked, ignoring the

question.

'Well first, I'd like you to confirm that you *are* Matthew Bridgefield, the son of Anthony and Amanda Bridgefield.'

'Yes,' Matt said sulkily, 'he was my father. But we didn't have anything to do with him, Mum or me, and he never had anything to do with us. I didn't even know he was coming here until I saw him in the meeting room. Look, what is this? What does it matter if he *was* my father? He was just another delegate at a meeting in the hotel as far as I was concerned. So long as the AV equipment worked OK that was all I was worried about. I didn't even realise it was Dad who'd been killed until I got home and Mum told me.'

'Alright, let's leave that for now,' Jonah said smoothly. 'Can we concentrate on the arrangements for the Awayday, for the time being? Bring one of those chairs over here and sit down, please.'

Matt pulled up another easy chair and positioned it between Andy and Bernie, who moved their own chairs to make space.

'Those are nasty marks on your hands,' Andy commented, looking down at a pattern of red stripes visible on both of Matt's palms. 'How did you do that?'

'That was the dog,' Matt explained sheepishly. 'She spotted a rabbit and I had trouble holding her back. She nearly jerked the lead out of my hand.'

'When was that?'

'During her morning walk. I always take her out before work.'

'Which day?' Andy persisted.

'Yesterday – no, it must have been Wednesday.'

'And speaking of Wednesday,' Jonah interjected, 'you set up the computer in the room first thing, is that right?'

'Yes. They'd booked a laptop to go with the display screen and also a spider phone for a teleconference. When the secretary arrived, she phoned Reception to say that the screen wasn't working properly. They sent me up to fix it.'

'Who was there when you arrived?'

'The secretary – Jessica, I think her name was – and an older woman.'

'And while you were there more of the Lichfield staff came in, including the bursar, your father?'

'Yes.'

'Did he speak to you then?'

'No. I don't think he recognised me. We haven't seen each other for about ten years. The last time we met I was still at school.'

'But you knew who he was?'

'Of course. Even if I hadn't, I'd soon have realised because people were talking about him before he arrived and then he came in and it all went very quiet.'

'What were they saying?'

'Oh just the usual stuff – usual for Dad, that is. Jessica and the other woman were joking about not wanting to sit next to him because of his wandering hands and then this man joined in and said something about how it wouldn't be so bad if it was only his hands that wandered.'

'And what made you think that was normal?' Andy asked, sharply. 'You said this was "the usual stuff".'

'He was notorious, wasn't he? Everyone knew what he was like. Even my gran knew. She used to say she couldn't understand where she'd gone wrong.'

'By your gran, you mean Bridgefield's mother?' Jonah asked.

'That's right. When I was a kid, she used to look after me while Mum was at work. She knew what Dad was like. That's why she stuck by Mum even after the divorce.'

'And what about you?' Jonah enquired. 'What sort of relationship did you have with your father when you were a child?'

'Relationship!' Matt laughed bitterly. 'We didn't have one. He was like, "why do I have to have this kid around all the time?" I just got in the way of him enjoying himself. And that's all he was ever interested in – enjoying himself!

He didn't want me, and he only wanted Mum for what he could get out of her.'

After this outburst, nobody spoke for a few minutes. Jonah, whose wife had been a busy trauma surgeon, had played a large part in bringing up his two boys, despite his own demanding job. He remembered the period when they had been young children as probably the happiest time of his life and found it hard to understand how a man could take no interest at all in his own son.

Bernie reflected on her own experience, as a single mother before her marriage to Peter, and felt sympathy for Mandy's struggle to bring up her child with a husband who was determined that she should carry the whole burden. She had worked hard to instil in Lucy an appreciation of her dead father; how did Mandy feel about knowing that her son despised his?

Andy wondered whether perhaps he should be grateful that his own father had absented himself from his life from the outset: better that than being there, but constantly reminding him that he was unwanted.

'You were, what? Ten years old when he left?' Jonah resumed. 'How did you feel about that?'

'Relieved.'

'Is that all?'

'Yes,' Matt answered sullenly. 'How else *should* I feel?'

'Angry, maybe?' Jonah suggested. 'I think I would have been.'

'Why would I be angry with him then? It was the best thing he ever did for us. Things got much better when it was just Mum and me. She wasn't always having to get meals for him that he didn't come home for and waiting up half the night for him when he had no intention of coming home and pretending to be pleased when he brought her flowers to make up for not being there when he'd promised he would.'

'So, after he left, you tried to forget all about your father?' Andy said, suddenly. 'Is that how it was?'

'Yeah – I suppose.'

'But with your mum still working at the college it couldn't have been that easy,' Andy suggested. 'His name would have kept cropping up in conversation, wouldn't it?'

Matt shrugged his shoulders.

'And maybe your mum sometimes complained to you about his behaviour? How he was still running after other women?' Andy persisted. 'How he only ever gave her the bare minimum from the divorce settlement to look after you? You must have hated the way he still managed to make life difficult for the two of you even after he'd left. It wasn't right, was it? He got all the fun and left people like your mum to live with the consequences.'

'No!' Matt burst out at last. 'It wasn't right. And, yes, I did resent the way he still somehow managed to manipulate Mum even after the divorce. I'm not sorry that he's dead. But it wasn't me that killed him. You've heard what he was like – there must be dozens of other people who wanted him dead!'

'Alright,' Jonah intervened. 'Let's get back to establishing the facts about Wednesday. We were talking about that morning. You finished setting up the computer and then left the room. Is that right?'

'More or less. I was just going, when the Master came in. He had his presentation on a USB stick and Jessica asked me to stay and help him put it on the laptop.'

'I see. And while you were there your father didn't give any sign that he'd recognised you?'

'He was too busy trying to chat up Jessica. She was too clever for him, though. There was this elderly guy came in about the same time as Dad. She sat him down next to her and told Dad that the Master was sitting on the other side of her so she could hand him his papers.'

'And after you left the room, was that the last time you went in there that day?'

'Yes – well, not quite,' Matt looked round as if trying to work out whether or not Jonah and Andy had already been told about his second visit to the room. 'I went up again at about one o'clock to check that everything was working OK. I saw the Master coming out just before I got there.'

'Tell us about what you saw when you went in.'

'I didn't really go in. I popped my head round the door and saw that Dad was there on his own, working on the laptop. It was obviously working OK so I decided not to bother and I went back down to the office.'

'Did you speak to him at all?'

'No. He didn't react when I opened the door, so I assumed he was concentrating on what he was doing and hadn't noticed me. So I just got out right away.

'Can you describe exactly how he was when you looked in?'

'What do you mean?' Matt asked, puzzled.

'Well, for a start, where was he sitting? Which way was he facing?'

'He was in the chair at the front of the room, by the laptop.'

'So, facing the door? How come he didn't notice you come in?'

'No. The chair was turned round so that he could see the screen. He was leaning back looking up at it – checking that it was displaying right, I suppose.'

'I see. That's very helpful. So you went back downstairs – what time was that?'

'I don't know exactly. Between one and half past, but I didn't look at my watch.'

'And how did you get down? Did you use the stairs or the lift?'

'The stairs.'

'Did you meet anyone on them? Or in the corridor at the bottom?'

'Not that I remember.'

'What did you do after you got back to the office?'

'I started working on some admin. There's a lot of paperwork involved in running a hotel.'

'You started but didn't finish?'

'The next thing I knew Mel was there saying she'd called the police because someone had died in one of the meeting rooms.'

'What did you do then?'

'I went out with Mel to the reception desk. I sometimes help out on the desk at busy times and she thought we'd better both be there when the police came. The manager was there too. We all hung around there waiting for what seemed like ages.'

'What did you talk about while you were waiting?'

Matt shrugged.

'Just how weird it was having someone die like that. We assumed it must have been a heart attack or something.'

'Alright. Thank you, I think that's all.'

'Just one thing!' Andy called Matt back as he turned to go. 'Going back to when you looked into the room at lunch time: is it at all possible that your father could have been dead when you saw him?'

'I don't think so,' Matt stared at him, wide-eyed with surprise. 'I mean, if I'd thought he was dead I'd have told someone then, wouldn't I?'

'Yes,' Jonah agreed, 'we know you didn't think there was anything wrong with him at the time, but the sergeant is asking you to think back to what you actually saw and tell us whether he could have been dead even though he didn't look like it. Try and picture it in your mind. Did you see him move at all, for example?'

'Not that I remember,' Matt said slowly. 'But I didn't really look very carefully. I just saw he was there and that the computer was on and then got out before he saw me.'

'So you couldn't swear to him being still alive when you went in?' Andy persisted.

'No. If you put it like that, I couldn't.'

'Thank you. You can go now,' Jonah dismissed him. 'I'm sorry to have kept you so long.'

Jonah and Andy looked at one another.

'Well, that certainly opens up some interesting possibilities,' Jonah muttered. Then in a louder voice as he headed towards the reception desk, 'Melanie! Can you tell me, were you on duty here on Wednesday between one and half past?'

'Not for the whole time,' the receptionist replied promptly. 'As I told your sergeant, I got back off my break at about twenty past.'

'Do you remember seeing a man and a woman sitting together in the reception area? Were they there when you got here?'

'No, there was a man sitting on that sofa under the window, but he was on his own.'

'Do you remember seeing this woman at all?' Jonah asked, turning his computer screen round so that Melanie could see a photograph of Ann Lambert, which Jonah had downloaded off the Lichfield College website.

'Yes, I met her at the top of the stairs as I was coming down.'

'How did she look?'

Melanie did not reply. She seemed puzzled by the question.

'I mean – was she agitated at all? Did she look as if she'd just heard some bad news, for example?'

'I'd say not so much bad news – she didn't look upset, more, well, angry.'

'I see. And did you see which way she went?'

'I think she turned left at the top of the stairs, but I couldn't be sure.'

28 THE LIAR

They went out of the front entrance and made their way through the garden to where they had left the car. As soon as the sliding doors of the hotel closed behind them, Jonah addressed Andy.

'Do you really think Bridgefield could have already been dead when the lad looked in on him at ten past one?'

'I just wondered, that's all,' Andy shrugged. 'It was the way the witnesses described finding him that made me think about it – that and Matt saying he didn't actually go in and speak to his father. Do you remember? Tom Carrington and Beverley Greenhalgh both said they thought at first he might have been having some sort of epileptic fit or something. And the position they talked about the body being in is just the same as Matt described just now. It was just a thought.'

'Indeed is was,' Jonah agreed, 'and one that the defence counsel would be bound to remind the jury of if we were to charge Matthew Bridgefield with the murder of his father without more evidence than we have so far that he was the only person who could have done it.'

'Do you really think it was him?' Bernie asked. 'What about Ann? We now have a witness that says she lied when she told you she stayed downstairs all through the lunch break.'

'You've changed your tune. I thought you didn't think that Ann was strong enough to strangle anyone.'

'I'm not saying she definitely did it,' Bernie protested mildly. 'I'm just pointing out that the jury would also, no doubt, have their attention drawn to the fact that a woman with a known relationship with the victim was seen heading in the direction of the crime scene, looking angry and having just been given some news which could well have made her think murderous thoughts towards him!'

'We need to speak to Ann Lambert again,' Jonah decided. 'and I also want to find out if anyone can confirm that those marks on young Matthew Bridgefield's hands were already there when he got to work on Wednesday morning or if they could have appeared during the day.'

'I could nip back and ask Melanie,' Andy suggested helpfully.

'No, I'd rather not risk letting Matt know we haven't bought the dog lead story. Let's get back to Lichfield and see if the ever-co-operative Jessica remembers seeing any marks on his hands when he was setting up the computer for her that morning.'

'So that's Ann and Jessica to see,' Bernie said, making a list of interviewees in her mind, 'anyone else? What about the Master? Do you want to grill him on the subject of whether Bridgefield really was still alive when he left?'

'Not unless we get some more evidence to suggest that he wasn't. It's all very well Andy here suggesting that the Master could have been the murderer, but Matt's statement that he thought his father was alive, but he can't be sure, isn't exactly overwhelming evidence against him, is it?'

'If he *is* our murderer then he must be an extremely cool customer,' Bernie observed. 'Why draw attention to the IT guy going in after him? It could have really backfired if Matt had said that he'd found Bridgefield's body.'

'Oh, but he didn't mention it until *after* he knew that Matt hadn't raised the alarm,' Andy said eagerly. 'He didn't mention seeing Matt when I took his statement on Wednesday. It was only when you spoke to him the next day that he remembered about it.'

'Let me get this straight,' Jonah said slowly, as they turned a corner and their car came into view ahead. 'You're suggesting that Grainger and Bridgefield had some sort of argument over the college accounts – maybe Bridgefield threatened to expose some illegal activity that Grainger had been up to – and Grainger killed Bridgefield. Then he leaves the room and, to his dismay, there's Matthew on his way in. But he holds his nerve and walks nonchalantly away, back downstairs to – where did he say he went after that?'

'The dining room, I think,' Bernie said, 'but I'd have to check my notes.'

'The dining room,' Jonah continued, 'which means that he crossed the lobby, in full view of anyone who happened to be hanging around there – did anyone mention seeing him, by the way? – and into the dining room for a relaxing cup of coffee before the afternoon session. All while he was expecting at any moment to hear the IT guy rushing downstairs to announce that he's discovered a body!'

'Like I said – a cool customer,' Bernie repeated, unlocking the car and opening the door at the back to let Jonah in.

'But you have to admit, it's not impossible,' Andy insisted, leaning into the car to get out the ramp and fix it ready for Jonah to ascend. 'It'd be worth asking Ann if she remembers seeing the Master crossing the lobby while she and Simon were sitting there. You never know, he may not have looked quite as cool as he seems to have been.'

Jonah drove his chair up the ramp and into the car. Bernie was just climbing in after him when her phone rang. It was Martin, sounding very confused and anxious.

'Bernie? Can we talk?'

'It depends. Is it about the murder? I've got Jonah and Andy here with me.'

'Yes. It's about Penny.'

'OK, fire ahead.' Bernie switched the phone to loudspeaker and Andy climbed into the car with them to listen.

'The rumours about her being pregnant had got back to the lab technicians and it was all anyone was talking about in the coffee bar at lunch time,' Martin went on. 'So that gave me the excuse to call Penny in and ask her to give me the real story.'

'And?' Bernie prompted, Martin having abruptly stopped speaking.

'Well, it doesn't make any sort of sense to me,' Martin began again. 'Penny says she *isn't* pregnant.'

Bernie gave Jonah a look indicating *I told you so* and Jonah grinned back.

'And she says she never has been,' Martin continued, in a tone of bewilderment.

'Go on,' Bernie urged. 'Did she have any explanation as to why Bridgefield might have told his wife that she *was*?'

'She says she made up the story to persuade Bridgefield to take her in.'

'It sounds more as if she took Bridgefield in!' Bernie snorted with laughter.

'She wanted better accommodation than the college would provide and she didn't want to have to pay for it.'

'It sounds as if Bridgefield had met his match at last,' Jonah commented drily. 'That's exactly what he did with Ann Lambert. As far as we can tell, she kept him for years.'

'Oh, but it gets worse,' Martin groaned. 'You'll never believe what else she said.'

'Try us,' Jonah advised, grinning at Bernie.

'She says that she told Anthony that it was Tom Carrington's baby, but he was too fixated with getting back together with his wife and kids to acknowledge it. She says that Anthony thought he was doing a noble act coming to the rescue when she'd been left in the lurch. She seemed to think it was very funny.'

'I suppose, to be fair to him,' Jonah murmured, 'everyone does seem to agree that he always *thought* that he was being chivalrous towards the women that he flirted with and patronised. Maybe he did fancy himself as a knight in shining armour coming to the aid of damsels in distress.'

'Or maybe he was just a typical macho man pleased to have people assuming that he'd fathered a child with a woman young enough to be his daughter,' Bernie grunted.

'So now I just don't know what to believe,' Martin declared in a voice of utter bewilderment. 'I'm not sure that I can trust a word the girl has said to me right from the beginning. I mean – did she have an affair with Tom at all? Or was she making the whole thing up? And then, when she moved in with Anthony, was she sleeping with him, or was that all just another made-up story? I just don't know what to make of her at all! I asked her if she didn't worry what people would think about her and she laughed in my face. She just doesn't seem to care.'

'I think she probably does care,' Bernie laughed, amused at her friend's discomfiture. 'Based on the way she spoke to Jonah when he interviewed her, she was probably trying to shock you. I think she wants to appear to us oldies as a liberated young woman who doesn't pay any attention to our out-dated moral codes and she gets rather disappointed when we aren't particularly horrified, just a bit bemused.'

'Anyway, I thought you ought to know what she said, in case it has any bearing on who killed Anthony. Make of it what you will.'

'Thank you, Dr Riess,' Jonah said. 'It certainly gives us food for thought.'

'OK. Right. Well, I'd better go. Be seeing you!'

'Bye, Martin,' Bernie called cheerily. 'Take care!'

She ended the call and put the phone in her pocket, giving a low whistle as she did so.

'Well!' she declared, 'that explains why Penny didn't look pregnant when we met her. What I can't understand is how she expected to get away with lying about it to Bridgefield. I mean – it's all very well trying to fool the outside world, but they were supposed to be lovers. Surely she couldn't have hoped to keep stringing him along for more than a few weeks before he realised that she wasn't actually having Tom's baby or his baby or anyone else's!'

'Maybe Dr Riess was right when he said that she might not have been having it off with Bridgefield after all,' Andy suggested.

'That's a thought,' Mused Bernie. 'Maybe she makes out that she's totally promiscuous to hide a complete lack of sexual experience! Nobody's suggested that she might have any *real* boyfriends, have they?'

'Carrington admitted to having sex with her,' Andy pointed out.

'Did he though?' queried Jonah. 'Weren't his actual words "one thing led to another" or something along those lines? We were led to believe that was what he meant, but I don't think he actually said it.'

'You're right,' Bernie agreed, 'but if he was leading us up the garden path about that – and I'm not sure I see why he would want to – she must have been lying when she told Bridgefield that Tom was refusing to accept his responsibilities. She couldn't possibly have even asked him, because he'd know the fictitious baby wasn't his.'

'I think we've established that we can't rely on anything that young woman says,' Jonah remarked, 'but I wouldn't put it past her to have told both Tom and Anthony that she was pregnant by the other one and just hoped that one or other of them would take pity on her and take her in. She was lucky that she picked up that job before either of them could be sure that she was making it all up.'

'Of course!' Bernie exclaimed. 'I've just realised what Anthony meant when he suggested to Ann that Penny might come to live with them. He didn't mean that Penny was going to be his mistress, but of course with his history that's what Ann assumed.'

'I think perhaps, we need to add Tom Carrington to our list of people we need to talk to again,' Jonah said. 'Bridgefield may have had words with him about his supposed desertion of Penny in her hour of need. And he is still the first person to see Bridgefield after he died.'

'And what about Beverley Greenhalgh?' put in Andy. 'We still have her confession to deal with.'

'Which has become somewhat less plausible now that we have evidence that Ann Lambert went to see Bridgefield during the few minutes available between when Matt left him and when Tom found him,' Jonah commented. 'It's starting to look as if the fellow was hardly alone in that room at all. He seems to have had a constant stream of visitors from the moment he got there to when he was found dead!'

29 THE DONS

When they arrived back at Lichfield College, Andy went off in search of Jessica, leaving Bernie and Jonah waiting outside the Porters' Lodge. Jessica's room in the administration suite was inaccessible to Jonah's wheelchair, being a few feet above the level of the quad and reached by means of stone steps leading to a narrow passageway.

'There's Bev Greenhalgh,' Bernie said, watching the don emerging from a door on the other side of the quad. 'Shall I ask her to come with us to the interview room?'

'No, I want to talk to Ann Lambert first. Let Beverley sweat for a bit longer, wondering whether or not we're taking her confession seriously.'

Beverley came towards them across the grass.

'Did you want to speak to me, by any chance?' she greeted them.

'Later perhaps. Where will you be in, say, twenty minutes?'

'Well, I was planning to go home, but I'll wait in my room. It's over there,' Beverley pointed back at the door from which she had come out of the building, 'staircase three, second floor.'

'Thank you. We'll try not to keep you waiting too long.

Ah! Here comes our escort.'

Jessica and Andy came out of a door on the left-hand side of the quad and started making their way towards the seminar room, which Jessica had confirmed was still booked out for police use. Jonah and Bernie hurried to join them.

Once inside, Andy showed Jessica to a chair while Jonah and Bernie settled themselves on the other side of the table.

'Sergeant Lepage said you wanted to ask me some more questions,' Jessica said, sounding a little anxious.

'Yes. Principally just one question,' Jonah answered. 'I'd like you to cast your mind back to Wednesday morning when you were getting the room ready for the meeting. A young man called Matt was there setting up the computer and the telephone. Do you remember?'

'Yes,' Jessica said slowly, looking puzzled.

'Do you remember noticing his hands at all?'

'What do you mean?'

'We've been over to the hotel this afternoon and we noticed that he had some red marks on his hand – like rope burns. Did you notice anything like that when he was working on the computer on Wednesday morning?'

'No.'

'And do you think you *would* have noticed them if they'd been there then?'

Jessica thought for a few moments.

'Well, I suppose it depends how obvious they were,' she began, 'but I do remember asking him to show me how to control the video screen, and he pointed out which buttons to press for different things. I must have looked at his hand then, mustn't I?'

'Thank you, Jessica, that's very helpful. Now, do you know whether Dr Lambert is in college at the moment?'

'I don't know, but I can check for you. I've got her mobile number in my phone. Shall I ask her to come here to see you?'

'If you would.'

Jessica rang Ann, who was in the Senior Common Room with several other dons for the ritual of afternoon tea, which still survived in the college as a convenient way of keeping the academic staff in touch with one another. A few minutes later Ann knocked timidly on the door and Andy let her in.

'Sit down, Dr Lambert,' Jonah invited her, inclining his head towards the seat opposite. 'Would you like some water?'

Ann nodded and Bernie filled a glass and set it down in front of her.

'Now Dr Lambert,' Jonah said pleasantly, 'first of all I'm hoping you can confirm one or two things that other witnesses have said in their statements. You and Mr Sutcliffe were in a rather strategic place sitting there in the lobby after lunch. You must have seen lots of people coming and going.'

'I don't know about that,' Ann said nervously. 'We were talking, not watching people.'

'But if people you knew came in, you'd probably notice them – they might even say "hello".'

'I don't remember any.'

'Try to think. Do you remember seeing any of the others coming out of the dining room after you, for instance?'

'I don't think so. Most of the others had already gone when we left.'

'Alright. What about going the other way? One or two people told me that they went *back* into the dining room for coffee later.'

'No, I'm sorry,' Ann said shaking her head. 'I really don't remember seeing anyone.'

'Very well, don't worry about that then,' Jonah said reassuringly. 'Now,' he went on in a more serious tone, 'I'd like you to consider whether you would like to make any changes to your statement about your own movements over Wednesday lunch time.'

'What do you mean?' Ann asked, wide-eyed, trying to feign innocence, but flushing red in the face as her heart started to beat faster.

'I'd like to remind you,' Jonah went on, his voice becoming harder now, 'that you have already changed your account once. Is there anything else that you forgot to tell us about earlier?'

'No – nothing,' Ann replied, her eyes darting from one face to another anxiously.

'Dr Lambert,' Jonah repeated with an air of exaggerated patience, 'we have a witness who says that they saw you going into the meeting room shortly before twenty past one. Now, would you like to amend your statement?'

'I – I -,' Ann looked around helplessly as if unable to think what to say. Then she closed her eyes and bowed her head for a moment before resuming in a tone of resignation. 'Yes, I did go in to see Anthony. I was furious with him – surely you can understand that?' she added looking straight at Bernie as she spoke.

'Oh yes,' Jonah agreed. 'I can understand. I can understand why you might want to kill him after the way he treated you.'

'But I didn't!' Ann wailed. 'I don't expect you to believe me, but he was already dead when I got there.'

'Go on – try me. What exactly did you see when you went in?'

'He was sitting there, not moving at all. I thought he must be concentrating on what was on the screen, but he still didn't move when I went up to him and more or less shouted in his face. Then I saw the mark on his neck and I realised that he'd been strangled. I was frightened, because I thought everyone would think that I'd done it, so I raced back downstairs and sat down again with Simon. I didn't tell you about it because I was scared. You do believe me, don't you?' she pleaded, looking with large, anxious eyes into Jonah's face.

'We'll need you to make a signed statement,' Jonah replied, ignoring her appeal. 'Go down to the police station on Monday morning and we'll get that all sorted.'

'You don't really think I killed Anthony do you?' Ann persisted.

'It's not a matter of what *I* believe,' Jonah replied remorselessly. 'I would simply remind you that you are likely to be an important witness in any murder trial that comes out of this investigation and that perjury is a serious offence.'

He paused to let his words sink in.

'Now, unless there is anything else that you would like to tell us …'

'No – nothing,' Ann said hastily.'

'Very well then, you're free to go.'

After the door closed behind her Jonah and Andy looked at one another.

'If she's telling the truth,' Andy said, 'then our choices of murderer are between the Master and the IT guy.'

'And if she's lying then it's because she's guilty,' Jonah agreed. 'Either way, it can't be Beverley Greenhalgh, so I suppose we'd better wheel her in and put her out of her misery. Bernie, could you go and fetch her over?'

Bernie got up to go and then turned back.

'But hang on a minute,' she said, 'didn't we say that Bev *might* have managed to do the deed between Matt leaving the room and Ann taking her call *provided* that he didn't stay long, which he says he didn't? So if he was right about his father still being alive then, well it's possible that Bev could still be in the frame.'

'I suppose so,' Jonah admitted grumpily. 'Well, let's get her here and see if she can convince me.'

A few minutes later, Beverley was sitting in the chair recently occupied by Ann Lambert. She looked across at Jonah with an expression of mixed anxiety and defiance on her face.

'Did you get my email?' she asked.

'I did indeed,' Jonah replied smoothly. 'May I congratulate you on a magnificent work of fiction?'

Beverley looked sulky but said nothing, so Jonah went on.

'Very well, Dr Greenhalgh, let's go through what you say happened.'

'Is that really necessary? I told you everything in the email?'

'Dr Greenhalgh, this is a very serious matter. If you are determined to go through with this confession business, we are going to need you to give us a signed statement. We have to get the details right. However, if you now want to withdraw what you said, then go ahead and we'll say no more about it. Please think very carefully. There's nothing noble about taking the rap for something you didn't do and allowing a murderer to go free.'

'Alright,' Beverley said wearily. 'Like I said, I walked about in the garden a bit and then I decided that the only way to make the world safe from Anthony's predatory sexual urges was to kill him. I remembered that strap in the car and thought that would be a good way of doing it. I went to the car and got the strap then went back through the garden to the side door and up the stairs.'

'Any idea what time it was then?' Jonah asked sharply.

'Not really,' Beverley shook her head. 'It must have been after one, but I didn't look at my watch so I can't say closer than that.'

'Did you see anyone in the corridor or on the stairs?'

'No.'

'OK. Go on. You went into the meeting room and Bridgefield was there on his own. How did he look?'

'Just as normal,' Beverley answered, looking puzzled.

'Sitting or standing? What was he doing? Did he say anything to you when you went in?'

'He was sitting in the chair under the display screen, where Tom found him later. He was busy with his presentation and didn't notice me go in. So I came up behind him and strangled him with the strap. Then I went back down the stairs and-'

'Did you meet anyone on the stairs? Or after you got downstairs?'

'No. I was lucky; there was no one about to see me.'

'What would you say if I told you that I have someone who claimed to have been sitting on the stairs from about quarter past one until shortly before you met Brampton outside the main entrance?'

For a moment, Beverley's face dropped and she looked confused. She thought for a few moments before replying.

'I'd say that this person must not have got there until after I'd gone downstairs and out of the door to the gardens. Perhaps they were mistaken about the time.'

'Alright. So you went out through the side door and back to your car. Did you see anyone on the path or in the car park?'

'No.'

'You put the strap back in your car. Is it still there?'

'No. I was afraid there might be traces of Anthony's DNA on it, so I went out for a walk that evening and threw it in the river.'

'How did you know about the side door?'

'What do you mean?'

'How did you know there was a side door that led to the path to the car park? Had you been to the hotel before?'

'I just saw the emergency exit signs and deduced that the door must open on to that side of the building.' Beverley started to sound flustered. This was a line of questioning that she evidently had not expected.

'The side of the building where you had conveniently left your car,' Jonah said, pressing his advantage. 'What made you choose that part of the car park when there were more convenient spaces available?'

'I – I,' Beverley stammered, clearly struggling to find a convincing answer. 'I thought it would stay cooler there, under the trees.'

'There are trees in the main car park in front of Reception.'

'Well I thought the shade was better in the side car park,' Beverley said defiantly. 'What does it matter why I went there?'

Jonah sat looking at her impassively. Beverley looked from his face to Andy's and back again.

'Alright,' she said at last. 'I parked there because I'd already thought about the plan to kill Anthony. I arrived early for the meeting and scouted round the outside of the hotel and found the side door. Then I moved the car from where I'd parked it in front of the main entrance, so that it would be convenient for getting the strap out when I needed it. I didn't dare take it with me to the meeting in case someone saw it and asked why I had it with me.'

'How did you know that there was going to be an opportunity for you to get Bridgefield alone?'

'I didn't. That was just luck.'

'In which case, it was hardly worth going to all that trouble making elaborate preparations for getting hold of the murder weapon during the lunch break,' Jonah commented. 'The chances were you'd never have had the opportunity to make use of it.'

For a minute or two, they all sat in silence. Beverley looked from Jonah to Andy, to Bernie and then back to Jonah.

'You don't believe I did it, do you,' she said eventually.

'No, I don't. Moreover, I strongly suspect that, if we check out the CC-TV footage of the camera that covers the main car park, it will show that your car never did move round to the side car park at all. Am I right?'

'Yes,' Beverley admitted, nodding. 'I'm sorry. I just hoped that if you could finish your investigations quickly you might not have to bother about reporting the irregularities with Nafisa's visa.'

'You thought,' Jonah said sternly, 'that I would be so

pleased to have made an arrest quickly that I would reward you by turning a blind eye to your other illegal activities. Contrary to popular belief, not all police officers are corrupt or out to get a conviction at any cost and regardless of whether the suspect is guilty or not.'

'I see that,' Beverley said humbly. 'I'm sorry. I suppose you'll be charging me with wasting police time?'

'We'll come to that later. Meanwhile, I'd like to know who *you* think did kill Bridgefield. I assume it must be someone with whom you have some sympathy or you'd hardly be shielding them.'

'I thought it must be Ann.'

'Any particular reason?'

'Well, she's got the best reason to hate him, hasn't she?'

'Possibly. Possibly not. Are you sure you didn't have any other reason to suspect her particularly?'

'She did look very odd when I saw her in the lobby when Charles Brampton and I came in from the garden.'

'How, odd?'

'Shocked and flustered, and she was sitting next to Simon trying to look as if she'd been there all the time, but she hadn't, because I saw her cross the lobby when I was just outside the door about to come in. It looked to me as if she was coming back from the passage that leads to the stairs.'

'I asked her if she was alright and she bit my head off – which is very unusual for Ann. She usually puts on a sort of icy calm if she's annoyed with you.'

'Would you blame her if she *had* killed him?'

'Not at all. He had it coming to him!'

'Now, there's one other little thing I'd like to know: when exactly did you really hear about Penny Green's alleged pregnancy?'

'Today,' Beverley admitted. 'It was all anyone was talking about in the SCR over morning coffee. It occurred to me then that it could have been *that* which made Ann want to kill him – assuming she'd heard about it before

Wednesday.'

'And would it surprise you to know that, according to Penny, Bridgefield was providing for her even though she'd told him that the baby wasn't his?'

'It would completely amaze me.' Beverley looked from Jonah to Bernie and back again as if trying to work out whether to believe what she had just been told. 'You mean he wasn't the complete bastard that we all thought he was?'

'So it would seem.'

'What'll happen to her now? Is there any chance of the real father taking on his responsibilities? I suppose it's probably some young postdoc or DPhil student who doesn't think he's ready for fatherhood.'

'I think you will probably find,' Jonah said drily, 'that the conversation over SCR coffee tomorrow morning is all about the fact that Ms Green now admits that there *is* no father because there never was any baby – except in her rather vivid imagination.'

'A false alarm you mean?'

'No – a calculated untruth to gain the gallant Anthony Bridgefield's sympathy. You and Penny ought to go into collaboration. Between the two of you, you'd probably produce some quite excellent works of fiction.'

'Yes. I really am sorry about that now. I just wanted to *do* something. I felt so helpless.'

'Alright. Well, unless you have anything else to tell us – or any other parts of your previous statements that you want to change – you can go.'

Beverley opened her mouth as if to ask a question, then thought better of it, nodded briefly and went out.

30 THE SON

'Who next?' asked Bernie, looking at her watch and hoping that the next interview would be shorter. She was determined to keep Jonah to his regular meal and exercise regime.

'Carrington, I think,' Jonah replied. 'I don't think he did it, but we can't rule him out – yet.'

A few minutes later Tom Carrington entered the room, ushered in by Bernie who had tracked him down to the Senior Common Room, where he had been listening uneasily to speculation from a group of his colleagues who had not been present at the Awayday as to who could have been responsible for the death of the bursar. He hoped that the business would soon be settled and they could get back to normal life. It was very nerve-wracking hearing your name bandied about as one among others who might be a murderer.

'Sit down Dr Carrington,' Jonah greeted him. 'We won't keep you long. I'd just like to know a bit more about your relationship with Penny Green.'

'Hardly a relationship! We just went out to a few concerts and meals together, that's all.'

'So when you said previously, and I quote, "one thing led to another". What exactly did you mean?'

'Well – you know.'

'Would it surprise you to know that Penny told Bridgefield that she was expecting your baby?'

Tom's jaw dropped. For a few moments, he was unable to speak. He looked wildly from Jonah to Bernie.

'That's impossible,' he said at last.

Jonah raised his eyebrows interrogatively.

'Whoever the father was,' Tom said, more decisively now, 'it definitely wasn't me, whatever Penny says.'

Jonah continued to look at him.

'Look,' Tom said irritably, 'we didn't, OK? If Penny says we did then she's making it up.'

'Like a lot of other things, it would appear,' Jonah said drily. 'Nevertheless, she seems to have convinced Bridgefield. Did he by any chance speak to you about it? Try to make you "do the decent thing" or whatever they call it these days?'

'No!' Tom stared round at them each again. 'Look: the first I even heard that Penny was pregnant was this morning in the SCR. Obviously I assumed Bridgefield must have been the father. Who else could it have been? And he never said a word to me about it before he died. So it's no good you trying to make out that I killed him because he was leaning on me to support Penny and her baby. In any case, I wouldn't have needed to kill him, because I know I'm not the father and Penny knew too, so she would have had to back down in the end.'

'Alright,' Jonah said, somehow managing to convey in his voice a slight dissatisfaction with Tom's answers. 'Let's go back to Wednesday afternoon, shall we? When you went up to the meeting room after lunch, did you use the stairs or the lift?'

'The stairs. I glanced at the lift on my way past, but it was on the fourth floor, so I reckoned the stairs would be quicker, and I was afraid I was going to be late.'

'You must have gone through the reception area to get to the stairs. Did you notice any of the Lichfield party there?'

'No. Were some of them there? I wasn't looking, because I thought I was late.'

'Dr Lambert and Mr Sutcliffe were sitting there and Dr Greenhalgh came in from the garden at about that time, accompanied by Mr Brampton. You didn't notice any of them?'

'No. Like I say, I wasn't looking. I suppose I was probably looking the other way – at the lift display to see whether it was worth waiting for it to come down.'

'I see,' Jonah said, still with the air of slight dissatisfaction. 'Well, thank you Dr Carrington. That's all for now.'

After Tom had left, Bernie looked accusingly at Jonah.

'You don't seriously think that Tom did it, do you?' she asked. 'It was mean leaving him thinking that he's under suspicion like that.'

'Well, you have to admit that it's odd he didn't notice any of his fellow Awayday-ers when he passed through the lobby – unless, that is, he passed through a bit earlier than he said, before Beverley and Charles came in.'

'Even so, he ought to have seen Simon,' Andy pointed out. 'And what about Ann? She was lingering in the passageway until the point at which she went up and found Bridgefield already dead.'

'Come on, Jonah,' Bernie reproached him, 'you know he didn't do it. Why leave him in suspense like that?'

'OK, I give in,' Jonah sighed, recognising the justice of Bernie's argument. 'Go after him and set his mind at rest. While you're about it, you might as well let him know that Penny's baby doesn't even exist. He'll hear sooner or later, no doubt, from your dear friend Dr Reiss. Then round up Amanda Bridgefield.'

Bernie went off happily, leaving Jonah wondering to himself why he had deliberately encouraged Tom to assume that he was a live suspect. He reluctantly came to the conclusion that he had a tendency towards jealousy of anyone with whom Bernie seemed to have any special relationship. Was it insecurity, he wondered, lest anything detracted from her devotion to caring for his needs?

A few minutes later, she returned.

'Mandy'll be along in about five minutes,' she

explained, taking her seat next to Jonah. 'She's in the middle of placing an online order on behalf of the college and can't interrupt it.'

'Is Tom a happy bunny now?'

'I don't know about that. He was very relieved to know that he's not really under suspicion of murder; but I almost think he was disappointed to hear that Penny's baby isn't real. I rather fancy he'd started working up a plan to offer to take her under his wing and start a new family to replace the one he so carelessly allowed to slip through his fingers.'

'Even though the baby wasn't his?' Andy asked in surprise.

'Why not? It happens all the time. Look at our Lucy and our Peter for example.'

There was a timid knock on the door and Andy strode across to open it. Amanda Bridgefield came in, looking nervously around.

'Dr Fazakerley said you wanted to see me,' she began.'

'That's right. It won't take long, Jonah promised. 'Sit down and make yourself comfortable.'

He waited while she took a few sips from the glass of water which Andy set down on the table in front of her.

'We were talking to your son Matthew earlier,' Jonah began. 'Did he tell you that he saw his father when he was at work on Wednesday?'

'He said he'd set up the computer for the meeting and Anthony was there,' Mandy replied cautiously. 'He said Anthony didn't recognise him though.'

'Good,' Jonah said encouragingly. 'That's what he told us too. Are you surprised that your husband didn't recognise his own son when he saw him?'

'Not really. I mean, it's a long time since they met and Matthew's changed a lot since then. I shouldn't think Anthony's seen him since he was twelve or thirteen.'

'And this was out of context, of course,' Jonah agreed. 'Did your husband know that Matthew worked at the hotel?'

'I shouldn't think so. *I* never told him.'

'Do you think any of the other Lichfield staff will have known who Matthew was? Ann Lambert or Simon Sutcliffe, for example?'

'No, why would they?'

'I just thought they might have seen Matthew with you sometime and recognised him.'

'No, I don't think so. Matt never came to see me at college because he didn't want to bump into his dad. Why do you want to know?'

'At the risk of sounding clichéd, *I'm* asking the questions,' replied Jonah, who had in fact merely been trying to avoid coming straight out with the one question that he wanted to ask, in the hope of making it seem less significant by hiding it within a sequence of others.

'When we were talking to your son, I noticed that he had some rather strange red marks on his hands. Do you know how they got there?'

'Oh yes!' Mandy said in a tone of relief. 'It was Dolly, our dog: she always pulls rather on the lead and on Wednesday evening she tried to get away from Matt to chase after a rabbit. He had to hold her back with both hands.'

'You were there?'

'No. He told me about it after he came in. Matt always takes Dolly out as soon as he comes home from work. I noticed the marks when he sat down to dinner and that was when he told me.'

'And you're sure he said it had happened that evening? It couldn't have been in the morning?'

'No. I've been taking Dolly for her morning walks this week because Matt had to be in work early. They're short staffed in the dining room at the moment and he agreed to help with serving breakfast. He can turn his hand to virtually anything in the hotel. That's why the manager's so pleased to have him.'

'I see,' Jonah said. 'That's cleared that up then. I'm

sorry to have to ask you so many questions. We always have to collect a lot of information, most of which turns out not to be relevant. Now I wonder if I could ask you about your telephone call to Ann Lambert?'

'What about it?'

'I was just wondering why you decided to ring her on the one day when she wasn't in college with you, instead of waiting until you could talk to her face to face. What was so urgent about telling her about Anthony's baby?'

'I don't know exactly,' Mandy said slowly. 'I suppose I was thinking over what Anthony had said to me the day before – I couldn't get it out of my mind, you see – and all of a sudden it occurred to me how devastating the news would be for Ann when it got to her. And I thought it would be better if I told her straight out than if she got to hear through rumours. And once I'd thought of doing it, I couldn't settle until I'd told her.'

'I see. So it wasn't anything to do with the idea that she might have been able to catch him alone while they were both at the Awayday and tackle him about it?'

'No, not at all. I just knew I wouldn't be able to settle to anything else until I'd put Ann in the picture.'

'I see. Thank you. I think I understand now,' Jonah said. 'And now I think that's all we've got to ask you, so you're free to go.'

After the door closed behind Ann, Jonah looked round triumphantly at the others.

'We've got him!' he declared emphatically. 'Those marks on Matthew Bridgefield's hands aren't from a dog lead at all. If they were, why would he tell us they were made in the morning, when he didn't take the dog out until the evening? They were made by the electric cable that he used to strangle his father. He must have been afraid that someone had noticed them during the day on Wednesday – maybe someone from the hotel even remarked on them – so he made up a story to account for them, but he had to tell a slightly different story to his mother, because she *knew* it didn't happen in the morning.'

'In any case,' Andy added, 'he told his mother *first*. 'He probably only started worrying about explaining how the marks came to be there during the day on Wednesday, once we started being interested in them.'

'Right!' Jonah exclaimed eagerly. 'So now let's get back over to the hotel and bring him in – or will he have left for home by now?'

'Whether he's left for home or not,' Bernie put in firmly, 'that's precisely what *we're* going to do now. Matthew Bridgefield isn't going to flee the country overnight. If you want to arrest him, you can do it just as effectively in the morning.'

'But if his mother tells him about our line of questioning he'll know we're on to him. If we go now we'll catch him before he has a chance to think up a good story.'

'*You* may be able to go on forever without a break,' Bernie complained, 'but I'm tired and hungry and it's past my knocking-off time.'

'Actually,' Andy put in, correctly deducing that Bernie was trying to prevent Jonah pushing himself beyond what his body could stand, and trying to find a way to back her up without mentioning this fact, 'I think it might work to our advantage if Matt *did* try to come up with an explanation. The more elaborate the lies, the easier they are to disprove. And when people get nervous they start making mistakes. I'd say: let his mother tell him we're interested in how he got those marks and see what state he's in after worrying about it overnight.'

'Peter and Lucy will be expecting us back,' Bernie urged, 'and I know Peter's making one of his special curries, which I for one don't want to miss!'

'Alright, I know when I'm beaten,' Jonah sighed with an air of resignation. 'We'll go round and see him at home tomorrow morning.'

'Well, actually,' Andy said sheepishly, 'I promised my mum I'd help her with the shopping tomorrow morning.'

'Tomorrow afternoon then,' Jonah said in a tone of exasperation, 'if you can both fit that into your packed social diaries. Andy – you come to our place at one thirty. We'll go together to see young Matthew Bridgefield, and – before you ask, Bernie – we'll make a point of being back in time for your Saturday High Tea. Is that alright with everyone?'

'Perfect!' Bernie declared, trying to keep any sign of satisfaction out of her voice at having succeeded in keeping Jonah to his agreed daily schedule. 'The afternoon suits me down to the ground. Lucy's going out with Martin in his boat and Peter's arranged a Skype call with Eddie and Crystal. So I'd be delighted to spend the afternoon hunting murderers!'

31 THE CAREGIVERS

'Thank you for not showing me up in front of Andy,' Jonah said to Bernie on their return home, as she climbed into the back of the car to release him from the fastenings that secured his wheelchair.

'How d'you mean?' she asked curiously. 'I wasn't aware of having been given the opportunity to do so if I'd wanted to.'

'Come on, Bernie, we both know the real reason why you wouldn't take me off to arrest Matthew Bridgefield this evening, and it's nothing to do with you being desperate to get back to Peter and his curry.'

'Oh that!' Bernie said dismissively as she continued with the process of preparing for Jonah for the descent from the car. 'Well, if you persist in believing that the only way of keeping the respect of your subordinates is to present yourself as some sort of superman who never needs to eat or sleep, it's not my place to undermine your position. I happen to think you're completely wrong about that, but that's another matter altogether.'

She fixed the ramp and Jonah drove his chair down it on to the drive.

'Bernie,' he said, as she bent down to fold up the ramp and put it back into its place inside the car. 'I never thought I'd say this, and I may well regret having said it afterwards, but thank you for being firm with me about not overdoing it.'

This unexpected speech pulled Bernie up short. It was extremely rare for Jonah to refer to his disability or to the restrictions that it imposed upon him. He often appeared to be determined to pretend that they did not exist and to assume that somehow his iron determination to do something would overcome any obstacle. She hastily finished stowing the ramp and then hurried round to stand in front of Jonah's chair, blocking his way to the front door.

'I'm sorry,' she said, trying to strike a light note so as to dampen the wave of emotion that she felt at hearing this surprising admission of weakness. 'I think there must be something wrong with my ears. Did you really say you were pleased that I wouldn't let you push yourself to the point of exhaustion in order to demonstrate that you can do everything that an able-bodied officer can do, and then some?'

'Much as it pains me to do so,' Jonah said, smiling up at her, 'I have to admit that, since Margaret died, there's been the distinct danger that there would be nobody left with the courage to stand up to me and remind me of my limitations. Of course, I should have known I could rely on you not to put up with any nonsense from me.'

'When it comes to straight talking and letting you have what's for, I'm definitely your man,' Bernie declared, crouching down so that her face was level with his. Their eyes met and both of them found themselves blinking back tears. Bernie put out her right hand and gripped Jonah's left. He responded by squeezing her fingers gently between his three working digits.

'Well, come along then,' Jonah said after a moment or two, 'what're you doing hanging around out here? I thought you were in a hurry to get to that curry.'

After the meal was over, Lucy turned to Jonah and addressed him sternly.

'Right!' she said, in the tone of a nanny dealing with a recalcitrant two-year-old, 'it's time for your physio. I suppose you thought you'd get out of it by staying out until teatime so there was no time before. Come along and I'll take you through your paces.'

'You really don't need to,' Jonah assured her. 'I often don't get time for it on Fridays. By the time Nathan's back from work and we've had dinner we just sit around and watch the telly most weeks.'

'But that's incredibly bad for you,' Lucy argued. 'You've been sitting around in that chair all day. It's time you got out of it and got moving or you'll be developing pressure sores.'

'Give me a break,' Jonah pleaded, feeling suddenly very weary. 'Just once won't make a difference.'

'I thought you said it wasn't just once!' Lucy cried triumphantly. 'Come along, the sooner we start, the sooner it'll be over.'

'Hang on, love,' Bernie intervened. 'I'm all for forcing Jonah to do his workout, but what about all that homework you were telling me about? Let me do Jonah's physio while you get on with that.'

'I can do that tomorrow. I need you to help me with the Physics anyway.'

'But tomorrow you're going to be out with Martin all afternoon.'

'Sunday then.'

'You shouldn't leave it to the last minute. *I'll* take Jonah for his physio and you do your homework now.'

'Tell me your secret,' Peter whispered loudly to Jonah. 'How do you manage to get women fighting over your body like this?'

'It's simple,' Jonah replied in a similar stage whisper.

'It's just a matter of getting someone to shoot you in the back of the neck – works every time!'

Lucy and her mother broke off their argument and looked at the two men.

'There's a simple solution,' Peter said in the silence that ensued. '*I* will take Jonah for his physio while you two go upstairs and sort out that Physics homework.'

'OK,' Lucy conceded, recognising that further argument was pointless, 'but it's still my week on duty, so *I'm* going be the one who puts Jonah to bed and sleeps in his room.'

'But the duty rota is only for weekdays,' Bernie argued. 'You've done your stint. Jonah doesn't usually stay with us for the weekend, so we need to go back to first principles. It wouldn't be fair if you just carry on for an extra day.'

'OK then, I don't mind doing that too,' Peter volunteered.

'But you're on duty next week,' Lucy pointed out, so the same argument applies from the other end.'

'Which means the most sensible thing would be for me to take over for the weekend,' Bernie concluded.

'Hang on a minute,' Jonah protested, hiding his amusement beneath a pretence of indignation. 'Don't I get a say in all of this? Don't forget it's me you're all haggling over.'

'Don't do it,' Peter warned, only half joking. 'You'll never hear the end of it if you choose which of them you prefer!'

'What I was going to say,' Jonah resumed, 'was that, since Our Bernie is going to enjoy the pleasure of my company for the whole of tomorrow afternoon, while we go off sleuthing together, whereas poor Lucy will be forced to spend the time confined to a boat on the Oxford canal with only Dr Martin Riess to entertain her, it would be only fair if Lucy is permitted to sleep with me tonight.'

Lucy raised her fists above her head in an exaggerated gesture of triumph while Bernie shook her head pretending to be disappointed.

'That settles that then,' she said. 'But we really must do something to work on your low self-esteem problem, Jonah.'

Bernie and Lucy went upstairs to Lucy's bedroom and Peter accompanied Jonah to his.

'I think I ought to apologise to you for stealing your wife away tomorrow afternoon,' Jonah said, as Peter lifted him out of the chair, his strong arms easily carrying the weight of his friend's slight frame. 'I shouldn't take advantage like that.'

'Don't be daft. Police work isn't nine to five; we both know that. And I knew perfectly well a year ago, when Bernie took over as your assistant, that it'd sometimes mean her being away for extra hours when there was a case on.'

'But when you signed up to that you didn't know I was going to end up living here with you as well. I still can't get my head round why you suggested that idea.'

'I told you at the time,' Peter joked. 'It was the only way I could think of to keep my wife and stepdaughter at home instead of gallivanting off to visit you all the time. I know I can never compete with you in the charisma stakes, so I have to resort to subterfuge. Now, are you ready for some serious exercise?'

For a few minutes neither spoke, as Jonah settled down to the strange sensation of watching his legs working the exercise machine, the muscles stimulated by external electric impulses.

'Of course,' Peter said quietly, standing behind Jonah so that he would not be able to see his face and there was no danger of them making eye contact, 'I have to admit that I probably wouldn't have suggested taking you in if I didn't like having you around the place anyway.'

Peter had become very fond of Jonah over the five years since his injury. The vague resentment that he had once felt towards his younger colleague had now gone and he no longer cared that Jonah had gained promotion ahead of him and so often achieved success through leaps of imagination, which by-passed the painstaking work of collecting evidence and piecing it together through reasoned deduction. Now that they were no longer in competition, Peter felt both admiration for Jonah's energy and determination, and compassion for his physical disability and, more recently, for his sorrow at the death of his wife. He did not, however, intend to show his feelings openly.

'Bernie tells me you've got a Skype session with Eddie organised for tomorrow afternoon,' Jonah said to break the awkward silence which followed. 'Do you have something special to talk about?'

'It's Angie's birthday.'

'I'm sorry. I didn't know.'

'Of course not. Why should you?'

'Our Bernie keeps telling me I'm part of the family, so I feel I ought to know about that sort of thing.'

More silence.

'Peter?'

'Mmm?'

'If you don't mind me asking, how long does it take to really sink in? I mean how long was it before you stopped expecting her to walk in the door any minute?'

'I'm sorry, I can't answer that. A long time – more than eleven years; that's all I can tell you.'

'Ah!' Jonah nodded, aware that Peter's wife had died a little over eleven years ago.

'And that's another reason why I'm so pleased to have you here to keep Bernie and Lucy amused. I know that if Angie *did* ever walk in the door, I'd walk out with her and leave them both behind without a thought. Now, are you done with that?'

'I thought you'd never ask.'

Peter switched off the machine and carefully detached the electrodes from Jonah's skin. Then he gently lifted him on to the bed, removed his shirt and began to massage his upper body.

'It does get better over time,' he said in a matter-of-fact voice, 'but it never really goes away.'

'That's what Our Bernie said too.'

'But then, you wouldn't want to forget, would you?'

'No ... I suppose we're the lucky ones, really. I mean, staying together till death us do part. We've never had someone walk out on us – like Amanda Bridgefield or Ann Lambert.'

'And you're sure now it was the boy who killed his father?'

'Yes.'

'And if he keeps his nerve and just denies it? Do you have enough evidence to convict?'

'I've got a witness that says Bridgefield was alive when he entered the room and another that says he was dead only minutes afterwards.'

'One of them could be lying.'

'And there are those marks on his hands.'

'For which he had an explanation.'

'Two inconsistent explanations.'

'Only inconsistent in the timing – a good brief would convince the jury that it was just an innocent mistake, the sort of memory lapse we all have from time to time.'

'You wouldn't be rushing off to make an arrest tomorrow, would you? Slow and sure Peter would have carried on gathering the evidence.'

'Yes, I probably would. In particular, I'd have been looking out for someone who would swear that those marks on Matthew's hands appeared during the day on Wednesday. But then,' Peter said, turning Jonah over on to his back and smiling down at him, 'I'd have been looking for an excuse *not* to have to work over the weekend.'

JUDY FORD

32 THE MURDERER

The following afternoon, when Andy rang the bell of the Bridgefield home, there was the sound of excited barking from inside, followed by a woman's voice calling to the dog to calm down. A few moments later, the door was opened by Mandy Bridgefield, struggling to hold it at the same time as gripping the collar of a Dalmatian, which was straining vigorously to get free. She looked at them in surprise.

'Is there some news?' she asked at last. 'Do you know who killed Anthony?'

'Can we come in please, Mrs Bridgefield?' Andy asked.

'Yes, of course,' Mandy looked down rather helplessly at the dog. 'Never mind Dolly, she's quite harmless. She just gets a bit excited when we have visitors. I'll shut her in the kitchen. Come along Dolly! Good girl!'

Andy watched as Mandy pushed the dog through a door at the end of the hall and closed it, shutting the animal inside. Then she turned and gestured to a door on the right of the passage.

'Come through here. I'm sorry about the mess.'

Andy followed her into a sunny sitting room furnished with a rather elderly-looking three-piece suite. Mandy

268

picked up a brush and frantically tried to remove the white dog hairs, which showed up clearly on the dark velvet fabric. Meanwhile Bernie set up the portable ramp and helped Jonah to make his way inside. Eventually they were all seated round a coffee table from which Mandy was hurriedly clearing a pile of magazines, a box of tissues and an assortment of dog toys.

'Can I get you a drink?' she asked, putting the things down in a pile on the floor in the corner of the room.

'No thank you,' Jonah replied, 'we won't keep you long. Is your son at home?'

'Yes. He's upstairs in his room. Would you like me to get him?'

'Yes please.'

Mandy disappeared and they heard footsteps going up the stairs then voices in a room above and two pairs of feet coming downstairs. A whining noise from the kitchen told them that Dolly was not best pleased at being shut away from the action.

'Mum said you wanted to see me,' Matthew said, coming into the room. He was dressed in jeans and a tee-shirt with canvas shoes, which had once been pale green but were now a muddy grey.

'Yes. Sit down please,' Jonah inclined his head towards the sofa and Matthew and his mother sat down on it, side by side. The whining from the kitchen grew louder and was accompanied by a scrabbling sound as Dolly scratched at the door.

'How're your hands now?' Jonah asked pleasantly, looking at them clasped together in Matthew's lap. 'No more trouble with the dog pulling on the lead?'

'They're much better now, thanks.' Matthew looked round at each of the visitors in turn as if trying to work out why they had come and where this question might be leading.

'You take the dog out every morning before work, do you?' Jonah asked.

'Yes, well most mornings.'

'Except this week,' his mother put in. 'Don't you remember? I said I took her out this week because Matthew had to be in work early.'

'So it was in the evening when she pulled away and made the marks on your hands?'

'Yes it must have been, mustn't it,' Matthew agreed, speaking in a low voice and glancing angrily at Mandy.

'But you told us that you injured your hands on Wednesday morning. Why did you say that, when you hadn't even been walking the dog that morning?'

'It was just a slip of the tongue,' Matthew muttered, looking increasingly discomforted. 'I meant the evening.'

'Yes, it was Wednesday evening,' his mother confirmed, looking round with a rather bewildered expression. 'Like I said: he went out the moment he got home from work and when he came back he told me about Dolly and the rabbit.'

'Is that right, Matthew?' Jonah asked sharply. 'Was it Wednesday evening?'

'No. Not Wednesday. It was Tuesday.'

'No, you're wrong there,' Mandy insisted. 'I know it was the day your dad was killed because I was waiting to talk to you about it and you rushed off without a word to take Dolly for her walk.'

'Matthew?' Jonah left the word hanging in the air, knowing that silence was often the most effective way of getting someone to speak.

For a full two minutes, the only sounds to be heard were Dolly's increasingly vehement complaints and her continued attempts to escape from the kitchen.

'It was Tuesday,' Matthew said at last. 'Sorry Mum. You must have remembered wrong.'

'Tuesday evening? That's your last word?'

'Yes.'

'You know, that surprises me,' Jonah said, looking straight at Matthew, who looked down quickly to avoid making eye contact. 'You see, I have a very reliable witness who is quite sure that you didn't have any marks on your hands by the time you started work on Wednesday morning. How do you account for that?'

There was another long period when nobody spoke. Mandy looked around wildly, trying to work out what these questions were all about and why her son seemed intent on lying about something so apparently trivial. Matthew stared down at the floor, maintaining a stubborn silence. Andy watched Matthew closely for any sign that he was about to speak. Bernie watched Jonah, wondering what he would do next. Jonah waited impassively, wishing fervently that he had taken the precaution of going back to question more of the hotel staff in the hope of finding someone who would testify to Matthew having the red marks on his hands on the Wednesday afternoon. That was a stupid mistake to make, he told himself, and Peter had warned him about it.

'Shall I tell you what *I* think,' Jonah said at last, having decided that Matthew was not going to answer spontaneously. 'I think that the story about Dolly and the rabbit was all just made up to account for the marks which were already on your hands when you got home on Wednesday evening. Maybe you told people who noticed them on Wednesday afternoon that your dog made them by pulling on her lead when you were taking her for her walk that morning, and that's what gave you the idea for how you were going to explain them to your mother when you got home. But you couldn't tell her that it had happened in the morning, because *she* knew that you hadn't walked the dog in the morning that day. So you went straight out as soon as you got home, to make sure she couldn't see your hands and ask about the marks until after you got back from Dolly's walk, and then you told her all about Dolly and the rabbit and hurting your hands on the lead. Am I getting close?'

Matthew continued to stare at the floor without

speaking, so Jonah continued.

'Shall I tell you where *I* think the marks came from?' he asked. 'I think they were made by the cable that you put round your father's neck when you went in to check the IT equipment and found him alone in the meeting room. And that's why, Matthew Bridgefield, I am arresting you for the murder of Mr Anthony Bridgefield. You do not have to say anything, but –'

'Wait!' Matthew interrupted. 'Let me tell you what actually happened.'

'It might be better to wait until we get to the station,' Andy advised him. 'And you have a right to have a solicitor present.'

'No. I want to tell you here. I want Mum to hear.'

'Very well,' Jonah said, 'but bear in mind that Bernie here is taking notes, which could be used as evidence later. Now, before you say anything more, I just have to finish cautioning you.'

He went on to repeat the legal form of words and then reiterated Andy's advice that Matthew should wait until they got to the police station and he had a lawyer to advise him.

Matthew swallowed a few times and looked anxiously at his mother, who put her right hand out and took hold of his left as it lay in his lap.

'When I got there,' Matthew began, 'I opened the door and looked in, and there was Dad, busy with his presentation on the computer. I saw everything was OK and I was going to just close the door and go away, like I told you before, but then he turned round and saw me. He said, "Do I know you from somewhere?" Just like that. He was my dad and he didn't recognise me. He just thought maybe he'd seen me somewhere before but he didn't know where. So then, I went in and closed the door; and I went up to him and I said, "I think you used to know my Mum. Her name was Amanda Bridgefield. Bridgefield! Now isn't that a coincidence – that's your name too isn't it?" He looked for a bit as if he didn't get it. Then he realised who I was and he laughed.'

Matthew held his mother's hand between his own two hands and sat for a moment looking down at them.

'He said, "I suppose your mother put you up to this," and I was like "what d'you mean?" He laughed again and said something about a deposit on a house, which I didn't understand. Then he said things about Mum always trying to scrounge from him and how it was time we both learned to stand on our own two feet, which made me angry because we've never gone begging to him. And then …'

He paused again, looking down at his mother's hand in his. She turned in her seat and put her other hand on his knee looking up at his bowed head.

'And then,' Matthew repeated, 'he said something about how we'd better get used to the fact that he wouldn't be supporting us any more because he was going to have another family. He seemed to think I already knew that he'd got some girl pregnant and he was planning to go off and live with her and bring up the baby together. He sounded proud of it!'

Matthew's voice rose as he remembered the injustice of what his father had said to him.

'He was full of how wonderful it was going to be for him to be a proper dad to this baby he was having; how much he was looking forward to it; and how he wouldn't have any time for Mum and me – as if he ever gave us any time in the first place! It made me so angry!'

Matthew looked up at Jonah, with an expression of desperate passion.

'At that moment I hated him more than I ever had before. There he was, so pleased with himself and so happy about this new family he was going to have, when he never cared about me or Mum and never did anything for us. And I just felt I couldn't stand it any more, so I grabbed the power cable off the laptop and put it round his neck and pulled it tight.'

'Did you mean to kill him?' Jonah asked quietly in the silence that followed.

'I don't know,' Matthew said helplessly, looking around as if in a daze. 'I don't know what I wanted except to shut him up talking about his wonderful new girlfriend and their wonderful baby.'

'Oh Matthew!' Mandy murmured, putting her arm around his shoulder and pulling him closer to her. 'He wasn't worth it. He wasn't worth it.'

'Anyway,' Matthew resumed, determined to finish the story now that he had begun. 'After a while, he stopped struggling and gasping for air and went very quiet. So I let go of the cable and he sort of slumped back into the chair. He didn't look how I expected a dead body to look. He looked as if he was leaning back looking up at the screen. But when he didn't move, I thought he must be dead. And then I got scared and I thought I'd better get away before anyone came.'

He stopped and looked Jonah full in the face, waiting for their eyes to meet before he went on, speaking very earnestly now.

'I wouldn't have let anyone else be sent down for killing him. If you'd charged someone else I'd have come forward. You must believe me!' he begged, holding Jonah in his gaze for a few moments before turning to his mother with a look of pleading on his face. 'You believe me, don't you Mum?'

She nodded, but seemed unable to speak.

'So what did you hope was going to happen?' Jonah asked. 'Did you think we'd just get bored and go away?'

'I didn't want to go to jail so I hoped this would be one of those unsolved crimes that you read about.'

'Leaving all the Lichfield College staff who'd been on the Awayday thinking it must have been one of them, but not knowing which one?' Jonah asked drily.

'I – I – I didn't think about that. I just hoped that

somehow I'd get away with it and no one else would go to prison either.' Matthew looked around wildly before collapsing into his mother's arms. 'I'm sorry, Mum,' he wept, suddenly appearing very young and vulnerable.

Andy rang for a pair of uniformed officers to come to take Matthew to the police station to start the formal process of charging him with the murder of his father. While they waited for them to arrive, Jonah turned to Mandy.

'Is there anyone who could come and sit with you, Mrs Bridgefield? A friend or family member, perhaps? I'm afraid time will seem to pass very slowly over the next few days. It would be better for you not to be alone.'

'I'll be alright,' Mandy shook her head 'I've got Dolly to keep me company.'

'I could ring Simon Sutcliffe for you,' Bernie suggested. 'It's his job to give pastoral care to members of the college.'

'No thank you.'

'Then how about Bev Greenhalgh? She's been wanting to do something to help. You'd be doing her a favour by making her think she's being useful.'

'How like Bev!' Mandy laughed. 'OK, you can ring her if you like. At least she won't offer to say a prayer with me or anything.'

'Talking of Bev Greenhalgh,' Bernie said as they drove off, 'have you decided whether or not to send a report to the Border Agency?'

'Why would the Border Agency want a report on a murder in an Oxford hotel?'

'No, of course not. Silly of me to ask.'

33 EPILOGUE

Some two hours later, they pulled up outside the house in Headington, glad that their weekend could now start in earnest. Peter came out to greet them, as Bernie and Andy folded away the ramp and locked the car. Bernie smiled and gave a thumbs-up sign when she saw him.

'I take it you've made an arrest,' Peter said. 'I hope that means you'll be taking the rest of the weekend off, seeing as you weren't supposed to be on duty in the first place.'

'Not merely an arrest,' Jonah confirmed with a smile of satisfaction, 'but a convincing confession as well. I'm pretty sure he'll go for a guilty plea, which will make things easier all round.'

He started to relate what Matthew Bridgefield had told them, but he had not got far when he was interrupted by the arrival of Martin Riess and Lucy on bicycles. They dismounted and Lucy wheeled her machine round to a position where she could look Jonah in the face.

'How did you get on?' she demanded. 'Have you solved the case yet?'

'We have indeed. Let's all go inside and I'll tell you about it.'

They went indoors and into the kitchen. Andy looked round at the crowd of people assembled there and started to understand what Peter had meant when he talked about

Bernie's 'family'. He was introduced to Stan and Sylvia, a Geordie couple in their seventies who, he was told, had moved to Oxford on their retirement in order to help look after Lucy when she was small. Exactly what their relationship with Bernie was remained unclear, but they were evidently old friends and very fond of both her and Lucy. Sylvia busied herself cutting up a large loaf of homemade bread while Stan sliced tomatoes and cucumber and washed lettuce in the sink to make a salad.

Sitting at the table was a small, white-haired woman who turned out to be Martin's mother, Eva. She spoke slowly with a very marked German accent. Lucy explained to Andy that she had completely forgotten how to speak English after having a stroke two years previously and was still in the process of re-learning it.

'Hello Andy, how're you doing?'

Andy turned at the sound of the familiar voice of pathologist Mike Carson, who emerged from the larder carrying an assortment of jars of jam and pickles. He too was evidently very much at home here.

As they sat round the large kitchen table, eating a high tea worthy of an Enid Blyton farmer's wife, Jonah related such parts of the investigation as could appropriately be revealed to the general public. Martin and Mike, of course, already knew much of what had gone on, and news of the arrest and charging of Matthew Bridgefield would be spreading rapidly by now within the university, so it was only some of the details that needed to be treated as confidential. Lucy obligingly expressed delight and amazement at the appropriate places and congratulated both Jonah and Andy on their remarkable detective powers. Sylvia, Stan and Eva while appearing suitably impressed were less effusive.

'Well,' Bernie said, smiling complacently as she leaned back in her chair at the end of the meal. 'I hope you've all taken note that I was right all along.'

'When you said it was the IT guy, d'you mean?' Jonah

asked.

'No, when I said that, whoever it was, I was pretty sure it would be someone a whole lot more likeable than Anthony Bridgefield.'

'Yes,' Lucy agreed. 'You can't help feeling a bit sorry for Matthew, after the way his father behaved to him and his mum.'

'I think I'm glad my dad never came back from Nigeria,' Andy muttered in an undertone, which only Peter and Jonah, who were his immediate neighbours round the table, could hear. 'I don't know what I might have done if he'd turned up on the doorstep one day.'

'But remember, even Anthony Bridgefield turned out to be less obnoxious than we thought,' Peter pointed out fairly.

'Oh yeah?' Bernie sounded sceptical.

'He was planning to make a home for Penny and her baby, even though it wasn't his.'

'Hmmph! He probably just realised, a bit late in the day, that he couldn't expect to carry on sponging off ever younger women for the rest of his life and that if he was hoping to be looked after in his old age he'd better establish a stake in the next generation.'

'Is that what made you decide to have me?' Lucy asked with mock innocence.

'That question presupposes that there was some sort of decision involved. I'm sure I've told you before: it wasn't anything like as organised as that.'

'Anyway,' Martin said, reflecting gloomily on the recent behaviour of his research assistant, 'whether you believe in Anthony's noble gesture or not depends crucially on whether we can believe a single word that Penny has said about her relations with him and Tom. I'm beginning to think that her whole story was a pack of lies from beginning to end.'

'Just count yourself lucky she didn't try to make out *you*'d fallen for her charms as well,' Bernie commented.

'She might have ruined your reputation! I agree. I just don't understand that girl.'

'I reckon she and Anthony deserved each other,' Mike said cheerfully. 'From what you tell me, they were both out for all they could get from anyone they came into contact with.'

'I'm not so sure,' Stan said thoughtfully. He had been listening in silence up to now and Andy had wondered whether he had been paying attention to the conversation about people and situations that were unfamiliar to him. 'Maybe everyone's been misjudging the man. Maybe he just couldn't come to terms with the expectations of the women around him. You keep saying that he went in for old-fashioned courtesy towards them: opening doors and pulling out chairs and that. Maybe that's all he really was – old fashioned. You say he sponged off the women, but maybe they insisted on it. Maybe they didn't want him to be the male provider. I've seen it over and over when the shipyards were in trouble and letting people go. There were men who felt humiliated at the idea that their wives were going out to work and they sometimes did strange things to prove they were still real men.'

'But this Anthony guy wasn't out of work,' Lucy objected. 'Why would he feel like that?'

'Didn't you say the college gave him a house because he got married? So he was dependent on his wife for that. And she said she'd been there for longer than him, so maybe she was earning more than he was. And she didn't give up work when the boy was born, which he might have seen as a reflection on his ability to support them.'

'It all sounds a bit tenuous to me,' Bernie said, unconvinced.

'No, but I can see where you're coming from,' Andy said eagerly. 'You're saying that the whole problem is a mismatch between the way Anthony saw things and the way the women he went off with did. They tried to keep him faithful to them by paying their way and not making demands, but he would have rather they'd allowed themselves to be dependent on him. Penny was the first one who just let him pay for everything.'

'Because she was a little gold-digger,' Martin observed glumly.

'I'm not sure it was really the money that was so important to her as much as the feeling of power,' Jonah suggested.

'But getting back to the idea of people looking at things differently,' Andy said earnestly, looking at Stan. 'What you said made me think. I suppose if you came from a society where it was quite normal for a man to have three wives, then it wouldn't feel so bad to be going out with another woman when you already had two wives at home. I mean, it wouldn't really be like adultery would it? Not from the man's point of view.'

Suddenly the room fell silent and Andy was aware that everyone was looking at him.

'And what made you think of that particular example, son?' Stan asked, with a puzzled frown on his face.

'My dad,' Andy explained, speaking in a low voice and feeling his heart suddenly beating faster. 'He was Nigerian. He came over here to do a postgraduate degree and he never told my mum that he was already married – twice! I always thought he was just, well, *using* her. But what you just said about Anthony Bridgefield made me think, that's all.'

'Maybe he was hoping your mum would go back with him and be wife number three,' Lucy suggested brightly.

'Well I for one am glad she didn't, because if you'd been brought up in Nigeria we'd have lost a good police officer,' Peter declared heartily, hoping to move the conversation off this difficult subject. 'Now, if everyone's finished ...'

Mike and Martin took charge of the washing up while Stan and Sylvia put away the remains of the food and wiped the table. Meanwhile Peter and Lucy accompanied

Jonah to his bedroom to get him out of his work suit and into something more comfortable. Bernie held the door open for Eva to make her way slowly into the living room. She walked in a lopsided way, steadying herself with a stick. One arm hung at her side with the hand curled at an awkward angle. Andy, his offers of help in the kitchen having been turned down, followed behind.

Gradually the rest of the party joined them and soon the spacious room was filled with the buzz of expectant chatter. Bernie clapped her hands to attract their attention.

'And now,' she said dramatically, 'if Miss Paige would please take her place at the pianoforte, the entertainment can commence!'

'I feel that I'm suddenly inside a period drama,' Andy whispered to Mike, who was sitting next to him on the settee.

'Or a Jane Austen novel,' Mike agreed with a grin. 'Don't worry, you won't be expected to perform – not on your first time!'

All eyes turned to the piano as Lucy began playing the introduction to a Gilbert and Sullivan duet while Bernie and Martin stood next to her listening for their cue.

'There is beauty in the bellow of the blast,' Bernie sang, 'There is grandeur in the growling of the gale, there is eloquent outpouring when the lion is a-roaring, and the tiger is a-lashing of his tail!'

'Yes, I like to see a tiger,' Martin responded dramatically, 'from the Congo or the Niger, and especially when lashing of his tail!'

'Volcanoes have a splendour that is grim, and earthquakes only terrify the dolts,' Bernie resumed.

'Appropriate, don't you think,' Mike whispered to Andy, 'what with Martin being an Earth Scientist.'

Andy nodded as Martin and Bernie sang together:

'If that is so, sing derry down derry! It's evident, very, our tastes are one. Away we'll go, and merrily marry, nor tardily tarry till day is done!'

Everyone seemed to have a party piece to contribute. Stan regaled them with a Stanley Holloway monologue, with which evidently his audience was very familiar, judging by the way they joined in with the words at appropriate moments. Mike unexpectedly turned out to be a proficient flautist and played a medley of Irish folk tunes to great acclaim. Sylvia read poetry and even Eva managed a one-handed piano recital with Lucy sitting next to her and filling in the missing part. To Andy, the greatest surprise was when the staid, one might almost say boring, Peter performed a sequence of conjuring tricks aided by 'my glamorous assistant' Lucy.

When it came to Jonah's turn, Lucy sat down at the piano, but he shook his head at her.

'I'll do this one unaccompanied,' he said and then, turning to face the waiting room, 'I think this expresses the work of a detective rather well.'

There was an expectant pause then he began to sing, softly but with a warm, full tone which was somehow very moving.

'Lead, Kindly Light, amidst th'encircling gloom, Lead Thou me on! The night is dark, and I am far from home, Lead Thou me on! Keep Thou my feet; I do not ask to see the distant scene; one step enough for me.'

This seemed to be the signal for Lucy and Martin to start handing out hymnbooks, which Andy noticed most of the company immediately started thumbing through looking for their favourites.

'You don't need to join in if you don't want to,' Mike told him in an undertone. 'Nobody will care.'

About nine hymns and half an hour later Bernie looked at her watch and declared that it was time for the party to break up.

'Oh Mam!' Lucy protested. 'It's not that late yet.'

'It's late enough; and we've all had a busy day.'

'Alright,' Lucy conceded suddenly realising that it was Jonah's presence that made it necessary to curtail the entertainment. It was nearly time to start the lengthy process of preparing him for bed. 'Just give us your rendition of the Liverpool Lullaby before we head off.'

'OK. Are you sitting comfortably? Then I'll begin.'

Everyone sat back to listen. Andy, to whom the song was new, wondered what was coming. Bernie began, putting on her strongest Liverpool accent. Andy looked round the room and saw everyone smiling gently. This was clearly a familiar favourite. One or two of the lines elicited brief laughter, despite the fact that everyone knew what was coming. As Bernie began the last verse, Andy looked across at Peter and saw that he was watching him keenly.

'Oh you've got your father's face,' Bernie sang.

Andy caught Peter's eye and smiled reassurance at him. What if he did have his father's face (as neither of Peter's children did)? It didn't matter anymore. His father was just a man – not perfect, but not the devil incarnate either.

ACKNOWLEDGEMENTS

I would like to thank the Spinal Injuries Association for information about living with spinal injuries, which I obtained from its website:
http://www.spinal.co.uk/page/living-with-sci.

I am indebted to WS Gilbert (1836-1911) for the lyrics to *There is Beauty in the Bellow of the Blast*, to Marriott Edgar (1880–1951) for his monologue *The Runcorn Ferry*, to Stan Kelly-Bootle (1929 – 2014) for his song *Liverpool Lullaby*, and to John Henry Newman (1801-1890) for his hymn *Lead Kindly Light*, which are mentioned in Chapter 33.

Every effort has been made to trace copyright holders. The publisher will be glad to rectify in future editions any errors or omissions brought to their attention.

A MESSAGE FROM THE AUTHOR

Thank you for taking the time to read AWAYDAY. If you enjoyed it, please consider telling your friends or posting a short review. Word of mouth is an author's best friend and much appreciated.

Thank you,

Judy

MORE ABOUT BERNIE AND HER FRIENDS

Bernie features in seven more books.

- **Changing Scenes of Life:** Jonah Porter's life story, told through the medium of his favourite hymns.
- **Despise not your Mother:** the story of Bernie's quest to learn about her dead husband's past.
- **Two Little Dickie Birds:** a murder mystery for DI Peter Johns and his Sergeant, Paul Godwin.
- **Murder of a Martian:** a double murder for Peter and Jonah to solve.
- **Death on the Algarve:** a mystery for Bernie and her friends to tackle while on holiday in Portugal.
- **My Life of Crime:** the collected memoirs of DI Peter Johns.
- **Mystery over the Mersey:** a murder mystery set in Liverpool.

Read more about Bernie Fazakerley and her friends and family at https://sites.google.com/site/llanwrdafamily/ or visit the Bernie Fazakerley Publications Facebook page here:
https://www.facebook.com/Bernie.Fazakerley.Publications

Follow Bernie on Twitter: https://twitter.com/BernieFaz.

ABOUT THE AUTHOR

Like her main character, Bernie Fazakerley, Judy Ford is an Oxford graduate and a mathematician. Unlike Bernie, Judy grew up in a middle-class family in the South London stockbroker belt. After moving to the North West and working in Liverpool, Judy fell in love with the Scouse people and created Bernie to reflect their unique qualities.

As a Methodist Local Preacher, Judy often tells her congregation, "I see my role as asking the questions and leaving you to think out your own answers." She carries this philosophy forward into her writing and she hopes that readers will find themselves challenged to think as well as being entertained.